P9-CEV-039

"Tell me about your night. You know you want to."

"Actually, it was over so fast, I can't really remember."

He gave a low, rather triumphant laugh and turned her to face him. "You haven't yet once managed to look me in the eyes and tell me how bad I was. Here's your chance, Molly. Give it to me."

See, that was the thing. She *did* want to give it to him, quite badly. *Naked* . . . Gah. She really hadn't seen this coming, but she deserved fun like anyone else, right? She looked at his mouth, desperately wanting it on hers. And then her body somehow mistook the fantasy for reality because she went up on tiptoes and . . . kissed him. Just a soft brush of her lips across his, gently and a little hesitant, but it was most definitely a kiss.

By Jill Shalvis

Heartbreaker Bay Novels

SWEET LITTLE LIES
THE TROUBLE WITH MISTLETOE
ACCIDENTALLY ON PURPOSE
CHASING CHRISTMAS EVE
ABOUT THAT KISS • HOT WINTER NIGHTS

Coming Soon
PLAYING FOR KEEPS

Women's Fiction Novels

RAINY DAY FRIENDS
THE GOOD LUCK SISTER (novella)
LOST AND FOUND SISTERS

Lucky Harbor Novels

ONE IN A MILLION • HE'S SO FINE
IT'S IN HIS KISS • ONCE IN A LIFETIME
ALWAYS ON MY MIND • IT HAD TO BE YOU
FOREVER AND A DAY • AT LAST
LUCKY IN LOVE • HEAD OVER HEELS
THE SWEETEST THING • SIMPLY IRRESISTIBLE

Animal Magnetism Novels

STILL THE ONE • ALL I WANT
THEN CAME YOU • RUMOR HAS IT
RESCUE MY HEART • ANIMAL ATTRACTION
ANIMAL MAGNETISM

JILL SHALVIS

hot winter nights

A
Heartbreaker Bay
Novel

AVONBOOKS

An Imprint of HarperCollinsPublishers

Excerpt from *Playing for Keeps* copyright © 2019 by Jill Shalvis.

HOT WINTER NIGHTS. Copyright © 2018 by Jill Shalvis. All rights reserved. Printed in the United States of America. No part of this book may be used or reproduced in any manner whatsoever without written permission except in the case of brief quotations embodied in critical articles and reviews. For information, address HarperCollins Publishers, 195 Broadway, New York, NY 10007.

First Avon Books mass market printing: October 2018
First Avon Books hardcover printing: September 2018

Print Edition ISBN: 978-0-06-274183-7
Digital Edition ISBN: 978-0-06-274184-4

Cover design by Nadine Badalaty
Cover illustration by Aleta Rafton
Cover and tip-in photographs by Shirley Green (couple); iStock/Getty Images; © Shutterstock

Avon, Avon & logo, and Avon Books & logo are registered trademarks of HarperCollins Publishers in the United States of America and other countries.
HarperCollins is a registered trademark of HarperCollins Publishers in the United States of America and other countries.

FIRST EDITION

18 19 20 21 22 QGM 10 9 8 7 6 5 4 3 2 1

hot
winter
nights

Chapter 1

#NaughtyOrNice

It took Lucas Knight longer than it should have to realize he had a woman in his bed, but to be fair, he had a bitch of a hangover. Even worse than that, last night was a blur, prompting him to take quick stock. One, there was a bundle of sweet, soft curves against him. Two, his head was currently threatening to secede from the United States Of Lucas. And three, his side hurt like . . . well, like he'd been shot.

It'd been two weeks since he'd gotten caught in some cross fire on the job and he hadn't yet been cleared for more than light duty—something he'd obviously managed to ignore last night given that he was palming a nice, warm, feminine ass.

Think, man.

Straining his brain, he remembered taking a pain med before going to O'Riley's Pub to meet up with some friends. A client had been there, someone he'd recently helped save from a multimillion dollar corporate espionage. The guy had ordered shots to toast to Lucas and . . . shit. Knowing better than to mix pain meds and alcohol, he'd hesitated, but everyone had been waiting on him, glasses hoisted in the air. Thinking just one shot couldn't hurt anything, he'd knocked back the drink.

Clearly, he'd been wrong and it'd been enough to mess him up big-time, something he hadn't been in years, not since his brother Josh had been killed. Shoving that away for another time—or never—Lucas cracked open one eye, but when his retina was stabbed by a streak of sunlight glaring in through the window, he immediately slammed it shut again. Taking a deep breath, he told himself to suck it up and opened both eyes this time, learning two additional facts.

He was naked and completely uncovered.

And the woman snugged up at his side was rolled up in his comforter like a burrito.

What. The. Hell.

A few more images slowly began to filter into his brain. Kicking ass at the pool table and winning two hundred bucks from his boss, Archer, who ran Hunt Investigations where Lucas worked as a security specialist.

Dancing with a sexy brunette . . .

And then making his way upstairs, but not alone.

His head was pounding too hard to remember

anything more, but clearly the brunette had not only come up, but stayed. She was cuddled up too close to see her face, especially with the way she had the entire blanket wrapped around herself. The only thing visible was a mass of shiny brown waves peeking out the top.

Holding his breath, Lucas slowly pulled away until he could slide off his bed.

The brunette's hair never so much as quivered.

Letting out a relieved breath, he shoved on the clothes he'd so thoughtfully left for himself on the floor—seriously, he was never taking another pain pill or drinking alcohol again—and headed for the door.

But unable to do it, unable to be the guy who just walked out, he stopped and detoured to his kitchen to make her a coffee. Leaving her caffeine was a nice gesture, right? Right, but . . . shit. He was out of coffee. Not surprisingly since he usually grabbed his from work because Molly, who ran the office at Hunt Investigations, made world-class coffee. And since one of the benefits of living on the fourth floor of the Pacific Pier Building and working on the second floor meant convenience, he texted the coffee master himself:

Any chance you'd send up a cup of coffee via the dumbwaiter?

A few seconds later, from his bedroom came a cell phone buzzing with an unfamiliar tone and he froze.

If his plan was to leave before the awkward morning after—and that was *always* the plan—he was on borrowed time.

Since nothing came back to him from Molly, he moved onto Plan B and scrawled out a quick note: *Sorry, had to get to work, take your time.*

Then he hesitated. Did she even know his name? Having no idea, he added: *I'm leaving cash for an Uber or Lyft—Lucas.*

He dropped some money next to the note and grimaced at himself for still being a complete asshole. He stared down at his phone.

Still nothing from Molly, which meant she wasn't going to save the day. She was smart, sharp, and amazing at her job, but for reasons unknown, she wasn't exactly interested in pleasing anyone, *especially* him. Locking up, he left his apartment.

The Pacific Pier building was over a century old and sat in the center of the Cow Hollow district of San Francisco. It was five stories of corbeled brick, exposed iron trusses, and big windows built around a legendary fountain. Retail and businesses took up the ground and second floors, with residential on the third and fourth. The fifth-floor penthouse belonged to his friend Spence Baldwin, who owned the building.

All of it was currently decorated for the holidays like it was about to star in a Hallmark movie.

Lucas jogged down two flights of stairs to the second floor, passing by the building manager's office and the offices of a nonprofit to get to Hunt Investigations. He was fully prepared to be blasted by Molly at her front desk—not just for his text, but for his appearance at all. Off duty since the shooting, he wasn't supposed to be back at work until next week, and that was *if* his doctor cleared him. But Lucas couldn't stay home another day, a fact that didn't have anything to do with the stranger in his bed.

Or at least not *all* due to the stranger in his bed.

He scrubbed a hand over his unshaved jaw, feeling incredibly tense, which for a guy who'd apparently gotten laid last night, didn't make much sense.

Nor did the fact that sitting on a bench outside of Hunt Investigations' front door were two old ladies dressed up as elves. Knitting elves.

The one on the left looked to be making a Christmas stocking. The one on the right was working on something too small to see. They smiled at him in greeting, lips coated in bright red lipstick. Left elf had a smudge of it on her teeth and her little elf cap seemed to quiver on top of her white hair.

Right Elf pulled out her phone. "I just got a text from Louise," she told Left Elf. "It says, 'Don't be late for work tonight, Santa's turned into Grinch. SMH.'" She blinked. "What does S-M-H mean?"

"Shaking my head," Left Elf said.

"Oh thank goodness," Right Elf said, putting a hand to her heart. "I thought it meant Sex Might Help."

They both cackled over that before they saw Lucas.

"Hello there, young man," Left Elf said. "We were hoping you were Molly. We've got a problem involving a bad Santa and she said to meet her here."

"A bad Santa," Lucas repeated, starting to wonder if maybe he was still in bed dreaming this day.

"Yes, we work for him. Obviously," Right Elf said, gesturing to herself.

"You're . . . Santa's elves," he said slowly. "And you work for him at . . . the North Pole?"

"Right." Left Elf snorted. "We work right here in the city like you, at the Christmas Village in Soma, in too tight costumes for too little money. Honey, didn't your mama ever tell you Santa isn't real?"

Okay, so they didn't believe they were *real* elves. That was a relief. Lucas had a great uncle who sometimes thought he was Batman, but that was only on the nights he drank away his social security checks with his cronies.

"Santa promised us half of the profits," Right Elf said. "To go to the charities of our choice. Last year we made enough to give big *and* hit up Vegas for a long weekend."

Left Elf nodded with a smile. "I've still got Elvis's underwear from that big impersonator party we were invited to, remember, Liz?"

Liz nodded. "But this year, we're not getting anything. Santa says there aren't any profits, that he's barely breaking even. But that can't be true because he just bought himself a brand-new Cadillac. Molly's my neighbor, you see."

Lucas didn't see at all. He was good at certain things, such as at his job of investigating and seeking out the asshats of the world and righting justice. He was good at taking care of his close-knit family. He was good, when he wanted to be, in the kitchen. And—if he said so himself—also in bed.

But he was not good in social situations, such as those that required small talk, especially with old ladies dressed up as elves. "This really isn't the sort of case that Hunt Investigations takes on," he said.

"But Molly said you're an elite security and investigative firm that employs finders and fixers for hire, whoever needs them."

Not *strictly* true. A lot of the jobs they took on were routine; criminal, corporate and insurance investigations along with elite security contracts, surveillance, fraud, and corporate background checks. But some weren't routine at all, such as forensic investigations, the occasional big bond bounty hunting, government contract work . . .

Nailing a bad Santa wasn't on the list.

"Do you know when Molly might arrive?" Left Elf asked. She was looking at him even as her knitting needles continued to move at the speed of light. "We'll just wait for her."

"I don't know her schedule," Lucas said. And that was the truth. Hunt Investigations was run by the biggest badass he'd ever met. Archer Hunt, and he employed a team that was the best of the best. Lucas was honored to be a part of that team. All of them, himself included, would step in front of a bullet for each other, and had.

Literally, in his case.

The lone woman in their midst was Molly Malone, equally fearless, though in other ways. She was the one to keep them all on their toes. No one would dare venture into her domain at her desk and put their hands on her stuff to check her schedule, but he could at least ask around. "I'll go check her ETA," he said and headed inside.

He found Archer and Joe in the employee room inhaling donuts. Grabbing one for himself, he nodded to Archer and looked at Joe, one of Lucas's best friends and also his work partner. "Where's your sister?"

Joe shrugged and went for another donut. "Not her keeper. Why?"

"There're two elves outside waiting to talk to her."

"Still?" Archer shook his head. "I told them we wouldn't take their case." He headed out front. Lucas followed because if his social niceties game was stale, Archer had *zero* social niceties game.

"Ladies," Archer said to the elves. "As I explained earlier, your case isn't the kind of case we take on."

"Oh we heard you," Left Elf said. "We're just waiting for Molly. She promised to help us personally if you wouldn't."

Archer looked pained. "Molly doesn't take on cases here. She's office staff."

The two elves looked at each other and then tucked

away their knitting. "Fine," Left Elf said. "We'll just go straight to her at home then."

Archer waited until they'd gotten on the elevator before turning to Lucas. "Why are you here?"

"Gee, good to see you too, boss man."

"Let me rephrase," Archer said. "How's your side? You know, where you have a GSW?"

"It's no longer a gunshot wound. It's practically just a scratch now. I'm good enough to get back to work."

"Uh-huh." Archer looked unimpressed. And . . . still pissed. Lucas had been hoping that he'd gotten himself out of the doghouse by now, but apparently not.

"I didn't get a report from your doctor clearing you," Archer said.

Lucas squelched a grimace. His doctor had told him—repeatedly—at *least* one more week. But he'd be dead of boredom by another week. "We're having a minor difference in opinion."

"Shit." Archer swiped a hand down his face. "You know I can't put you back on the job until he clears you."

"If I stay home another day, I'll lose my shit."

"It's only been two weeks since you were shot and nearly bled out before we got you to the hospital," Archer said. "*Way* too close of a call."

"Practically ancient history."

Archer shook his head. "Not even close. And I told you to abort. Instead, you sent the team out to safety and then you alone hauled ass deeper into the yacht, knowing it was on fire thanks to our asshole perps trying to sink it for the insurance payout."

"I went deeper because there was still someone on board," Lucas reminded him. "Their lead suspect's teenage kid. He'd been holed up and had fallen asleep watching TV. He would've died if I'd left him."

"And instead *you* almost did."

Lucas blew out a breath. They'd had this argument in the hospital. They'd had it twice since. He didn't want to have it again. Especially since he wasn't sorry he'd disobeyed a direct order. "We saved an innocent. You'd have done the same damn thing. So would any of us."

Archer looked over at Joe, who'd been silent through this entire exchange.

Joe lifted a shoulder, an admission that yeah, he might've done the same thing. And so would Archer, and Lucas damn well knew it.

"Shit," Archer finally said. "Fine. I'll unground you, but only for light duty until I hear from your doctor personally that you're one hundred."

Lucas didn't dare smile or pump a fist in triumph. "Deal."

Archer went from looking pissy to mildly amused. "You don't know what light duty I'm going to make you do yet."

"Anything would be better than staying at home," he said fervently.

"Glad to hear you say that." Archer jabbed a thumb

at the door. "Molly's going to want to take those elves seriously. She's been asking to take on a case for months now, but our cases have all been too risky."

Lucas rubbed his side. Wasn't that the damn truth. "And?"

"And *your* 'light duty' job is to make sure she turns those elves down," Archer said. "She's not ready yet."

Joe nodded his agreement on that and Lucas let out a mirthless laugh. He understood why Molly's boss might tell her not to take on a case, but her brother should know better. "Hello, you've met her, right?" Lucas asked them. "No one tells Molly what to do."

"Improvise," Archer said, unmoved. "And keep in mind, you're still in hot water with me. So be careful." He looked at Joe. "Give us a minute."

Joe looked at Lucas and left the room.

"You've got something else to say?" Lucas asked Archer.

"Yeah. Don't screw this up. And don't sleep with her either."

Granted, Lucas had never been all that discriminating when it came to the fairer sex, but this was Molly they were talking about. She was the baby sister of his friend and coworker, which meant she was *not* on his radar. At least not during the day.

The nights were something else altogether because there'd been more than a few times where she'd starred in his fantasies—his own deep, dark secret since he liked breathing. "I wouldn't sleep with her."

Archer looked behind him to make sure Joe had left. "Elle and I saw you at the pub last night, flirting with her."

This had Lucas's full attention. "What?"

"Yeah, and what the hell were you thinking? You were lucky Joe was late."

He'd flirted with Molly? Was he crazy? He'd long ago learned to ignore the undercurrent of electricity between them because he had zero interest in mixing business and pleasure, and even less interest in hurting her.

And he *would* eventually hurt her.

Not to mention what Joe would do to him after he did. And if Joe failed in this new mission, Archer would happily finish him off, and they'd both have every right. But Lucas wouldn't go there, ever. His job had come between him and The One a few times now, so he'd shifted his priorities. He still loved women, just not one woman—and he was good with that and who he was.

Except . . . sometimes, like two weeks ago when he'd almost died on the job and had been forced off duty, he knew he was fooling himself. He'd been left feeling far more alone than he liked to admit. He looked at guys like Archer and Joe, both who'd managed to make love work for them just fine, and he wondered what the hell he was doing wrong.

Drawing a deep breath, he thought of the woman in his bed two flights up. Maybe for starters, he should try to remember the name of the women he'd just slept with. "Trust me," he said. "Nothing happened with Molly last night."

"Uh-huh."

"No, really. Apparently, I was preoccupied with someone else."

Archer went brows up. "The new brunette at the bar?" He then clapped Lucas on the shoulder. "Glad to hear you're not going to have to die today."

"Yeah, well, when Molly finds out you've put me on babysitting duty, she's going to kill us both."

"That's why she's not going to find out."

Lucas stared at Archer, a very bad feeling coming over him. "I'm supposed to keep it from her?"

"Now you're getting it."

Lucas didn't know much about Molly's past other than something bad happened to her a long time ago and she still had a limp from whatever it'd been. Joe had kept a tight lid on his and Molly's rough childhood. Both brother and sister had some serious trust issues. He shook his head glumly. "This is *worse* than monitor duty."

"Is it worse than dying?" Archer asked mildly.

Shit. Lucas went back upstairs. He needed a shower, fresh clothes, and a clear head before he faced Molly, as well as a good story because apparently he couldn't tell her the truth. He hoped to hell that a long hot shower would clear his brain enough to come up with something believable, because something else Molly was—sharp as they came. He stalked through his bedroom, hit the switch on the wall and froze.

The brunette was still in his bed.

At the bright light flooding the room, she gasped and sat straight up, clutching the sheet to her chin, her hair a wild cloud around her face.

And not a stranger's face either.

Molly's face.

Molly was in his bed and his first thought was *oh shit*. His second thought tumbled right on the heels of that—he *was* going to die today after all, slowly and painfully.

Chapter 2

#TheyDontKnowThatWeKnowTheyKnow

Molly Malone didn't have a lot of experience at the whole morning-after scenario. She wasn't big on going out much, mostly because all she wanted to do after a long day of work was take off her work clothes, chill, and *not* get dressed up and go out on some date with a guy who thought that by date three he should get laid.

Last night had been different for several reasons, one of which happened to be standing at the foot of the bed, his short, silky dark hair tousled; scowl on his very hot, unshaven face; hands on his lean hips. He wore rumpled cargoes and the same black T-shirt he'd worn last night, the one that hugged all his sinewy strength and could make a woman's mouth water.

But not hers. Instead she lifted her chin into his

terse silence. Lucas was a man of few words. He could say more with an annoyed exhale than anyone she knew. "What?" she asked.

"I'm . . . confused."

Probably not an easy admission for a guy who always knew what to do or say. But she had to admit, seeing him a little off his axis, something she'd bet the tough, hardened investigator rarely allowed anyone else to see, made her want to mess with him. Yes, sometimes she liked to live dangerously. "And you're confused about . . . ?"

His warm, deep brown eyes met hers, but he didn't answer.

"You didn't seem confused last night," she said with more bravado than she felt.

He scowled. But more interestingly, he also paled. Which, considering he'd gotten his sexy bronzed skin tone from his Brazilian mother, was quite the feat.

"Maybe you should tell me what happened last night," he said.

"You first. What do you remember?"

"We were at the pub." He frowned. "And then I woke in bed with you."

Oh boy. After one of Hunt's longtime clients had shown up and had lifted his glass with "this one's for Lucas, who saved my ass and my life," he'd tossed back his drink, clearly expecting Lucas to do the same.

Which he had.

Shortly after that, Lucas's constant sharp edge had softened, though she'd been the only one to notice. To make sure he got upstairs to his place safe and sound, she'd taken him herself. He'd been both a smartass and a pain in her ass as she'd bossed him to bed, asking if she'd been mean Nurse Ratchet in another life.

It'd been a direct hit because she'd played the hard-ass nurse nearly all of her life to her dad. She'd had to.

"Molly," he said tightly now, clearly out of patience.

Fine. He wanted to know what had happened. A recap might be fun. "Well, for starters," she said, "you told me you had a crush on me."

"Bullshit."

Okay, fine, he hadn't. And *ouch*. "You're so sure about that?" she asked, knowing he wasn't. He couldn't be. By the time she'd gotten him here, he'd been really out of it. Having never seen him anything less than 100 percent in control of himself and everything around him, she'd been worried about him.

And had been ever since he'd gotten shot two weeks ago on the job, the memory of which still made her heart clutch. According to Archer and Joe, Lucas had continuously denied being anything but "fine," but there'd been shadows in his eyes last night and a new hollowness that she recognized.

Deeply buried pain.

Being shot had brought back some bad memories for him and no one understood that more than she.

Still standing at the foot of the bed, hands on hips,

his expression dialed to Not Happy, he blew out a breath. "Tell me what else."

She'd grown up in a house made of testosterone. It'd been just her dad, her brother, and herself, and she'd learned early on how to handle the male psyche. Her best strategy had always involved humor. "I don't know if I should say. You look ready to have a mantrum."

He scowled. "What the hell's a mantrum?"

"It's like a tantrum, only worse because a grown-ass man is having it." She smiled.

He did not. The muscles in his jaw ticked. "I don't have mantrums. I want to know exactly what I said." He paused. "And did."

So he really didn't remember, which was both a disappointment and an opportunity. "You said, and I quote . . ." She lowered her voice to imitate his low base tone. "'I'm gonna rock your world, baby.'"

He closed his eyes and muttered something about being a dead man walking . . .

But she couldn't help noticing he didn't doubt that he'd come onto her. Interesting. Maybe even . . . thrilling. Not that it changed a thing. She wasn't interested in him, period. To be interested meant putting herself out there and being willing to fall. And to do those things, she had to be vulnerable.

Not going to happen. Not ever again.

Nope, at the ripe old age of nearly twenty-eight, she was done, thank you very much. Not that this stopped her from starting to feel a little bit insulted at

Lucas's attitude. "I'm not sure I see what the problem is," she said.

"Are you kidding me?" His voice was morning scratchy and sexy as hell, damn him. She could tell he hadn't had any caffeine yet today.

And neither had she. And worse, she'd not taken off her makeup the night before out of worry and stress over the man currently glaring at her, so she probably looked like a raccoon.

A raccoon with really bad morning bed head.

Ignoring him, she tossed back the bedding. And it was some really great bedding too. She'd need a raise from Archer before she could afford anything close to this quality.

Lucas seemed to suddenly choke on his own tongue, prompting her to look down at herself. Not wanting to sleep in her one and only party dress, she'd . . . *borrowed* one of his T-shirts last night. It hit her at mid-thigh and was softer than any T-shirt she'd ever had and the truth was, he wasn't going to get it back.

"Is that my shirt?" he asked.

"Yes." The funny thing was that on the job, Lucas was the steady, unflappable, stoic one. Nothing got to him, nothing penetrated. He was "it's all good" Lucas Knight. But he wasn't all good now. He thought they'd slept together and though he was doing a great job at hiding it, he was freaking out.

Craning his neck, he eyed the chair, and her dress on it. Her heels lay haphazardly on the floor, her champagne lace bra on top of them. Closing his eyes, he ran a hand over his scruffy jaw. "Just shoot me now."

She crossed her arms over her chest. "You don't remember any of it?"

He paused, dropped his hand and opened his eyes on hers. "Just how much of *'it'* was there?"

"Wow," she said in her best pissy tone. She had no idea what she thought she was doing poking the bear like this, but his clear unhappiness at the thought of them being together felt like an insult.

"Just, please God, tell me it was all consensual," he said, not playing. In fact, he was more serious than she'd ever seen him.

Well, if he was going to go all hero-like on her . . . She sighed. "Of course the evening was entirely consensual."

He nodded and sank to the chair holding her dress.

"Hey," she said, adding temper to insulted. "I didn't say it was *bad.*"

"How about we say it didn't happen at all?"

Oh no. No way was she going to let him off the hook that easy. She arched a brow. "Or did it?" She desperately wanted to get off the bed and dressed, but here was the thing. In the mornings, her right leg was particularly unaccommodating. Numb from her knee to the top of her thigh, it always took her a long few minutes to stand up first thing. And a cane, which she kept by her bed and hated more than green vegetables, and she hated green vegetables a lot. The whole thing involved a lot of whimpering and gasping with pain as she stretched and worked and coaxed the leg into working.

But hell if she'd do that with an audience. Pride before the fall and all that. "I think I hear your cell buzzing from the other room," she said.

"Shit." He turned to the door, but not before pointing at her. "Don't move."

Right. The minute he was gone, she slid out of the bed. Her right leg predictably didn't hold and she dropped to her knees. "Dammit," she whispered as nerve pain shot through her thigh in a series of bolt lightning blasts. "Dammit . . ." She grimaced through the cramp and slowly rose, breathing through the pain in short little pants as she'd learned to do.

"My phone wasn't ringing—" Lucas broke off and then he was there, right there, steadying her with hands on her hips. "You okay?"

"Yes!" She shoved his hands away and tried to push his big body back too, but he was an immovable tree when he wanted to be and he stayed right here, supporting her until, finally dammit, she got her leg beneath her. She probably would have even relented and used her cane if it'd been here, not that she intended to admit it. "I've got this," she muttered, stepping free, incredibly aware of how little she was wearing and how much he was.

And worse, the look in his eyes didn't have anything to do with sexy times, but *pity*. "I said I'm fine."

He lifted his hands. "I heard you, loud and clear."

"But you don't believe it."

"Hard to when you're pale from pain," he said. "Sit down."

"No."

"Molly," he said in that frustrated voice again. But then he hit her with a zinger she didn't see coming. "Please," he said quietly.

Well, hell. She sat at the foot of the bed, and the fact that she did it just before her leg gave out again was her own little secret.

"There's something I need to talk to you about," he said very seriously.

"I'm not going to rate your performance last night."

"That's not—" He paused, his eyes sharpened. "Wait. What does that mean?"

"Nothing."

"So you're saying I *did* suck."

She had to laugh. "Well, if you can't remember it, how good could it really have been, right?"

She was only teasing of course, but he frowned like the possibility that he hadn't been heart-stoppingly amazing had never crossed his mind until that very moment. "What did you want to talk about?" she asked.

Still looking distracted, he shook his head. "Two elves were waiting on you at the office this morning."

She raised a brow. "Are you still drunk?"

"No, really. It was your neighbor and a friend. They were talking about their bad Santa."

"Mrs. Berkowitz," she said, remembering. "She's

been working at a small pop-up Christmas village in Soma and thinks there's something nefarious going on."

"You can't take this case on, Molly. You've got to turn her down."

She raised her eyebrows. "I know you didn't just tell me what to do. Even if we did sleep together."

She meant him to react to that and he did, with a grimace. "Okay, first, this"—he waggled a finger between them—"*didn't* happen."

"And you're so sure about that, are you?" she asked.

Assuming by the way his mouth opened and then closed, he wasn't sure of anything right about now. Now that they were both irritated, she got up again and dammit, Dammit, her leg still hurt. She paused, but didn't see any way around letting him see her limp over to her clothes.

But for the record, she hated it.

Incredibly aware of his quiet gaze on her as she moved, she didn't look at him. *This* was why she didn't do morning afters. Well that and morning breath.

"Do you wake up like this every morning?" he asked quietly.

"No. I usually wake up with a good attitude, but then idiots happen."

"I meant your leg," he said, ignoring her outburst. "You're hurting."

She sighed. Honestly, she was *always* hurting. "I'm fine." She stepped into her dress and pulled it up under his T-shirt, working like a trapeze artist to not flash him as she got it into place. Leaving his T-shirt on—she was so keeping it—she moved to the door. "Gotta go."

"Wait." He caught her at the door. "About last night."

"I know. You don't want it broadcasted blah blah."

"Whatever happened last night," he said, eyes very intense. "It can't happen again."

Something deep inside her quivered in . . . disappointment? And here was the thing. She knew what had happened last night. Nothing. But it still made her mad, so she snorted. "Don't worry. With lines like 'I'm gonna rock your world, baby,' it most definitely won't happen again."

He started to nod, but stopped. Winced. "Did I— *Shit*." He stared down at his work boots for a moment before meeting her gaze again, his disarmingly concerned. "I made it good for you, right?"

Her every single erogenous zone got a little wiggly at the thought, which annoyed the hell out of her. She shrugged.

He looked horrified. "I didn't?"

The truth was, if he set his mind to it, she had no doubt he could make it *good for her* without even trying. Not that he was going to ever get the chance. Yes he was smart, resourceful, confident, and incredibly quick-witted. On the job, he was doggedly aggressive with razor sharp instincts that rarely failed him, things that no doubt suited him in bed as well—and the women lucky enough to be there with him. All very sexy, attractive traits in a man . . . for a normal woman.

But she wasn't normal. So she gave him one last vague smile and reached for the door.

He put a hand flat on the wood, holding it closed.

"Move," she said.

"You're still wearing my shirt."

And if she wore it to work, everyone would know they spent the night together. She yanked it off, threw it at him and tugged open the door.

"Molly."

There was a touch of exasperation in his voice, and also possibly regret. Since both made her want to punch him, she kept going.

"The elves," he said to her back. "The bad Santa case. Tell me you're not taking it on."

"I can't tell you that, since I'm no longer talking to you." She made her way down the stairs and to the courtyard, walking past the pet shop, the office supply shop, and the new day spa, heading right for The Canvas Shop. One of the people who worked there, Sadie, had given Molly her one and only tattoo, and a friendship had been born of the experience.

Sadie waved at her. She wasn't alone. Ivy was with her. Ivy operated the taco truck on the street along the back of the building. Like Molly, Ivy sometimes ducked into The Canvas Shop for some calm sanity, which Sadie always provided along with a side of sarcasm.

Both women had become new friends even if it felt like they'd known each other forever.

"How's things?" Molly asked.

"Given that it's a work day . . ." Ivy shrugged. She

hopped down off of the counter and headed to the door. "Try to have a good one!" she called back before vanishing.

"And you?" Molly asked Sadie.

Sadie gazed at the shop's small Christmas tree, under which were a nice stack of wrapped presents, and sighed. "Well, none of the gifts with my name on them have barked yet, which is disappointing . . ." She took in Molly's appearance and her eyes widened. "Whoa. Wait a minute. You were wearing those same clothes when I last saw you. Yesterday. Am I witnessing the rarest of creatures, Molly Malone making the never before seen *Morning Walk of Shame*?"

Molly grimaced.

And Sadie grinned. "Yay, Christmas came early for me. Did all your parts still remember how to work?"

"Okay, it's not what it looks like."

"Bummer," Sadie said.

"Can I borrow your shower?"

"Absolutely," Sadie said, nodding so that her jet black hair, streaked with purple, flew around her face. "And in exchange for the deets, I'll even throw in some clothes."

This was a good deal because Sadie had amazing clothes. Today she was in a pretty flowy top, skin-tight jeans, and some seriously kickass ankle boots that would have had Molly drooling if she wasn't already completely thrown over the night and morning she'd just had. "No deets," she said firmly. "But I'll buy you a coffee and muffin from the coffee shop on my first break if you have Advil."

Sadie pulled a small bottle from her purse. "Welcome to adulthood, where having Home Advil and Purse Advil is everything. Who was he?"

"Who?"

Sadie rolled her eyes and Molly sighed. "I'm not telling."

Sadie cocked her head and studied her. "Lucas."

"What the actual hell," Molly said.

Sadie's eyes nearly popped out of her head. "Are you serious? I'm right?" She laughed with sheer delight. "Nice choice," she said approvingly.

"No. No, he's not a 'nice' choice, or any choice," Molly said. "He's . . ."

"Hot?" Sadie inquired.

Well, okay, yes.

"Perfect?" Sadie asked.

"No," Molly said quickly. *"Not* perfect."

"Good," Sadie said. "'The One' should never be perfect."

"And he's not The One either," Molly said. "That's absurd." For many, many reasons, not the least being that while Lucas was incredibly serious on the job, off the job he was . . . not. He joked around nonstop and women tended to flock to that charming flirt thing he had down pat. But not her.

Never her.

She had . . . trust issues with that kind of guy, big-time.

"Okay," Sadie said, nodding. "You're not ready for The One. Make him The One for a night then. Before someone else comes along and snags him up."

Molly opened her mouth and then shut it, afraid to let anything out. Such as how much she hated the idea of Lucas sleeping with another woman. Which wasn't a comfortable realization at all. Get over it, she told herself firmly, and fast.

By the time she walked into Hunt's office twenty minutes later, she'd lost her amusement for the game of letting Lucas think they'd slept together. Mrs. Berkowitz was no longer waiting on her, but a million other things were, including a battle with Hunt's health insurance company over some of the coverage from Lucas's medical care.

Normally, she loved her job. There hadn't been money for her to go to college, and her plan to get a track and field scholarship had died when she'd wrecked her leg. Out of desperation she'd gone into admin work while Joe had been away in the military. She'd moved around a bit, gathering skills, until Joe had come home and landed at Hunt Investigations, bringing her into the fold as well.

But after two years behind the front desk, she wanted more. She'd begged Archer to let her also take on the background checks and research that overloaded his men, and he'd been all too happy to comply. She'd kicked ass too, providing them with superior intel all year. Yeah, they had their resident IT person—Lucas himself—but she could be just as good as him with some training.

Probably.

In any case, she'd loved getting a foot in the investigative door, but instead of satisfying her, she only craved more.

She wanted to go out in the field.

Archer had told her point-blank that while she had a brilliant mind and he was grateful for it, he couldn't let her get hurt. Joe had been far less diplomatic, flatly refusing to discuss it with her. And that's when she'd realized that when they looked at her they didn't see brilliant investigation work, they saw vulnerability and weakness. And she got it. Appearance made a strong impression, and her physical appearance suggested weakness, not strength.

There was nothing she could do about that but prove them wrong.

"Need you to fax us the paperwork," the insurance guy said in her ear after being on hold for thirty minutes. "I told you this already, last week."

"Right," Molly said. "I'll just jump into my De-Lorean and drive back to 1987 to get my fax machine. Can't I just scan you the pages?"

"We don't accept scans. They must be faxed or snail-mailed."

She needed more caffeine for this, and after her call, she hit up the staff room, where she came face-to-face with Archer. She pointed at him. "You turned away those two sweet little old ladies who needed your help."

"We don't take those kinds of cases."

She glared at him. "You mean old people cases?"

In typical Archer fashion, he refused to engage. "We're booked up solid for the next five months. I don't have the manpower available."

"Or the interest?"

Archer didn't sigh, but he looked like he wanted to. "Look, I know you're bored. I know you want to do more. I get it. I'm working on it. But I'm not going to throw you into things without the proper training and field experience before you're ready. You'll eventually get a caseload of your own. I promise you that, but when it's right. Okay?"

She sighed. "Okay."

"You're a valuable part of this company, Molly. I'm not just placating you here. All I'm asking for is a little patience on your end until you're ready."

"Are you sure it's not the other way around? That you're not ready for me?"

At that, she got a rare smile and a low laugh. "The world isn't ready for you." Archer let his smile fade. "But they will be, and when things happen, you'll be prepared, and safe because of it."

"And in the meantime?"

"I'm bringing you in on two new cases where we need your research and intel. They're in your in-box waiting on you."

She knew this was a bone, but she'd take it. And though she appreciated the vote of confidence, she was having trouble accessing her patience. Especially when she ran into Joe a few minutes later.

"You're not taking on any cases," her brother

said flatly while stuffing a huge sandwich down his throat. He'd just come in from a takedown that had involved the entire team and he had three minutes before he had to head back out again for surveillance on another job.

His job rocked, dammit. "I think I have a right to do whatever job I want to do," she said coolly.

Joe sighed and put down his sandwich. A rare occurrence, letting go of his food, signaling he was very serious. "Molly, listen to me. I can't think of you in this job that I do, in the thick of it, with the constant danger."

"And yet *you* do it. Do you think I don't worry? Or that Kylie doesn't?" she asked, referring to Joe's better half.

"I just don't want you to get hurt," he said stubbornly.

The unspoken word being *again*. Because they both knew what he was *really* referring to, which was the one time she'd been involved in his world and she'd nearly died. She still carried the scars, inside and out.

He blamed himself.

But she did not. "Look," she said softly, wanting to make him understand and end this discussion once and for all. "I'm smart. I'm resourceful. I'm resilient."

He nodded his agreement, which warmed her just a little bit. "All things I learned from you," she said and squeezed his hand, smiling at the look of surprise on his face. "You've always taken care of me, Joe. *Always*," she repeated fiercely. "And I'm thankful and grateful for it. But I'm good, okay? I'm better than good. And it's time for you to let me go, to let me make my own decisions."

"I don't know if I can," he admitted. "But I'll try."

"Try real hard," she suggested.

Chapter 3

#BadSanta

By the time Molly got home that evening, she was completely done in. She lived in Outer Sunset, about twenty minutes from work on a good day with no traffic.

But there was always traffic.

When she walked up the few steps to her apartment building, she found three elves waiting for her.

Seemed they'd multiplied.

The shortest elf was Mrs. Berkowitz, her neighbor. The other elf was Mrs. White, Mrs. Berkowitz's knitting partner. Molly had never seen Elf Number Three before, who was younger than the other two by a good decade. "Evening, ladies," Molly said, getting her first real smile of the day. "Looking good."

"Thank you, dear," Mrs. Berkowitz said. "But your boss said he wouldn't take our case."

"I know. I heard. I'm sorry—"

"We really need your help. Santa's stealing from us."

Molly leaned against her porch railing. "You know for a fact that he's actually stealing?"

"Yes. He's saying there aren't any profits to pay us from, but he has money. Bingo alone brings it in, I've seen the piles of cash. We need your help," she said so earnestly that her little elf ears quivered.

Molly looked over at Mrs. White, who nodded. And then Elf Number Three.

"That's Janet," Mrs. Berkowitz said of the sweet-looking, softly rounded woman. "She heard us talking about the money and wants to join the cause."

"The cause?" Molly repeated.

"Yes, the Santa Claus cause," Mrs. Berkowitz said with a straight face. "We worked hard all year. We won't stand for being ripped off, it's not right."

If true, it wasn't right at all. The men in her life might not understand her need to step in, but they should. It'd been from them that she'd learned to do the morally right thing even when no one else believed. "We'll get to the bottom of this," she promised.

Mrs. Berkowitz looked relieved. "Oh, thank you, we so appreciate it. And of course we want to pay you, but until we can get our hands on our money—"

"It's okay," Molly said. "I'm not officially an investigator anyway. But if we get to the bottom of this case, I might be able to convince my boss to let me be one, so see, we're helping each other."

"Thank you," Mrs. Berkowitz said fervently. "You're a godsend."

Several hours later, Molly sat in her bed staring at

her laptop. She'd researched the Christmas village, the owners, and the bingo hall. The hall itself was leased by the same company that leased the adjoining lot and parking area for the Christmas village. St. Michael's Bingo. Near as she could tell, in spite of the company's name, it wasn't affiliated with a church or specific charity. And Mrs. Berkowitz had been right. According to Yelp ratings and other reviews, it did appear that bingo brought in lots of business and was extremely popular.

So why hadn't Santa been able to pay his elves?

And why couldn't she find the names of the people associated with running St. Michael's Bingo? The website was one page consisting of nothing more than a pic of the village with their hours and address listed. No contact, no number.

Molly called Mrs. Berkowitz. "Who runs the village and the bingo hall?"

"Santa."

Molly rubbed the spot between her eyes. "Does Santa have a name?"

"Santa."

Molly had to laugh. "The guy who puts on the Santa suit. What's his name?"

"Oh. We call him Crazy Nick."

"As in . . . St. Nicolas?" Molly asked.

"No, as in Crazy Nick."

Okay, she'd bite. "What makes him crazy?"

"Well, he's had four wives, for one. And they all work for him even though they hate him. That's what makes him crazy. He's always grumpy. If I had four ex-wives, I don't think I'd want them working for me."

"Does Crazy Nick have a last name?" Molly asked.

"Probably, but I don't know it. I could ask one of his exes for you on my next shift. But I've gotta go, dear. *Jeopardy*'s on."

Molly disconnected. She needed to dig deeper, but for that she needed her work computer and superior programs. Telling herself she'd get up early, she went to bed.

And dreamed of warm, deep brown eyes the color of her favorite thing in the world—chocolate. She dreamed of a wicked smile to go with, and hands that had pulled her close, but not to sleep . . .

The next afternoon, Lucas was dividing his time between peering out through his binoculars and eyeing the screen of his tablet, which was streaming a live feed from the bugged building they were surveilling. He was doing his damnedest to concentrate on the job instead of how cruel life was that he'd slept with Molly but couldn't remember a single minute of it.

Was her body as warm and curvy as it seemed in those sexy business dresses she always wore?

And what did she wear underneath? Lace? Silk? He had absolutely zero preference; he loved any of it. Had she slowly stripped out of everything and then run her hands all over his body? Had he gotten his mouth on hers? Did she taste as good as he imagined she would—

"It's effing hot in here," Joe muttered.

Since the guy had been complaining for hours, Lucas didn't respond. Especially because it *was* hot in here.

"I'm hungry," Joe said.

Lucas lowered the binoculars and pulled out an earbud of his headset. "Anything else?"

"My ass is numb."

"And you want me to what exactly?" Lucas asked.

"Just saying," Joe muttered and blew out a breath. "We've been here forever."

Here, being the inside of a surveillance van. They were an hour north of San Francisco, in Sonoma at the Sonoma Raceway. And yeah, for December, the day was unseasonably warm and it *was* effing hot, and they'd run out of food a few hours ago.

He was there for surveillance and to record any evidence, but had been ordered to stay away from any real action, with Joe as backup on the off chance things were sour.

Lucas was ridiculously grateful to be on the job at all.

"I'm just saying," Joe said.

"What are you just saying?"

Joe gave him a look. "Why aren't you listening?"

Because I'm fantasizing about your sister naked and under me, moaning my name . . .

"This isn't going to happen today," Joe decided, pulling off his headset. "Intel was wrong."

Intel on today's surveillance had come from

Molly's research, research that Lucas had gone over with a fine-tooth comb. "My gut says otherwise," he said. And his gut was almost always right. He'd honed his instincts at his previous job with the DEA, where he'd worked undercover for five years. Several of his cases had involved huge insurance fraud schemes, and it'd been one of those jobs to cost Lucas the love of his life, however indirectly.

Not that he was going there.

In any case, *this* job was going to be textbook. Their client, a major car manufacturer, had a problem. Some of their employees had been working overtime when a drive shaft had slipped, sending a truck axle crashing to the floor. Seven employees had claimed a variety of injuries, though no one had been hit. Three of the employees were back at work. Four employees were still off and had instigated a civil suit against the car manufacturer.

Lucas had dug deep, and in fact he'd done so with Molly's help, discovering that the four employees went way back with each other and were old friends whose lives were entwined to the point that they'd all vacationed together. They each had doctor documentation saying they were unable to work, and yet Molly had tracked credit card records that put all four of them at the Sonoma Raceway for three consecutive weekends.

They were taking race car lessons.

"Maybe you're right about tonight," Joe murmured as two cars pulled into the lot. Two men came out of each car, the four of them meeting the descriptions and photos they had of the "injured" employees. "Damn," he said looking through the lens of his camera, snapping still shots. "You getting this?"

"Yep," Lucas said, filming their entrance. "Still want to leave?"

"Shut up."

When the men vanished inside the racetrack, Lucas and Joe exited their vehicle to get better coverage. And to make sure that the men actually got into race cars.

"I always forget how good she is," Joe murmured as they took their seats in the stands as spectators. "Molly."

Lucas didn't answer. Because he never forgot how good Molly was.

Well, except for the other night . . .

Chapter 4

BahHumbug

It was late afternoon the next day before Lucas and Joe were able to show everyone in the team meeting the footage of the supposedly injured employees joyriding in race cars. The whole team was in a conference meeting doing post op; Archer, Joe, Lucas, Max, Reyes, and Porter, along with Carl, Max's hundred-pound Doberman. Everyone was still dressed from their last job—meaning they were all loaded for bear, having come straight off a high-stakes takedown that had gone down without a hitch.

Lucas hadn't been in on the action, but once again tasked with running the surveillance van, which was bullshit. But Archer had been a stone wall on making sure he saw zero action until his doctor fully cleared him, something the guy had refused to do for another full week.

Lucas thought about having Molly call his doctor and tell him that he'd managed to see *plenty* of action in bed several nights ago, but with his luck, she'd tell the doctor the action hadn't been worth the effort.

Now they were debriefing, each giving an oral report of the mission.

"Nice job," Archer said when he'd heard everything they'd done. "Couldn't have closed this one down as fast as we did without your help on the intel."

Lucas opened his mouth to say thanks, but realized Archer had been talking to Molly.

She beamed at the rare compliment from their boss, and Lucas shook his head to himself, once again thinking that Archer and Joe were wrong by trying to clip her wings.

The meeting ended and everyone filed out, leaving for the end of the work day. Lucas stayed seated, opening his laptop as it was his job to type up the report. Another reason to hate his doctor. When his phone buzzed an incoming call from his mom, he hit answer on speaker so he could keep typing.

"Lucas Allen Knight," she said. She'd been in the states for forty years but she still had a slight accent from her homeland, Brazil, and the sound of her voice always made him smile.

Well, usually.

"You've been ignoring me," she said.

He blew out a sigh. "Hi, Mom. And I haven't been ignoring you, I've just been working long hours—"

"Honey, don't even try. I know that this job—unlike your last—doesn't keep you out of commission for weeks at a time."

True, which was part of the reason he had a life again, although he wasn't wholly sure he fully deserved it.

"So how are you, baby?"

He hadn't told her he'd been shot, or that he was on light duty. If he had, she and his older sister, Laura, would have descended on him like dogs on a bone. Sweet, loving dogs, but still . . . "I'm fine, I promise. I'll call you this weekend to catch up."

"You mean you'll come *see* me this weekend."

He heard a snort and turned to find Molly standing there, unabashedly eavesdropping. "Mom." He pressed the heels of his hands into his eye sockets. "I'm overworked here. Where's my sympathy?"

"I have plenty of sympathy. For all the mamas whose sons don't visit them. Did you know that Margaret Ann Wessler's son visits her? And Sally Bennett's son visits her too—"

"I'll come visit you," he said and put a finger to the twitch in his eye.

"For our family Christmas party next weekend."

"Mom—"

"Everyone will be there, Lucas. Even my ex-husband."

"You mean my dad?" he asked wryly. His parents had been divorced for closing in on two decades now and were friends. Well, mostly. In any case, they'd co-parented to the best of their abilities, including co-holiday-celebrating when feasible.

"Yes," his mom said on a sigh. "And if you don't show up, people are going to ask me why *my* son doesn't come visit."

Now both eyes were twitching. "Yes, fine. The Christmas party. I'll be there."

"And Christmas Eve two weeks after that. And Christmas morning too, because—"

"Mom—"

"Don't tell me you're going to be working. If you tell me that, I'm going to call your boss myself. Don't think I won't."

He pictured his mom calling Archer to bitch him out and actually smiled. "I'll be there."

"Okay then." Her voice softened and warmed, as well it should since she just got what she wanted in the first place. "And bring a date to the party—"

"Sorry," he said. "Can't hear you, bad connection—"

"Lucas!"

"Going through a tunnel . . ." He made a staticky sound in his throat before disconnecting.

"Need a little more phlegm in that static," Molly said, clearly amused. "Do you always lie to your mom?"

"Whenever I can get away with it." He pushed his laptop away and met her gaze. "You telling me you never give either of your parents a little fib here and there to keep your sanity?"

"That's what I'm telling you."

"Come on," he said in disbelief. "Never?"

"Well, my dad isn't someone you lie to. He's got one of those top-notch inner lie detectors," she said, tapping her temple. "And my mom . . . she passed away a long time ago."

He stilled and then shook his head at his own stupidity. "I'm an idiot. I'm sorry."

"You didn't know."

"I didn't. But I'm still sorry."

She shrugged and turned to go.

"Molly—"

"Turn off the lights when you're done in here," she said. "I'm shutting down for the night soon."

"Molly."

She turned to him.

"Did the elves come to you?" he asked.

She hesitated. "Yes."

"And you told them what?"

"That I'd help," she said as if he was very dense.

She walked out of the room and he took a deep breath. His mom might be nosy, bossy, manipulative, and couldn't seem to help herself from butting into his life, but she was also loving and protective and would fight to the death for any of the people she considered hers. He couldn't imagine his world without her in it.

But Molly didn't have any of that because her mom was gone.

Not for the first time, he cursed the fact that Joe, as good of a friend as he was, rarely opened up and *never* talked about his family life. In any case, Lucas wished he could take back the last few minutes. Hell, as long as he was rewinding, he'd like to go back a few days to before mixing a shot of bourbon with his pain meds and then sleeping with Molly.

Although if he could remember the sleeping with Molly part, he definitely wouldn't want to take away the memory . . .

He shut off the lights and headed down the hall.

Archer was perched on the edge of Molly's desk going through a file. Joe and Reyes stood near the front door talking.

"You out?" Archer asked Lucas.

"Not yet. Going to finish the report."

Reyes looked at Lucas. "You never did say which chick you ended up with the other night."

Lucas froze. There'd been a lot of times where living or dying had depended on his next move and yet in that instant, all skills deserted him.

"Let me guess," Reyes said. "The stacked brunette at the end of the bar, right? She's new, never seen her before."

Lucas had to strain to remember the brunette. The brunette who hadn't been Molly. He glanced at her and found her staring at him like the cat with a canary.

"It could've been the hot redhead at the pool table," Joe said.

It was a predicament. For one thing, Lucas's alibi was sitting right there, not that he'd point the fin-

ger at her. He'd never do that, and not just because
it would mean his certain death, but because it was
no one's business who she slept with. "Yeah," Lucas
said. "Sure."

"Sure to which?" Reyes asked. "Bar brunette or
pool babe?"

Molly propped her chin in her hands like she was
watching the most fascinating show ever.

"Both?" Joe asked hopefully.

"Pig," Molly said to her brother, who shrugged.

"He's single," Joe said. "Gotta live vicariously
through him now."

"I'll be sure to let Kylie know you think so," Molly
said. "Also, that 'hot redhead' at the pool table has a
name. It's Ivy and she's pretty great."

"Right," Reyes said, pointing at Molly. "Ivy's the
taco truck chick—you know that new taco truck
parked on the corner now? She makes amazing food."

No one answered because everyone was looking
at Lucas, waiting on his answer.

"None of your fucking business," he told the room.

Archer let out a rare laugh and pushed off of
Molly's desk, heading back to his office. "Elle's vote
was that you ended up with no one."

Lucas opened his mouth, caught Molly's gaze, and
then shut it. Elle was going to have to think he was a
loser who made women up in his mind, and it wasn't
because Joe and Archer would kill him. It was because he wouldn't rat out Molly for anything.

Joe and Reyes said their goodbyes and left, and

Molly immediately stood up and grabbed her purse, looking to be suddenly in a hurry.

In a hurry to avoid him, he bet.

"'Night," she said.

"You can run but you can't hide," he said quietly.

She laughed, but still left. When the door closed behind her, Lucas took a step to follow her and then realized someone was watching him.

Archer was back, leaning against the doorjamb. "So . . . how did things really go?"

Lucas knew he wasn't asking about today's job, but it was worth pretending. "Felt good to be out. I'm more than ready."

"Good to know," Archer said. "Now answer the question I asked."

Lucas blew out a breath and gave it to him straight. "I'm not sure Molly can be deterred from taking the bad Santa case. The old ladies hit her pretty hard for a sympathy vote."

"Are you telling me that a couple of old ladies are better at the game than you?"

"Hell no."

"Good," Archer said. "Cuz I've got a new job for you."

"Why am I not feeling excited about this," Lucas muttered.

"If she dives in to help the elves without asking me or Joe for help—"

"Are you kidding me?" Lucas asked. "She's not going to ask you for help. She'll never ask anyone for help and you know it."

"I do," Archer said. "So you're going to *offer* to help her, and keep her safe while you're at it. And since I value my life, you're not going to tell her I put you on the case."

"So . . . if she finds out, I'm the only one who's going to die?"

"Correct," Archer said.

Good to know everyone's six was being protected except his own. He went back to his office. Not feeling all that great about the state of affairs of his life at the moment, he leaned back in his chair and studied his ceiling. Things had been much less complicated before he'd gotten shot. Before he'd slept with the woman who he was supposed to be protecting and keeping safe—without her knowing about it.

Most days after work, he hit the gym or went on a run. But his doctor hadn't cleared him for any of that. His doctor hadn't cleared him for jack shit—including whatever he'd done with Molly . . .

Hold up . . .

If he'd had wild and crazy sex, wouldn't his side hurt like a son of a bitch? He scrunched his abs. A twinge, yes, but no real pain. Inconclusive, dammit. Because chances were, for sex he'd have fought through any pain.

Hmm. He opened his laptop. He wasn't supposed to be able to access his fellow employee files. No one was supposed to be able to. But he'd been hired for his dubious IT skills so it wasn't a stretch for him to locate Molly's home address.

He left the offices and strode through the courtyard that was decorated for the holidays with garlands of evergreen entwined with twinkling white lights in every doorway and window frame, not to mention a huge Christmas tree between the entrance and the alley. He entered the alley, and as expected found Old Man Eddie sitting on an upside-down empty crate. The guy was a sixties throwback with a shock of long white hair that tended to stick up around his head like Einstein's. Everyone, including Spence Baldwin, the owner of the building and Eddie's actual grandson had tried to get Eddie off the streets. All efforts had been met with sweet but steely resistance. Today Eddie was on his phone playing a game, presumably against the man sitting on another crate across from him.

Caleb was in a suit, an expensive one by the looks of it, and yet seemed perfectly at home in the alley.

"Fucker," Eddie said fondly.

Caleb snorted. "Your problem's that you play with your heart, old man."

"Right," Eddie said. "I forgot that you don't have one."

Caleb nodded a quick greeting at Lucas, still playing the game. He was a venture capitalist, some kind of a tech genius, and a longtime client of Hunt Investigations. Lucas had been tasked with guarding the guy's back on several occasions now, and since one of those occasions had involved a near and not accidental mugging where Caleb had entirely held his own with some impressive MMA-like skills, Lucas had nothing but respect for the guy.

"Feeling better than you were the other night?" Caleb asked Lucas.

"Yeah, man, cuz you were looking pretty out of it," Eddie said. "That's probably why that cutie-pie from your office walked you up to bed." He slid him a sly smile. "She didn't leave until morning, so I'm guessing it was a good night for you."

Caleb went brows up and finally gave up the game to stare at Lucas. "Wait—Molly? You spent the night with Molly? You have a death wish or something?"

Or something. "How much for you to never repeat any part of that story?" Lucas said to Eddie, ignoring Caleb for now. He wasn't worried about Caleb. Caleb knew the value of secrets and kept plenty of his own. But Eddie loved and adored nothing as much as some good gossip.

Proving it, the old man smiled slyly and held out his hand.

Shit. Lucas fished out a twenty.

Eddie just kept smiling.

Lucas added a second twenty.

Eddie's hand remained out.

So Lucas added a third twenty, and then a fourth.

"That should do it," Eddie said.

"Sucker," Caleb said with a shake of his head.

Chapter 5

#DefineNice

Lucas drove to Molly's place, trying to concentrate on the radio and the Cal football game playing. He'd gone to Cal State Berkley because that's where the scholarship had been. Also, his dad had gone there; it's where he'd met Lucas's mom—who hadn't been a student but worked at one of the campus cafes. Lucas had never been all that passionate about school, but he was definitely passionate about football. Like his dad, he'd played as a wide receiver for a year, although mostly as a bench warmer, before blowing out his ACL, which had required surgery, but he still loved the game.

But even that love couldn't keep his mind on the Cal broadcast. Instead he was trying to figure out how best to handle Molly. Keeping anything from her was sheer stupidity, but telling her the truth would only make her go undercover and on her own. He couldn't risk that, couldn't risk her.

She lived in Outer Sunset, a district of San Francisco that was the most populated in all of San Francisco. Streets were narrow, buildings old and worn and overfilled, but well cared for.

Her building was no exception. There were eight units, four on the bottom, four on the second floor, which, thanks to the heavy fog, was nearly invisible. Molly lived on the ground floor in one of the units facing the street. Her lights were on, but no one answered his knock. He noted that her neighbor—not one of the elves—was staring at him from behind her curtains with a pinched look on her face, so he sent her what he hoped was a harmless smile and knocked on Molly's door again.

The door still didn't open, but Molly's voice sounded from a hidden speaker. "What do you want?"

"To talk to you." He looked around and spotted a small camera above her porch light. She never failed to surprise him. "Smart," he noted. "Now open up."

"I don't think so."

He stared into the camera. "We need to talk."

"So talk."

"Not happening while I'm standing on your porch with your non-elf neighbor staring at me with her phone in her hand."

"That's just Mrs. Golecky. And she's probably calling the police because you look like a bad guy in your all-black SWAT gear."

He thunked his head against the wood of her door.

"I'd hurry and start talking before the cops arrive," she said.

"You're really going to make me say it out here?"

Silence.

"Okay," he said. "Fine. We'll do this your way, but heads-up, Mrs. Golecky just opened her window so she's getting all of this."

More silence. Never let it be said that Molly took her stubbornness lightly.

He blew out a breath and opened his mouth to tell her that he'd partner up with her on the elf case, but that's not what came out. "I need to know what happened the other night," he said instead. Because he was an idiot.

The door opened and Molly stood there, brows raised. "You sure you want to hear it? I mean . . . suppose you were really bad. And not the good kind of bad."

"I was not." Hell. "Was I?"

"Well, it's a little hard to remember," she said. "Since it didn't take but a minute."

From behind him and across the hedge bush between their front doors, Mrs. Golecky snorted.

Having had enough, he nudged Molly aside and let himself in.

She was grinning at him as he shut and locked her door and faced her. "Looking pretty pleased with yourself," he said.

She shrugged. "I'm just surprised you're being so

persistent on this line of questioning given your level of . . . performance."

"Are you going to keep insulting me or tell me the truth?"

She laughed, and damn, it was a nice sound. "Can't I do both?" she asked.

He gave a single shake of his head and looked around. Her place was small. Tiny, actually, but neat and warm, filled with comfortable-looking furniture and lots of personal touches like pictures and books and thriving plants.

He'd never kept a plant alive in his life. When he'd been with Carrie, they'd shared a place during the times he hadn't been undercover. She'd loved plants too and he'd been banned from touching them, claiming his bad attitude killed them dead.

He hadn't cohabitated with a woman again.

Or owned a plant.

"About the other night," he prompted.

"What about it?" Her eyes were sparkling with amusement. Clearly, she was enjoying the hell out of this.

"I—" He broke off, catching sight of her kitchen table. There were three elves sitting there drinking tea.

"Tell me this is a tea party," he murmured to Molly. "And that you're not figuring out their bad Santa situation."

"Of course I'm trying to figure things out for them. I told them I'd help."

And that's when he realized they were far more alike than he could have imagined.

Molly gestured to the first woman. "You've met Mrs. Berkowitz, my neighbor. And Mrs. White, her knitting partner. And that's Janet, one of their co-workers."

"Here," Mrs. Berkowitz said, holding out a cup of steaming tea toward him. "It's ginkgo. It'll help you with your memory problem."

"And you can take kava and ashwagandha for your, er, not being memorable problem," Janet said.

Then they all cackled while Lucas did his best not to bash his head against the wall. "Any new developments?"

"None of your business," Janet said.

Great. Terrific. With Archer's directive in his head—watch after Molly, don't let anything happen to her—he pulled her aside and hopefully out of ear-shot range. "If you're serious about this—"

"I am," she said, no longer smiling, looking very serious indeed. "And there's something else."

"What?"

"You're going to help me."

Which is exactly what he'd come here to do, but he was curious—and highly suspicious—about why she'd ask. Actually, she hadn't asked at all; she'd told. She was nothing if not Joe's sibling. "What makes you think so?" he asked.

"Because if you don't, I'll tell Archer and Joe about us."

Lucas took a deep inhale. "So you hate me and want me to die."

She laughed. "No." Her smile faded. "But I'm not stupid, Lucas. Or reckless. I can do the legwork on this, but I also want to go to the village and poke around. I need to get a feel for the place and hopefully find someone to talk to, someone who knows Crazy Nick's last name, for one. But I need backup. A partner. Someone who's smart, resourceful, and not afraid to bend a few rules."

"You have my attention," he said.

She smiled. "Do you happen to know anyone else with those attributes besides yourself?"

Shit. He looked into her pretty but sharp-as-hell hazel eyes and knew he was sunk.

She turned from him and moved across her living room to the kitchen to sit at the table with the ladies, clearly still favoring her right leg. In the past, he'd tried asking her about it, several times actually, and she'd always brushed off his concerns while at the same time making it clear it was none of his business.

There was no one more proud or stubborn than Molly.

Well, except for maybe him.

But as time went on, he found himself not just wanting to know what had happened to her, but *needing* to know. He had the feeling it was bad, but as his own past wasn't exactly filled with happy memories, he'd never pushed because he knew what that felt like.

He had the means to dig into her past. At Hunt,

they had the best of the best search programs. Some were so intense and invasive, he could have found the day she'd been conceived and how many cavities her dad might've had at the time. Lucas had used those programs without remorse or regret when it came to work and digging into the scum of the earth as needed.

But he'd never been able to bring himself to dig on Molly. He couldn't justify, even to himself, the invasion of her privacy.

None of which lessened his curiosity any.

Knowing when to fold, he joined the ladies at the table. Mrs. Berkowitz nudged a cup of tea in his direction. He looked at it. It was green, with some flecks swimming around in it. Great. He took a sip and burned his tongue. On top of that, it tasted like ass. "Okay, ladies. Talk to me."

Everyone started talking at once.

He shook his head and held up a hand. "One at a time. You," he said and pointed at Mrs. Berkowitz.

"We work all year long," she said, pulling out her phone. "I have a ledger of work details—Hold up, where are my glasses?"

"On your head," Mrs. White said.

"Oh. Right." She put them on her nose. "Better. Anyway, as you know, we've not been properly paid and we think Santa's guilty of fraud and money laundering."

"Do you have any evidence?" Lucas asked.

"What is it with you and the police always needing evidence?" Mrs. Berkowitz asked. "Isn't that *your* job?"

"So you did already go to the police," Lucas said.

"Yes, but they wouldn't help us without some sort of evidence. The thing is, I know we're right. And then there's the fact that Santa's brother is always around, acting like he's in charge."

"What's wrong with that?" Lucas asked. "Maybe it's a family business."

"It is a family business," she said. "Forty years ago, Santa's brother was a crime boss."

"How can you remember forty years ago when you just forgot where you put your glasses when they were on your head?" Lucas asked.

She glared down that nose at him. "Boy, my long-term memory's like a steel trap."

Molly slid him a small, amused glance. He'd just insulted one of Santa's helpers. Definitely he was on the naughty list.

"Do you have a real name for this guy?" he asked.

"The brother? Tommy Thumbs," Mrs. Berkowitz said. "Back in the day, rumor had it that if you crossed him, he'd cut off your thumb and feed it to his pet snake. He was just a low-level mob guy back then, but he had ambitions. Hence the thumb thing. He wanted to stick out."

Lucas shook his head. "Tommy Thumb was indeed a low-level mob guy in the eighties, but he was killed in a warehouse explosion in the early nineties. His legend's been kept alive by the old-timer loan sharks pretending to be him in order to keep their people in line with the threat of losing their thumbs."

"Wrong," Mrs. Berkowitz said. "He's not dead."

Lucas got serious real fast. "No one's seen Tommy Thumbs in years, and believe me, a bunch of people have been looking. Why do you think it's him? Did you recognize him? And how?"

"Oh, well, I slept with him a bunch of times in the late nineties." She gave a small smile. "And maybe once or twice in the new century as well. *What?*" she said when Mrs. White and Janet gave her a shocked look. "Back in the day, I was a little slower to recognize a horse's patoot when I saw one."

Lucas did his best to block images of Mrs. Berkowitz and Tommy Thumbs getting laid, but he wasn't entirely successful. He pressed the heels of his hands to his eyes and took a deep breath. "Do you still . . ." Shit. He couldn't even say it.

"Do it?" Mrs. Berkowitz asked with a smile. She shrugged. "Not nearly as much these days. First of all, men my age no longer look as good naked, if you know what I mean."

Lucas wished to God he didn't.

"But no, I don't still sleep with Tommy," she said. "He got old and cranky, and mean as a snake. I don't stand for that. I'm a feminist, you know."

Lucas rubbed his temples.

"Headache?" Molly asked.

Worse. Because if Tommy Thumbs was still alive, with his fingers in the hard-earned cash of this Santa

Village bingo money, then shit. These elves actually had a legit case—which meant he had zero chance of changing Molly's mind and getting her to walk away from this. He knew Archer and Joe would have his neck for not calling them in on this, right now. And that was definitely the smart way to go if he loved his job. And he did. But he also knew he could handle this case and keep Molly safe without backup, at least at this point. And more than that, if he called in the troops, he had no doubt that Archer and Joe would come in hot and play hardball, immediately removing her from the case.

She'd never forgive him.

So for better or worse, he was going to let the bad Santa case be Molly's secret, which meant he was in now, all the way in, and not because Archer had asked him to be. He was going to help her however he could and keep her safe at any cost.

And hopefully not lose his job while he was at it.

Or his thumbs.

Or, he thought, meeting Molly's see-all gaze, his heart.

Chapter 6

#MerryElfingChristmas

Molly watched Lucas's face as he listened to the elves. They had a viable case and he knew it. And if there was one thing she knew about Lucas, it was that he was always willing to fight the good fight.

The ladies stayed late, appearing happy to knit away their evening at Molly's table. Lucas had planted himself as well, the intent in his steely gaze telling her he planned to outwait the elves to have a little chat.

But she wasn't feeling like chatting.

And so the standoff had begun. Luckily for her, Lucas's work phone went off around ten p.m. He slid her an unreadable look and jerked his head toward the door before heading that way, apparently certain she'd follow.

Which of course she did.

He pulled her outside onto her porch and shut the door to get away from three sets of curious, nosy eyes. Then he nudged up her against the wall and tilted her chin up, staring down into her eyes. "Okay," he said. *"Uncle."*

At the feel of his warm, hard body against hers, her nipples had gotten very happy. She ordered them to cool it. "Uncle?"

"Yeah," he murmured, eyes on her lips. "I cave. I'm no match for the likes of you. I'm in."

She tried to hold in her triumphant smile and failed.

He gave her a head shake. "Before you say I told you so, we're going to make a deal."

"You think so, huh?"

"Yes," he said, tone final.

"What kind of a deal?" she asked warily.

"The kind where you don't go off without me. We're partners on this, Molly, or no go."

That night she'd slept in his bed with him, he'd been warm as a furnace. Twice she'd woken up wrapped around him as if her body knew what her mind didn't want to accept, that she wanted him. Bad, too. Both times she'd forced herself to scoot away.

Tonight, he was just as warm. And hard with lean, sinewy muscle. She had to remind herself not to wrap around him again. "And if I don't agree?" she murmured.

His gaze never wavered. "Then I bring in Archer and he takes over. Joe as well."

She stared up at him, wanting to call his bluff but not wanting to risk it. Lucas was a man of his word. He would do exactly as he'd just said. He'd rat her out in an instant and Archer would bench her. Of that she had no doubt. "Fine," she said. "Deal."

He nodded and backed up a step, leaving her body feeling annoyingly bereft. His gaze slid over her features, stopping for a beat on her lips, and as if he was magic, they trembled open.

His hot gaze lifted to hers, and then with a slight quirk of his lips, he was gone.

When she finally went to sleep that night, it'd been to dream about a future with a man she couldn't, *wouldn't*, have.

The next morning she was up early and at the gym. She had a specific routine she put herself through, given to her by her physical therapist and designed to keep the strength up in her weakened leg.

"Ready?" asked a male voice behind her.

She got up and swiped the sweat from her brow, facing Caleb. Besides being a client of Hunt Investigations, he was some kind of a tech genius, a venture capitalist, and . . . her secret sparring partner.

Caleb had his reasons for keeping the secret. He was a closed book for one, a complete mystery to everyone, and kept his own counsel.

Molly had never told anyone about the training he gave her, because she'd started working out to regain her strength after her last surgery and it'd become almost a religion for her. A *very* private one. Keeping strong physically kept her strong mentally. No one could touch her.

Or so she liked to tell herself.

Stepping into the ring with Caleb, she smiled.

He went brows up. "You look like you're looking forward to kicking my ass today."

"I am."

He laughed low in his throat and planted his weight when she came at him. She swept his legs out from beneath him, but at the last second he snagged an arm around her calf and took her down with him.

"Damn," she said breathlessly from flat on her back.

"You had a good move," he told her, immediately taking his weight off her and reaching a hand down to pull her up. "But you led with your eyes, so I saw you coming."

Holding his gaze in hers, she nodded and . . . went for him again.

This time he went down like a sack and lay there, grimacing.

"Oh shit," she breathed and dropped to his side, putting a hand on his chest. "Are you okay—"

The rest of her sentence vanished with an "oomph" from her as he rolled and flattened her.

"That's just mean," she said on a laugh.

"That's real life," he said seriously. "Don't get taken advantage of because you're soft."

"Hey!"

"I mean that in the best way possible," he said and did one of those moves only really fit people could do; he popped up to his feet without using his hands.

A low whistle had them both turning. Sadie stood ringside. "Thanks for recommending this gym. Just bought a day pass." She then looked at Caleb, her eyes going hooded and unreadable.

He looked right back but didn't say a word, which was impressive in its own right. As far as Molly knew, the two hadn't had much, if any, interaction, which made *this* interaction all the more fascinating.

"Sadie," Caleb said lightly in greeting.

"Suits," Sadie said back, not nearly so lightly.

At the moment, Caleb was wearing basketball shorts and a tight long-sleeved performance t-shirt over his extremely well-honed body, but it was true that, away from the gym, he was rarely seen in anything but a suit.

"That insult's getting old," he told Sadie.

Sadie lifted a shoulder. "Just making sure you realize that one of your suits would probably feed the entire homeless population in San Francisco for a year."

Caleb's eyes went a little hot, and not in a good way. "Making assumptions about me?" he asked quietly.

Sadie shrugged.

Caleb studied her for a long beat. "Maybe we could start this little game over. What are the chances of that?"

"I'd say a pretty solid zip," she said and moved to the weights.

"Wow," Molly said, watching her go. "She's usually got a really long fuse. What did you do to piss her off?"

"Breathe air."

She didn't believe that for one second. Clearly there was something in their past. No one got that better than Molly. Her own past had affected her in a very large way, which she thought about as she showered and headed to work.

She'd grown up with two bossy males, so she was naturally pushy and always willing to fight back. In fact, not knowing when to back down had been a lesson she'd learned the hard way at age fourteen.

Joe had gotten himself in with a bad-news group of guys, one of whom was Molly's first crush. Darius had been charming and way too old for her at age eighteen but he'd flirted with her and she'd been ridiculously smitten. What she hadn't known was that Darius's buddies had wanted Joe to steal a car for them and when he'd refused, they'd decided to force his hand.

By kidnapping Molly.

Initially, she'd misunderstood the severity of her situation. They'd snatched her right off the street on her way home from school, Darius among them. She could still feel the terror, taste the blood from where she'd bitten her lip, refusing to cry or show her fear. They'd shoved her into a van and brought her to an abandoned house, ordering her to sit the hell down and keep her trap shut.

Something she hadn't been capable of doing.

She just hadn't been coded for passive. She'd been a sassy teen who literally hadn't been able to shut up to save her own life. She'd *had* to fight back.

Which hadn't worked out so well for her; all memories she shoved deep. But here it was nearly fifteen years later and she was still pushing back.

Half an hour later she was at the Pacific Pier Building, letting herself into the offices of Hunt Investigations to open up for the day.

Not three minutes later, the door opened and testosterone personified entered in the form of Archer and his entire alpha pack, all dressed in SWAT black and loaded with enough weapons to protect a developing nation.

They'd been investigating another insurance scam, this one a complex fraud scheme regarding the manufacture and distribution of compounded medications. The fraud had involved material misrepresentations to health insurance providers, and illegal payments to coconspirators and medical professionals—generating in excess of five million dollars in criminal proceeds.

Molly took a moment to take in the impressive sight of a bunch of really hot, really fit guys wearing their gear like they'd been born to it, every one of them dangerous *and* dangerously sexy in their own right.

Even if only one stuck out to her.

"Solid intel," Archer told her when she looked at him. "Good job."

Wow. Two compliments in one week, and Molly felt the pride fill her. "You have a problem finding your way around in Hunters Point?"

Hunters Point was San Francisco's radioactive basement. The decommissioned Hunter's Point Naval Shipyard and the surrounding area was not exactly the sort of place you wanted to go in without knowing every nook and cranny and dark spot.

Something that both Joe and Molly knew all too well, having grown up there. The warehouse they'd been looking for had been in a literal maze of warehouses, each on a more dangerous corner than the next.

"No real problems," Archer said.

Which wasn't much of an answer but whatever had happened out there, they'd apparently gotten past it. Still, she knew she'd have been valuable on the ground. "If you'd let me come along, you'd have had an extra set of eyes other than Joe who knows that place like the back of his hand."

"Maybe next time," he said.

"Liar."

This got her another rare smile. "We'll find you the right case."

She returned the smile. She'd already found the right case . . . She slapped a stack of mail against his chest as he walked by.

Behind him was Lucas and he slowed at her desk to look her over.

She looked right back. Black knit cap, black long-sleeved T-shirt snugged over his broad chest, black cargoes on his long legs, kickass boots. Body loose, not tense, his dark eyes sharp and maybe slightly wary. He looked tall, dark, and edgy, and just about the opposite of everything she might want in a man—if she'd wanted one—which didn't stop her heart from skipping a beat or two.

Or three . . .

The corner of his sexy mouth curved and she felt heat flicker through her veins.

Joe was behind Lucas, and on his phone. Without looking up, he gave his partner a shove. Lucas didn't budge, holding his ground for another beat, most likely being a male through and through and therefore making it clear that he wouldn't move until he was good and ready. When his point was apparently made, he shifted out of Joe's way.

Molly had to draw in a careful breath, telling herself she was at work and shouldn't be ogling Lucas.

"Hey," Joe said with a frown. "You're all flushed."

She put her hands to her cheeks. "I was . . . exercising."

From behind Joe, Lucas arched a brow. She looked away.

Archer poked his head back in from his office and narrowed his eyes at her. "You're sick?"

Joe reached out to touch her forehead and she

smacked his hand away. "I'm not sick!" she said, maybe yelled.

"She's hot," Joe said.

Lucas coughed and she knew it was to hide a damn laugh. She was hot alright; she was hot for him and dammit, he knew it. She went hands on hips and gave her boss and brother each a hard glare. "Listen carefully, you Neanderthals. I'm not sick. I was working out before work and I'm still"—she refused to meet Lucas's gaze—"overheated."

"You work out?" Joe asked doubtfully.

She tossed up her hands. "You know what? If I died and went straight to hell, it would still take me a damn week to realize I wasn't at work anymore! Now go away and leave me to my work. All of you."

Archer and Joe shifted away with some various muttering. But not Lucas.

She stared at him.

He stared right back. "Are you working out?"

She sighed. "Yes. I'm not exactly the faint of heart, delicate little snowflake you all seem to think I am."

He gave a low laugh that set butterflies to flight in her belly. "You're a lot of things," he said. "Most of them pretty fucking great, but being a faint of heart, delicate little snowflake isn't one of them."

Molly let out a reluctant smile. "That might just be the nicest thing anyone's ever said to me," she admitted.

"So what kind of workouts are you doing?"

Because she was still looking at him, she could

see it wasn't concern or doubt prompting his question, but genuine curiosity. "I go to the gym on Van Ness Avenue," she said. "I do some weights and take an assortment of classes when I can fit them in."

"Van Ness? Caleb owns a gym there."

"I know," she said. "Sometimes I work out with him."

There was a beat of surprise from Lucas. "Caleb is a martial arts expert, and badass in his own right."

She smiled and shrugged. "He's a good workout buddy."

Lucas's gaze slid down her body to her right leg, as if trying to decide if she was yanking his chain or not. "He doesn't baby me," she said pointedly.

Something changed in Lucas's eyes at that, and if she didn't know better, she'd say it was jealousy.

"What does he do?" he asked, voice flat, eyes just a little bit . . . hot?

"He works me out hard," she said.

There was that flash again. Good God, it *was* jealousy. This pleased her way too much. To hide her smug smile, she turned to her computer.

"I wanted to let you know I'm free tonight," he said to her back, still sounding slightly out of sorts.

Aware that he couldn't see her face, she let out a small victorious smile. "Sweet of you," she said lightly. "But I'm not going to date you."

"You know that's not what I meant."

Yes, she did. And maybe that's why she was still playing this game, keeping up the ruse instead of letting Lucas know nothing had happened between them. Because deep down, she would have liked for that night to be real and he didn't return the sentiment. Swiveling in her chair to face him, she affected a hurt expression. "So now that we've slept together, you're done? You don't want to see me anymore?"

He grimaced and looked behind him to make sure they were alone, seeming to be at about a twelve on the one-to-ten stress scale. "Are you *trying* to get me killed?"

She laughed and went back to her computer. Yeah, it was mean and she was going to have to let him off the hook and soon, but . . . not today.

He came up behind her, leaning in until his mouth brushed her ear. "Paybacks are a bitch, Molly."

This gave her an entire body shiver that she ignored and forced herself to get to work. Or at least pretend to get to work. This lasted about three minutes before she caved and took a quick peek.

Lucas was gone.

But there was a steaming mug of coffee waiting for her.

Well played.

Chapter 7

#Pivot

At lunchtime, Molly's friends came into the office. Elle, Sadie, Pru—whose husband, Finn, ran the downstairs pub—and Haley, the optometrist two doors down from Hunt Investigations. Elle was carrying a tote that smelled like heaven on earth and had Molly's mouth watering.

"You texted that you were too busy for lunch," Elle said. "But as the manager of this entire building and the person who sleeps with your boss, I'm over-riding him." She smiled. "Or just *riding* him."

Sadie grimaced. "Have a care for those of us not getting any, would ya?"

"We all know you could be getting whoever you want," Pru told her. "You're just too picky."

Sadie shrugged. "I don't need a guy's drama."

"Sorry, but women are just as dramatic," said Haley, who should know since she dated women.

"Okay, that's probably true," Sadie said. "But my point is, without a significant other, I don't have to wear pants. Although, I do miss cuddling. Sometimes I just need to be kissed and spooned, you know? I deserve that, I'm a decent person, I recycle."

Everyone agreed that she was a good person and deserved a cuddle.

"I bet you could download an app for that," Haley said.

"Yeah," Sadie said. "But I make due with Amazon Prime."

Molly's mouth was watering from the scent coming from the bag of food Elle had brought. "What's for lunch?"

Elle smiled. "You'll love this. Aged organic milk tossed over seasoned tomato puree spread on baked whole wheat."

Molly blinked. "You mean pizza?"

"Well, if you want to get technical," Elle said and pulled out the pizza.

"Oh my God," Molly moaned, stuffing her face. "I missed breakfast."

"I don't get it when people forget to eat," Pru said. "How in the world does one forget to eat?"

To be fair, Pru looked to be about twenty months pregnant and was hungry all the time. "Stress," Molly said.

Pru shook her head and refilled her plate with piece number three *and* four.

Willa, who ran the courtyard pet shop, popped in

with a bag of muffins from the coffee shop. They all promptly pounced on these like they were the secret of life.

"What's the occasion?" Elle asked Willa.

She smiled. "Keane and I set a wedding date."

They all squealed in delight, as Willa and Keane had been engaged for what felt like forever.

"What was the catalyst?" Elle asked.

Willa smiled. "We're redoing the kitchen and I want new stuff."

Elle smiled. "Look at you, thinking ahead. I'm so proud."

Sadie shook her head. "I think when you get married, you should have to give gifts to your guests. I mean you found lifelong love, right? That means I deserve a blender far more than you do."

Willa grinned. "I'll keep that in mind." She took another muffin and sighed. "I wish everything was as easy as getting fat."

They all agreed on this very sage comment and then went back to their respective jobs. Molly's afternoon flew by. She put out fires, answered phones, filed reports, and did background and security checks. At five o'clock, with most of the guys still gone on various jobs, she switched gears and pulled out her own personal laptop.

Time for *Project Bad Santa*.

Another look at the Christmas Village's website didn't yield any new information. But she did find ads on Facebook and Craigslist and a few other places advertising the village's bingo, along with the claim that all profits went to charity. One of the ads noted that additional information for *private parties* was available upon special request. Hmm. She called the number listed. "I'm interested in a private party," she said when a man answered.

There was a beat of silence. "Bingo night?"

She had no idea. "Yes. Who do I speak to?"

"Me."

"Okay," she said. "And you are?"

"Doesn't matter. What are you looking for?"

Since she had absolutely zero idea, she hung up. And then researched the number. It was a cell phone registered to a Nicolas King. She wondered if she'd just found Crazy Nick. But when she searched that name, she hit a brick wall.

The guy didn't exist.

"Well, that's not suspicious at all," she said and tried a different angle, searching Tommy Thumbs. His given name was Thomas Russolini. Once she had that, she hit pay dirt. As Lucas had told her, he was indeed presumed dead, but before that he'd been wanted in five different counties for fraud, money laundering, and embezzling.

She leaned back. *Think. What do you know?* Well, she knew Santa and Tommy were brothers . . . On a hunch, she typed in what she imagined Tommy's brother's name might be: *Nicolas* Russolini.

There was one Nicolas Russolini in San Francisco. The address listed was in Soma, a stone's throw from the Christmas Village. "You and your brother have been very bad boys," she murmured, smiling in triumph. "You're officially on the naughty list."

"I'd go on the naughty list if it'd make you smile at me like that."

She jerked around and found Lucas propping up the doorjamb, arms crossed, watching her. "What are you doing here?"

"We've got a date, remember?" he asked, voice low and sexy and . . . teasing.

If he only knew. She turned back to her computer and saved everything she'd found, all while incredibly aware of the man watching her every move.

"What did you find?" he asked.

"Crazy Nick's address. Maybe."

He pushed off the wall and came over. Reaching out, he opened her laptop and leaned over her to read her screen.

She stilled. He had a hand flat on her desk on either side of hers. If she turned her head, her mouth would brush against his inner biceps, a fact that did something quivery to her belly. And how was it that he'd been working since before the crack of dawn and he still smelled disarmingly delicious?

Long before she could gather herself to push him away, he straightened and looked down at her. "What's your plan?"

"To go check out the village."

He nodded. "With me."

Here was the thing. She knew it was smart, and

she really had no intention of going without him. But it rankled that he felt like he had to remind her, like maybe he believed she would be stupid enough to sneak off and go it alone.

"Molly," he said into her silence. "It's my way on this, or I hand you over to Archer and Joe and let you all fight it out."

She refused to be intimidated. "We have a damn deal and I don't go back on my word, so see that you don't. You don't tell them I'm on this case, and I don't tell anyone we slept together."

A muscle in his jaw ticked, which was fascinating. She'd never seen it do that until the other night. Clearly she was on his last nerve.

"We didn't sleep together," he finally said.

She just smiled. "You keep telling yourself that."

He dropped his head and rubbed the back of his neck. "Look, I'd rather 'fess up than have you in danger."

"Okay," she said agreeably. "So you're going to tell them what happened the other night?"

"*Nothing* happened."

"Uh-huh. And you're willing to bet your balls on that?"

He blew out a breath. "I really wish I knew what you have against my balls."

She had to laugh. "For the record, I was working here at my desk, waiting for you. So you can stand down, soldier."

He narrowed his eyes and searched hers as if looking for signs of deceit. "We're doing this together," she said and a thrum of adrenaline went through her at the thought of her first real case.

At least she told herself that was what her excitement stemmed from.

She stood and then sucked in a breath and shifted her weight to her good leg as her other did its usual frustrating thing where it sent nerve pain screaming up the IT band along the outside of her thigh from knee to hip.

Lucas reached out to steady her; soon as she was good, he let go and backed up.

She'd been prepared for him to hover and coddle, but she should've known better. Lucas wasn't a hoverer or a coddler. In fact, unlike everyone else in her world, he never looked at her like he felt sorry for her, or peppered her with questions she didn't want to answer.

She liked that.

He trusted her to know when and if she was okay, and she liked that too. Way too much. They'd shared a bed and for her, the sober one, it had felt shockingly intimate, especially given the fact that she hadn't shared a bed with a man in . . . well, a damn long time. She was attracted to him, and he was attracted to her too, and . . . damn. She wanted what she *hadn't* had the other night.

"You're staring at me funny," he said.

Probably because she was confused over how badly she wanted him. Okay, not so suddenly, but

still, denial had been her friend and now that friend
had deserted her. "No, I'm not."

"Yes, you are. You're staring at me like . . ."

She turned her back on him and grimaced to herself, knowing *exactly* how she'd been staring at him.
"Like I'm annoyed by your presence?" she asked.

"Like I'm dinner."

She closed her eyes. "Oh, please," she said on a
low laugh. "I've slept with you now. Trust me, I don't
need a repeat."

"So you keep saying."

His voice sounded right in her ear now. He'd
moved, shifting close enough that his chest nearly
brushed the entire length of her spine. She could feel
the heat of him and nearly moaned. *Nearly.* But she
caught herself. It was just that his body heat was
soaking into her and she found herself wanting to
back into him. He smelled amazing and he was still
dressed from his job, and that was a shocking turn-
on too. As was the sexy smirk she heard in his voice.

Which didn't make any sense. From the time she'd
come into her sexuality as a teenager, complete with
all the baggage of her kidnapping still hanging over
her head, she'd only ever felt comfortable when *she*
was the one doing the charming and chasing. She'd
dated guys here and there, all very different from her
brother and men like Lucas. They'd been . . . beta.
Not pushovers, but nonthreatening. Nice and sweet.
Emotionally available.

The exact opposite of Lucas.

But the truth was, no one had ever really invested in her, and she wasn't sure Lucas was the investing type either. In fact, she was fairly positive he wasn't, but it still felt a little bit like he was chasing her and she wasn't at all certain what to do with that.

"Tell me about our night," he said. "You know you want to."

"Actually, it was over so fast, I can't really remember."

He gave a low, rather triumphant laugh and turned her to face him. "You haven't yet once managed to look me in the eyes and tell me how bad I was. Here's your chance, Molly. Give it to me."

See, that was the thing. She *did* want to give it to him, quite badly. *Naked* . . . Gah. She really hadn't seen this coming, but she deserved fun like anyone else, right? She looked at his mouth, desperately wanting it on hers. And then her body somehow mistook the fantasy for reality because she went up on tiptoes and . . . kissed him. Just a soft brush of her lips across his, gently and a little hesitant, but it was most definitely a kiss.

He froze, and she didn't know if it was horror or shock. Maybe both. To find out, she pulled back slightly and stared at him.

His eyes were closed, but they opened now, the deep brown holding hers prisoner as she held her breath. Beneath the hand she'd set on his chest she could feel his heart steady and sure. And maybe a little too fast.

"Molly," he breathed and shifted so that his forehead rested against hers. Sliding his hands into her hair, his fingertips against her scalp, he held her in place. "Do that again," he demanded, his voice soft steel.

Letting out a breath of relief, she leaned back in, but he beat her to it, closing the distance, his mouth taking hers in another heart-stopping kiss that released something wild in her, something she'd kept locked deep inside. But suddenly she couldn't get close enough to him or enough skin contact.

But he pulled back, one hand still cupping the back of her neck, the other under her long sweater, so low on her spine that he had a palm full of her ass as he stared down at her with a look she couldn't quite read.

"What?" she whispered.

He gave a single, slow shake of his head. "We didn't sleep together."

She blinked. "How do you know?"

"Because I could never have forgotten this."

Chapter 8

#SharingIsCaring

Lucas had never been so sure of anything in his life as he stared down into Molly's slightly dazed face, waiting for her response, his heart still thundering in his chest.

Because holy shit. That kiss.

If it'd been anyone else, he'd have had them both naked and halfway to satisfaction by now. But it wasn't just anyone else, it was Molly. Joe's threats had been pretty effective, but sleeping with his good friend's baby sister wasn't the mental holdup. Neither was her being a coworker. Or the fact that she was someone he instinctively knew he couldn't have just once and walk away—which was his current MO these days. Yeah, all of those things added up to a Hands-Off situation, but the truth was none of it was stopping him.

What *did* was that she thought he was on her side. That he was helping her because she'd asked-slash-blackmailed, when the truth was he was helping her because it was literally his job to do so. But even more importantly, he was helping her because he was worried about her being out there on her own, when even he and the guys were never on their own. They always worked as a team, that was the only way to do this job.

But Molly wouldn't care about any of that. She'd care only that he was—as she'd see it—babysitting her, and that he hadn't told her about it up front. It'd piss her off in a large way and he fully understood that, but he still couldn't tell her or she'd get herself yanked off this case. Lucas figured he at least owed it to her to see it through.

Given how complicated it all was, he wouldn't further complicate that with . . . emotions.

So he really needed to not muddy the waters. He needed to not want her as badly as he did. And most of all, he needed to keep his hands and mouth and other various body parts off of her.

Which he knew would be the hardest job he'd ever have. "You lied to me," he said.

She started to pull away, but he held on, bending his knees to catch her gaze. "Why? Why did you let me think we'd slept together?"

She closed her eyes.

"Talk to me, Molly."

"Talking's not my strong suit."

"Bullshit," he said. "I've seen you talking with the

girls for hours on end without so much as taking a breath."

"Hey," she said, and then sighed. "Okay, maybe true. But talking about . . . feelings aren't my strong suit."

"Try anyway."

She looked up at him thoughtfully. "What do you remember of the other night?"

He lifted a shoulder. "I'd tried going out for a run that day, the first time since getting shot, and got home hurting like a son of a bitch. I took two pain pills. Then I received a text to come down to the pub because a client had shown up to meet us and I'd forgotten. He bought a round of drinks and toasted to me, and I drank." He shook his head. "A stupid decision, but that's it, that's all I remember until I woke up with you all over me."

"I wasn't all over you—" She broke off when he arched a brow. "Fine," she said. "I was all over you but you sleep like a damn furnace and I was cold, that's all."

"Or," he said.

"Or what?"

"I don't know, Molly, you tell me. But I want the truth. And it's not that we had sex, because that kiss . . ." Just thinking about it got him hot all over again. "That was most definitely our first. I'd have remembered any other, and I'd have remembered anything that followed." He waited until she met his gaze. "And so would you."

She blushed, but also rolled her eyes. "Fine. We

didn't . . . *sleep* together," she said. "I'd never have taken advantage of you that way."

At this very unexpected comment, he paused, surprised.

"I was already at the pub when you arrived," she said. "You seemed fine until you had alcohol. Then you got pale and shaky, and when I asked you if you were okay, you said you wanted to go to bed. The pub was packed and everyone was either playing pool, darts, or dancing. No one else seemed worried about you getting upstairs okay, so I walked you."

He reached out and cupped her jaw, tilting her face up to meet his. "And then . . ."

"I got you upstairs."

He gave her a go-on gesture.

She grimaced. "You hit the sack, tumbling me down with you."

He froze. "I forced you into my bed?"

"No! No, nothing like that," she rushed to tell him. "You were being playful, joking around about me wanting to tuck you in and suddenly you closed your eyes and were out. It happened so fast it scared me. So I stayed where I was."

"In my bed."

"Yes," she said.

"Because you were worried about me."

"Yes." She nodded earnestly.

"So I didn't . . . try anything."

She bit her lip.

Oh, Christ. He had. Visions of being slowly murdered by Archer were filling his head when she said, "It wasn't you, it was me."

He felt his brows vanish into his hair as a relieved laugh escaped him. "*You* tried something?"

"No, I didn't try something. I just . . . wanted to."

He felt the smile curve his mouth and she gave him a little shove. "Would you be serious?"

Something about her sincerity grabbed him by the throat. And the gut. She cared about him. And he cared about her. This wasn't just fun and games, and he needed to be honest with her. Because no matter what his body wanted, he wasn't ruled by it, and this wasn't going to happen.

Ever.

She was looking up at him with her feelings on her sleeve, seeming half embarrassed at her admissions and half braced for rejection, and it was that which snaked in past his defenses and detonated his walls.

He dropped his forehead to hers. "We can't."

She closed her eyes and pulled back, turning from him. "Right. Of course not. That would be stupid. So stupid. I have no idea what I was thinking. I *wasn't* thinking." She grabbed her purse and made a beeline for the door.

He snagged her hand and reeled her back in.

"Don't you dare say it's because you feel sorry for me," she ground out.

He stroked a finger along her temple, tucking an errant strand hair behind her ear, making sure she was looking at him when he spoke. "I don't feel sorry for you. I feel sorry for me for missing out."

"Well so do I," she said, tugging free. "Because I'd have rocked your world. I'm going now, off to solve my case."

She shut the door before he could say another word and he had to admit, he was pretty fucking impressed. There weren't very many people who could render him stupid.

But she managed it effortlessly.

He followed her out. Normally he took the stairs to the courtyard after work, where he'd grab dinner, either from Ivy's taco truck outside on the street or at the pub. There was a new sandwich shop and also a pretty good food truck on the street.

But Molly had called for the elevator. Another indicator that her leg was especially bothering her. He followed her into the elevator, searching her face.

She was good at hiding when she wanted to be, but the pinch of pain in her expression didn't escape him. When she glanced up and caught him looking her over, he smoothly pulled out his phone and looked at the screen.

"You don't have to pretend not to notice," she said as the elevators doors opened to the courtyard. It was a frosty cold night but Molly headed right into it, slowing at the alley to wave at Old Man Eddie, who was sitting on his crate. He wasn't with Caleb this time but a woman, which was new. Her hair was silver leaning toward light blue, her skin the texture of an apple doll, and she and Eddie were laughing at something one of them had said.

"This here is Virginia," Eddie said in introduction. "She's my new girlfriend. We met when she stopped by for some of my special mistletoe."

Eddie's "special" mistletoe was most likely pot and if Archer caught the old man selling it to the geriatrics again, he and Spence would get into it like they did every year. "I thought you agreed to stop selling your . . . mistletoe," Lucas said.

Virginia smiled at Eddie. "He's not charging me. Today's our one week anniversary."

Eddie winked at her. "Just wait, I'm saving my good stuff for week two." He looked at Molly and gestured to Lucas. "This guy treating you right?"

Molly took a quick glance at Lucas. "Oh. It's not like that."

"Huh." Eddie sent a disappointed look to Lucas. "I thought you had more game than that."

"Game?" Virginia asked on a laugh. "Honey, last night you kissed me and farted at the same time."

"It was the tacos from the food truck. Tacos gives everyone gas. But hey. I can still kiss, right?"

Molly laughed and kept walking. Lucas followed, slowing a minute later at the courtyard fountain. It'd been here since the mid-1800s, back in the days when there'd actually been cows in Cow Hollow. The building had been constructed around it, and legend stated that if you stood before the water and wished for true love with a true heart, it'd happen for you.

The myth was perpetuated by the fact that there were more than a few couples who either lived or worked in this very building who claimed the legend had come true for them, some of them being his good friends. Because of that, he liked to give the fountain a wide berth.

So of course Molly stopped in front of the fountain.

She stared at the water for a minute, her hands shoved in her pockets, where he could hear the jingle of a few coins. Was she going to wish for love? He hoped not, but something of his thoughts must've shown on his face because she arched a brow.

"Nervous?" she asked.

"Of course not." Skill Number One for his job— being able to lie his ass off.

"Ever been in love?" she asked.

He paused, not wanting to go there. But in the end, he figured she deserved a real answer. "Yes," he said.

He could tell by the look on her face that this wasn't what she'd expected. "You're surprised," he said.

"Yes."

"You don't think I have emotions?"

"I don't think you admit to them very often."

"I don't." He shrugged. "But it doesn't mean it hasn't happened."

Taking this in, she cocked her head. "So you've been in love. What went wrong?"

"She was killed in a car accident."

"Oh my God." She shook her head. "I'm so sorry. How long ago?"

"Eight years."

She nodded and took a step closer. "Is that why you don't do anything too deep relationship-wise now?"

He shrugged. "I've had some losses but I've also let people down that I care about. I don't like that feeling, so I guess I've just conditioned myself to not get invested past a certain level. Like you."

"How do you know what I do or don't do?" she asked.

"We've worked together for two years," he said. "I've never seen you invest yourself. Am I wrong?"

She hesitated and then shook her head. "You're not wrong."

"Molly!"

They both turned in time to see Molly's friends coming out of the coffee shop calling out for her.

"Whoa," Sadie said as the women came close, looking into Molly's face. "Your skin's glowing."

Molly slid a quick glance at Lucas, confirming that she put the "glow" blame firmly on him.

Sadie slid her speculative gaze from Molly to Lucas, who she stared at for a long beat. Not much got by her. There was a warning in her eyes, one he understood perfectly.

Hurt her and you'll die slowly and painfully.

He got that, but she had no idea that there was already people waiting to kill him if he hurt Molly, and she'd have to get in line behind Archer and Joe.

Molly had put her hands to her cheeks. "I'm not glowing. That would be weird."

"Not weird," Haley said. "It's nice. You look pretty. But you also look . . . different, that's all. You haven't glowed like that in a long time."

"It's just windburn."

"Wouldn't mind some of that windburn," Haley said wistfully.

"We're having dinner," Pru said, rubbing her big baby bump. "You two want to join?"

"I'm still working," Molly told her.

Sadie smiled and squeezed her hand. "Just take it easy, okay?"

"No worries, I'm fine," Molly said and then the two women exchanged a long look.

Lucas did his best to read it, but even having a sister and his mom, he was most definitely not fluent in Women Speak. He knew people sometimes saw Molly as a fragile little flower, but in his mind she wasn't fragile like a flower at all. Not even close. She was fragile like . . . a bomb.

"I just pushed myself a little too hard in the gym this morning, that's all," Molly said.

"You need to come do yoga with me sometime," Elle said.

"Maybe," Molly said. "If it's cold yoga and I get to wear sweatpants and just lie on the floor."

Elle laughed. "Sweats are a cry for help."

"Hey, there's no reason a cry for help can't be comfortable. 'Night, guys." Molly walked off and Lucas followed, feeling all the eyes following them. But Molly didn't seem to give it a second thought.

A few minutes later they were buckling into his car when his phone rang. Seeing it was Joe, he clicked off his blue tooth so it wouldn't blast the conversation into the interior of the vehicle. "Talk," he said.

Molly looked over at him, brows raised. She always complained about the guys and their phone manners, but the truth was, they were just usually in a hurry and trying to be efficient, and he didn't get the problem with that.

"I'm at the pub with Kylie," Joe said. "Saw you leave the courtyard with Molly. She's not answering my call. What's going on?"

Shit. What was going on? Well, let's see. Fact number one: he'd kissed Molly until he'd nearly forgotten his own name. Fact number two: she'd kissed him back. Fact number three: that kiss—no, better make that kisses, as in plural—had been the best thing to happen to him in recent memory, and all he could think about was hauling her over the console and into his lap and taking more of what she'd so sweetly offered. "I'll have to get back to you," he said.

"Negative," Joe replied. "Tell me now."

Right. Okay then. He held up a finger to Molly signaling that he needed a moment and stepped out of the car, shutting the door and walking a few feet away so as to not be overheard. "I already told Archer. She's taking the case outside of work and there's no stopping her," he said quietly.

Joe was quiet for a beat, then he said something, muffled. Lucas realized he was talking to Archer.

Perfect.

Joe came back. "And you're not going to tell her what you're up to."

"What is this, sixth grade?" Lucas asked. "Why can't you guys just tell her I'm here to have her back?"

"Because then she'll think we don't trust her."

"As you clearly don't."

"It's complicated," Joe said.

No shit.

"Look, just take care of her, okay? It's simple."

It wasn't simple. Nothing about this was simple. And neither was Molly. She was simple like . . . like quantum physics. "Tell me what happened to her."

"Why?"

Lucas pinched the bridge of his nose and drew a deep breath. Brother and sister were more alike than either of them wanted to believe. "Look, you want me to keep her safe, I'm going to keep her safe. But I'm missing some key intel here."

Joe was quiet for a beat. "It's a long story," he finally said. "And it's not my story to tell. But I can say that her getting hurt . . . that shit was all on me. She used to run track. Wanted to be an Olympian. That was her dream, it was her way out. And none of it happened. So yeah, I go a little crazy when I think she could get hurt again. I know that."

Not an apology, but Lucas didn't need one. He understood guilt. And he understood the gut-clenching, heart-stopping fear of someone he loved getting hurt. "I've got her back," he said gruffly. "You know I do. I'll watch over her."

And he would, or die trying. But if Joe knew the truth, that Lucas had had his mouth on Molly's, and also his hands, there was every chance that his partner and good friend would kill him dead where he stood with absolutely zero remorse, and Lucas would expect no less.

Chapter 9

#JingleAllTheWay

Molly watched Lucas end his call and slide behind the wheel.

"What's your plan?" he asked, clearly having no intention of talking about his phone call. The call that had agitated him, even though he was still looking his usual calm, implacable self.

A reminder that while they appeared to have added kissing to their repertoire, they weren't exactly friends.

Or lovers.

Got it.

"My plan," she said, "is to go look around the Christmas Village, but first I want to check out Bad Santa's home address. Stealthily, of course. I just want to get a feel for him. Something's weird to me." She gave him the addy and he started driving.

She looked resolutely out the window and not at him because that was the only way to get through this, not looking into his face. She didn't know how to go back to before the kiss, didn't know how to un-want him.

When he spoke a few minutes into the silence, he startled her. "I've got a question," he said.

She hesitated, feeling more than a little wary. "Okay."

"Your leg seems to bother you more on the cold days."

She looked over him in the dark, ambient lighting of the interior of the car, surprised. People who'd known her for years hadn't caught onto that. "Yes. It does."

"What happened? What can be done so you don't have to be in pain?"

"That's more than one question," she said, turning back to the window.

He snorted and the sound made her want to smile, but she held it because she didn't want to talk about this with him. Or anyone. Ever.

"I'd like to know," he said quietly, the amusement gone from his voice. "Because I'd like to know more about you."

"I tried to let you know more about me and was shut down."

"No fair," he said softly.

Okay, he might be right on that one. She shrugged. "Hey, if you want to play a game of questions, I'm all for it. But I get to go first."

"Fine. Hit me," he said.

"You said you'd let down those you've loved. How?"

He glanced over at her and then turned his attention back to the road. "I started out as a medic but I hated that, so I went into the DEA. I did a lot of undercover and was gone all the time, and when I wasn't, I still wasn't good about being there for the people in my life."

"So that's how you let them down? By being a workaholic?"

He gave a short nod.

"Being a workaholic isn't the worst thing," she said.

"It is if you love one," he said. "My turn. Tell me what happened to you."

The injury had actually been her back, not her leg. She'd broken her back in three places falling out of the window making her great escape all those years ago. She'd had multiple spine surgeries but the nerves in her right leg still hadn't come back. While the stabbing, burning, constant nerve pain had thankfully faded, left in its placed was . . . a nothingness. Her right leg from knee to hip was entirely numb. Like gone-to-the-dentist-and-been-doped-up-with-Novocain numb.

It drove her crazy. But it was better than the constant pain. The only time she felt that was when she was stupid and vain enough to wear a set of her beloved heels, or if she sat too long. Or stood too long. Or forgot to stretch daily. Or moved wrong.

In other words, lived.

It was just a way of life for her now. One she kept mostly to herself about. There wasn't anything anyone could do about it and she also hated when people felt sorry for her. She had a very serious thing about that. Her first boyfriend had freaked out when she twisted her leg on his stairs and then couldn't walk for a week. They'd gotten past that only to have him freak out again their first time in bed, when he'd seen her surgical scars. And he hadn't even known that there were more surgeries in her future, which weren't guaranteed to help what was now a degenerative condition and would likely continue to worsen.

Her second boyfriend had bailed even faster.

It'd left her leery of revealing too much of herself, naked or otherwise. The funny thing was, in spite of everything, she still felt whole. Or mostly, anyway. But while she was okay with her body just how it was, she couldn't expect anyone else to be. "It's residual nerve damage from an old injury when I was fourteen."

"What happened?" Lucas asked.

"I was stupid." She pointed out the windshield. "If you turn here instead of at the next light, it's faster."

Lucas looked frustrated at the subject change but didn't comment further as he made the turn. He parked in front of an apartment building that looked like its heyday had long ago come and gone. "Which apartment?"

"It's 105, bottom floor." She got out of the car, not at all surprised when Lucas moved fast enough to come around and offer her a hand. He didn't say anything when she straightened her leg and gave it a minute before trusting it to hold all her weight. Soon as she nodded, he stepped back.

They headed up the walk of the apartment complex, a steep set of stairs that left her in the unhappy position of dragging her leg where it didn't want to go. She could tell Lucas had set his pace to hers which piqued her pride, but facts were facts. It was a bad nerve day, it happened, and she'd long ago learned to deal with it. She was still working on accepting it.

Night had fallen, and while there were lights on the street, the building itself seemed dark. She glanced around, trying to be aware of her surroundings, but felt grateful to have Lucas with her. "Seems a little sketch."

"The whole street is sketch." He took her hand, walking very slightly ahead of her, clearly in protector mode. Fine by her, she wasn't going to ever be the stupid chick in the horror flick.

"Let's walk around back," he murmured, leading the way along the side of the building. In the back was an alley and a few dark windows and one lit.

The lit window was suddenly raised and a woman stuck her head out. She was a hundred years old if she was a day, and had a been-smoking-for-six-decades voice. "What are you two up to?"

"We're here to visit a friend but he's not home," Lucas said smoothly. "In 105."

"St. Nick?" the woman asked.

"Yes," Molly said. "You know him?"

"I play bingo at the village, even though I have yet to win, that fucker. Now's not a real good time to catch him. He's probably sleeping. He's nocturnal, you know. And he had a long night last night with his latest girl."

"Long night?" Lucas asked.

"Yeah, and either he's great in bed or he just likes her to agree with him. A lot."

Lucas grimaced, thanked the woman, and walked silently with Molly back to the car.

"I'm not sure what it says about me that a sixty-year-old Santa is getting more than I am," she said.

"Money or sex?"

"Probably both."

Lucas was wise enough not to comment as he drove but she sensed amusement. When his phone buzzed an incoming call, he glanced at the screen and blew out a breath. "I'm sorry," he said. "I have to take this one too. Brace yourself."

Before she could ask why, he'd connected the call. "Hey, mom. You're on speaker."

"Don't you hey me. And you're on speaker too."

"Hi, Lucas," came another female voice.

"Sis," Lucas said.

"Where are you?" his mother asked. "And don't say at work!"

"Okay, I won't say."

"You suck," his sister said. "I'd say worse, but your nephew's asleep on me right now and he has tender ears."

"Laura," Lucas's mom admonished and Molly caught a very pleasing to the ears hint of her Portuguese accent. "And I know you haven't forgotten that it's game night," she said to Lucas. "Tell me the truth. Did you take on another case just to avoid it?"

Lucas nodded his head yes to Molly but to his mom, he said, "Of course not."

"Fine," she said. "I get it. You hate game night. But Laura says you still have the Cards Against Humanity game in your trunk from when she borrowed your car a few week ago. Drop it by?"

"You have other games. A whole cabinet of them."

"We want that one."

"Or this is a trick and you just want to see me."

"Are you calling your mama a liar?" she asked sweetly.

Lucas blew out a breath. "Fine. But I can't stay."

"Baby, you have to eat dinner."

"No can do tonight, sorry."

"I made *cozido a portuguesa*."

Lucas groaned. "The big guns."

"No, the big gun is the *bolo de bolacha* I made for dessert. And if you don't come by, I'm going to let Laura and my grandbaby take them all home."

"You're evil to the bone."

"And don't forget it. You love me anyway."

"I do." Lucas glanced Molly's way and she did her best to look like she hadn't been very busy eavesdropping. "I'm five minutes out, but I can't stay, I really am on a job." He disconnected and blew out a breath.

"Don't not stay on my account," Molly said. "I don't know what it was she was cooking, but it sounded amazing."

"Portuguese stew and cookie cake."

Her mouth watered. "Well, far be it for me to be the reason you miss out."

Molly could cook. If she had to. But she didn't enjoy it at all and tried very hard not to do it unless she had no other choice, such as it was the end of the month and she was low on funds or if there was a zombie apocalypse. Joe cooked, but only because he'd discovered women thought a man in the kitchen was sexy. Molly had inherited her dislike of cooking from her dad, whose idea of cooking was opening a can of Chef Boyardee. "Sounds like you've got a nice, normal family."

He glanced over at her and caught her looking at him. A small smile touched his lips as he turned his attention back to the road. When she didn't say anything more, he glanced over again. "Was that a personal question?"

Was it? "No." Liar . . . "Maybe."

"Well for starters, I wouldn't exactly use 'normal' to describe my family," he said. "They love loud, but also fight loud. At any given moment, my mom could throw her shoe at you or hug you. It's always a calculated risk to let her get too close until you know if you're in good standing."

Molly smiled. "Sounds nice."

Again he looked over at her. "You and Joe are close."

She shrugged.

"I've seen you smack him upside the back of his head so hard that he nearly swallowed his tongue," Lucas said. "I've also seen the look on your face when he's hurt. Like on that job last year when he took a bat to the skull, you lost it. Understandably, of course."

It'd been one of the scariest moments in her life, and that was saying something. He'd fully recovered, but there for a while it'd been touch and go, and the memory of that, the gut-clenching, heart-wrenching fear that her brother might die and leave her alone in this world with no one but her dad, had terrified her to the bone. "Yeah, we're close," she said. "But it's a different kind of close. It's like we've had to be in order to survive."

He glanced over at her. "I get that. More than you might think."

It was her turn to look at him, but he was concentrating on the road. He made a few quick turns and ended up on a street that was well lit and lined with older Victorian homes, well lived in but all extremely well taken care of, many of them decorated for the holidays in holly and garland and twinkling lights.

Lucas stopped in front of a house that was lit up from top to bottom, complete with reindeer cutouts on the grass. The driveway held six cars. Two more were parked on the lawn with the reindeer. The street was filled with cars.

"Holy cow," Molly said.

Lucas squeezed in between the reindeer and the cars. "Family game night's pretty popular."

She stared at all the vehicles. "How many people are in your family? All of San Francisco?"

"Not quite, but still way too many." He looked over her. "I'll be two seconds, tops."

The message was clear. *Stay here*. Instead, she got out with him.

He grimaced. "Listen, you heard my mom and sister on the phone. My entire family is like that. Certifiable, really. It's too late for me, but save yourself and wait here."

"Not a chance," she said as he grabbed the game from the trunk.

The front door opened and people spilled out. A woman in her fifties was the leader of the pack, looking a lot like Lucas with his dark eyes and dark hair, though hers was sprinkled through with gray. Two younger women flanked her, also dark hair and dark eyes.

"My mom, my sister, Laura, and cousin Sami," Lucas said to her. "Brace yourself."

"What for—" Before she could finish the sentence, Lucas's mom had bounded down the walk and engulfed him in a hug. The other two women each hugged Molly in turn, smiling and saying how nice it was to meet her.

Then the Knight women all switched spots and it was Lucas's mom's turn to hug Molly while his sister and cousin pounced him. An arm full of each, he turned to catch his mom hugging Molly. "Mom, stop abusing my coworker's space bubble."

"Oh." His mom looked so disappointed as she pulled back from Molly. "I was hoping she was your girlfriend."

Lucas blew out a breath, grabbed Molly's hand and rescued her from his mom. "We work together."

"Is there a policy at Hunt that forbids coworkers from dating?"

"Don't answer that," Lucas told Molly when she opened her mouth. "Trust me."

"There's not!" his mom said gleefully.

Laura and Sami both laughed.

"It's because we're both married, you see," Laura said to Molly. "And I've even provided a grandchild." She waved a baby monitor, which presumably would lead to a sleeping kid. "Now Mom's luckily focused in on Lucas to provide *more* grandchildren."

"Do you like children?" his mom asked Molly. "Are you single?"

"We've talked about this, Mom," Lucas said. "You were going to stop accosting strangers and trying to recruit them to marry me."

"Well, Molly's not a stranger now, is she? She's your coworker." She smiled at Molly. "Lovely to meet you. You're also Joe's sister."

"Yes," Molly said. "You've met Joe?"

"Only briefly when I made Lucas stop by a few months ago and Joe was with him. I fed him. He appreciated my food." She shot a mock glare at Lucas. "Unlike some people."

"Mom, I appreciate your food so much I have to run four miles every morning."

Lucas's mom slipped an arm around Molly and turned her toward the front door. "You're chilled. Come in with me, I have—"

"Mom," Lucas said. "Back away from her. We're working."

"Well you have to eat."

"We're not hungry." He handed his mom the game and then wrapped his arms around her in a very warm, loving hug, brushing a kiss to her temple. "Love you, you crazy person."

Her arms squeezed him tight. "Someday I'm going to be dead and you're going to be sorry you were so mean to me."

Lucas just laughed and kissed her again. He hugged Laura and Sami, gently patted Sami's baby belly and then took Molly by the hand. "Good night," he said firmly.

They headed back to the car, Molly deep in thought. Her family wasn't anything like Lucas's warm, loving one. She and Joe had been raised by a single dad who suffered from war PTSD. He hadn't been able to hold a job for long, which left them perpetually scrambling for a roof and food. Safety and security had been in short supply. She'd learned early to count on herself and no one else.

And God knows, that had certainly stuck with

her as she'd gotten older. There'd been lots of bumps along the way and she'd been bruised and scarred, inside and out, literally and figuratively. Her trust issue was a fifteen-foot-thick brick wall around her heart, and not much penetrated.

But Lucas, who also had been bruised and scarred, didn't seem to have that brick wall, and it wasn't a comfortable realization.

He cranked over the engine and met her gaze. "You survived that pretty well. Thanks for being so nice about it."

"Your family," she murmured, still a little over-whelmed. "They're . . ."

"Crazy. I know."

"No," she said, shaking her head. Not even close. She could still feel their warmth, their closeness, their unconditional love. "They're . . ."

"Nosy, manipulating, pushy . . . ?"

"Stop," she said on a laugh, knowing he was teasing by his fond tone. He knew what he had, how wonderful they were, and her smile faded. "You're lucky, Lucas."

His smile faded too. "I know. I take it you aren't as lucky?"

"No, I'm lucky too," she said, thinking of how much Joe and her dad meant to her. "Just in a very different way."

Chapter 10

#UnderTheMistletoe

Molly took in the sight of the Christmas Village as Lucas pulled into the lot. It had been constructed on a part of a large parking lot at the marina and was lit within an inch of its life with an old-fashioned feel to it. She wasn't sure if that was on purpose or if the decorations and lights had just been around for half a century.

Lucas parked and turned to her. "We're going in as paying customers. Just a couple out on the town, having a good time," he instructed.

She gave him a long look. "You should know, I typically only take alpha orders in bed." It was a total bluff, of course, pure bravado. And okay, maybe she was trying to goad him into kissing her again.

"Molly." He took a deep breath. "You can't say things like that. I'll take advantage."

"Promises, promises."

He shut his eyes and groaned. "Killing me."

"Am I? Cuz it seems like you've resisted pretty easily."

"Trust me," he said, voice low and gruff. "Nothing easy about it."

"Uh-huh."

"Molly, look at me."

Oh boy. She inhaled a deep breath and turned to face him. They were no longer playing around. His expression was serious, very serious, as he stroked a finger along her temple, tucking an errant strand of hair behind her ear. "You're incredible, and you should know that it's been a long time since I've felt so tempted by someone."

"Come on," she said on a scoff. "You don't expect me to believe that when you went out with that red-head from the pub like two weeks ago."

"Not the kind of tempted I meant."

She stared at him, trying hard not to read too much into that statement. "What does that even mean?"

"It means I want you, and I'm tired of resisting. But when I get you naked, it won't be in an office where anyone can walk in, or in my car, and it sure as hell won't be something one of us can't remember."

All her girlie parts quivered and she ordered them to behave. "You said when, not if," she murmured.

The fingers he'd just run over her temple sank into her hair. Pulling her face to his, he kissed her long and slow and most definitely not sweet. By the time he pulled back, she'd forgotten what they were talking about. Hell, she'd forgotten her own name.

"When," he repeated in a voice that made her toes curl. "Definitely *when.*"

Okay then. With hands and knees shaking a little bit, she got out of the car and headed to the entrance gate of the Christmas Village. They had to pay ten bucks to get in. "Yikes," Molly said to the older woman staffing the ticket booth dressed in an elf costume complete with pointy shoes, pointy ears, a little green dress made out of a cheap material that couldn't help but cling, and matching cap that didn't quite hide the fact that she was about three decades past looking good in anything little and stretchy. "Ten bucks seems kind of steep for an empty Christmas Village."

And it was true. The village wasn't exactly hopping.

"Hence the ten bucks," the woman said in a bored tone, hand held out for the dough. "Each."

Lucas handed her a twenty and she winked at him. "Thanks, handsome."

They stepped inside the village, their senses immediately assaulted by the scent of popcorn, the bright lights stretched across and along the individual stands, and the odd quiet. The temps had dropped and the fog had rolled in, playing peekaboo with the night.

"I feel like we're in a horror flick," Molly whispered. "If a clown jumps out at us, you'll shoot him for me, right?"

"Absolutely." Lucas took her chilled hand in his warm one and led her across a lane lined with hay towards a popcorn and hot dog stand. It was run by yet another elf. Lucas bought two dogs and two lemonades and gave the woman a flirty smile. "Slow night, huh?"

She smiled back. "Honey, they're all slow when bingo's running," she said. "Everyone's keeping warm while playing in the big old building at the end of the aisle."

They ate their hot dogs and popcorn and walked most of the aisles. Or rather, Molly ate popcorn and hot dogs. Lucas strolled along with her, looking casual and laid-back, although he was anything but as his sharp gaze took everything in. "You're not hungry?" she asked.

"Oh, I'm hungry."

She looked up from her hot dog and met his hot gaze. His smile was pure sex and she swallowed hard and went back to her food, which felt far safer. Somehow it'd been a whole lot easier to resist him before he'd put his mouth on hers.

The craft stands held some beautifully created things and Molly used that to instigate some conversation with the two elves in charge.

"Holiday shopping," Molly said with a friendly smile and picked up a small reindeer knitted cap. "Cute."

"It's for dogs," one of the elves said. "I make them. My own Fluffy was the model for that one."

"Cute," Molly said and bought it for her dad's new emotional support dog. And to hopefully encourage some more chatting. "What a fun job this must be."

"Used to be," the elf said wistfully. "I've been doing this with my girls for years now. Last year we made enough to go to Vegas Eleanor, my sister, she married an Elvis impersonator." Her smile faded. "But this year's different."

"How so?" Molly asked.

"Well, for one thing, the big boss isn't paying us nearly what he should. He's claiming he's not making any money this year."

Lucas looked around. "That might actually be true."

The elf waved this off. "Everyone's just in seven o'clock bingo right now. Emptying their social security checks and pockets into Santa's coffers. Trust me, he's making plenty. It's just not trickling down, the bastard."

"Alice," the elf in the next booth called out. "Loose lips sink ships."

Alice rolled her eyes and went back to her knitting.

Molly and Lucas moved down the aisle, but though the few other elves working were friendly, they didn't open up in spite of the fact that Molly bought another hat, a scarf, and a throw blanket.

At the beginning of the next aisle of stands, there was a sign.

ELVES WANTED

And another at the end of that row too. This sign was out in front of a large trailer, the kind that construction sites used as offices. Molly stared at the trailer and then turned to Lucas.

"No," he said.

She crossed her arms. "I don't know if you realize this or not, but when someone tells me no, I tend to rebel for rebelling sake."

"Good to know," he said and gestured with his hand. "Then by all means, apply to work for a guy who's a known asshat and also a possible felon."

"His brother's the felon," she said.

He shook his head. "I stand corrected. Go to work for two known asshat felons."

"Sounds like a plan." Thrusting her lemonade at him, she headed to the office door.

"Shit," he muttered to himself. "You walked right into that one, Ace." He tossed her drink into a trash bin and started to follow her.

She held out a hand to stop him. "You're waiting here."

He came forward enough that her hand bumped into his chest. "Like you did at my mom's?"

She left her palm on him. She had no idea how he did it, but he was always warm, and given the even steady beat of his heart, always collected. "You have to," she said. "They're not going to hire me if I have a big, badass bodyguard with me."

His hand came up and covered hers still on him. "I'd be happy to guard your body any day of the week, but don't forget you made a deal. We're partners in this."

"I know," she said. "So *I'm* going to follow this angle and *you're* going to follow another, and we'll meet up and compare notes." She started to pull back to walk off but he still had a hold of her hand.

"Molly—"

"Don't say I can't do this."

"Actually," he said. "You're smart, resourceful, and incredibly crafty about getting your way. I think you can do anything you set your mind to. But tonight, you're limited."

She stiffened. "I'm not—"

"You're favoring your leg," he said quietly. "In a big way. If you have to run—"

"I can run. I pass Archer's fitness test every year like the rest of you," she said hotly, as he was currently standing on her biggest, most rawest nerve point.

"But you're in pain," he said.

"So what?" She gave him a push. "I'm almost always in pain. I deal with it, so you can too."

He drew in a deep breath, as if the thought of her in pain caused a mirroring pain in him. But that resonated a little too close to pity for her and she went hands on hips. "I've got this," she said. "Unless you think I can't handle it."

He was a smart man and he apparently knew a dare when he heard one. He wisely let go of her hand. And she walked into the office and found another elf behind a counter, whose fingers were racing over the keys of an ancient adding machine.

"Hi," Molly said. "I'm here about an elf job."

The woman looked up. Like the others, she too was at least seventy, which Molly was really hoping wasn't a requirement for getting hired.

"You want to be an elf?" she asked Molly doubtfully.

"Yes."

"But you're like . . . *twelve*."

"I'm twenty-eight," Molly said.

The elf blinked. "But you're not even getting social security for at least a million years."

"Or never," Molly said. "Given the current political climate and all."

The woman didn't crack a smile.

"My name's Molly. And you are . . . ?"

"Louise."

"Well, you're right, Louise, I don't get social security checks. Is that a requirement?"

"No, being on social security isn't a requirement. It's just usually what it is," Louise said.

"And what do the elves do exactly?"

"They follow Santa's orders. The elves in the white caps are the worker bees. They've created the goods and work the booths and sell food. The elves in the green caps run bingo. I'm assuming you don't knit, crochet, sew, or embroider?"

"Why would you assume that?"

"Because no one under fifty does those things."

Right. "Okay, so I'd have to be a green capped elf," Molly said. "Am I hired?"

"Do you have any elf experience?"

"Well, I've got experience with bossy, alpha men and getting them to do whatever I need them to do," Molly said honestly. "And I look good in green."

She hoped.

"Those things are indeed a plus," Louise said and slid off her stool. She stretched, popping her neck and back. "Lord, if only I was sixty again." She grabbed a clipboard and handed it to Molly. "Fill out this form."

"And *then* I'm hired?"

"If you can fit the last costume we have in stock." Louise looked Molly over critically and then went to a closet and pulled out a hangar from which hung a few scraps of green shimmery stretchy material. "It's extra small because the last woman to wear it was like four foot ten on a good day with heels, so not sure it's going to cover all your business."

Oh boy.

She was directed to a bathroom, where she locked herself in and glanced in the mirror. "For elves everywhere," she told herself and began to strip.

Lucas had walked the entire length of the village while waiting on Molly to come out of the office. He'd been smiled at, winked at, and even propositioned by one particular feisty elf running a cotton candy booth.

He had to give these ladies credit. Either they were taking their replacement hormones and vitamins every day, or he'd stepped into the *Twilight Zone*.

He'd texted Molly twice with a question mark. She'd answered him back with two exclamation marks.

He had no idea what that meant.

By the time the office door finally opened again, he'd eaten three hot dogs and two soft pretzels and he'd been groped by the elf who'd served him.

Molly stepped out of the office wearing . . . Christ. The smallest elf costume known to man, complete with elf ears, an elf cap, and a little green spandex dress that appeared to be shrink-wrapped to her body. A body that had his mouth going dry.

She flashed him a self-deprecating smile and he was struck dumb and mute for so long she managed to come down the steps, cross the aisle, and come toe to toe with him before his wits returned.

"Do *not*," she muttered.

"Do not what?"

"Do not tell me what you think."

He shook his head. Deal, because what he thought was that he wanted to pick her up and sling her over his shoulder and take her caveman style back to his place, where he'd unwrap her from that green spandex one inch at a time, making sure to kiss every single one of those inches as he did until she was begging him for more.

And if she wanted to scream his name while she did it, he was all for it.

"Okay," she said, staring up at him. "I changed my mind. Tell me."

Not even if someone was holding a gun to his head. "You look . . . green."

She rolled her eyes. "Funny." She started walking down the first aisle. She got several feet in front of him, enough that he could admire the back view every bit as much as he'd admired the front view.

Realizing he wasn't following her, she turned in exasperation. "You coming?"

Unfortunately, no. There'd be no coming for him any time soon. "Where are you going?"

"I'm working eight o'clock bingo. Thought you'd want to buy in and sit in the back and check things out."

"Bingo," he repeated.

"Yep. You've got yourself a real live wire for the evening. You ready for this?"

He looked down into her eyes and had to laugh. He considered himself a man who'd seen and done it all, but he'd never felt so out of his league in his entire life. He was in no way ready for this. Not for bingo. Not for working so closely with her. He wasn't close to ready for any of it, but especially not ready for her. "Lead the way," he said.

She flashed him a smile that dazzled him even more than her skimpy elf costume. "Follow me."

As if he could do anything but.

Chapter 11

#BingoBabe

Molly learned two things about herself that night. One, bingo wasn't some sweet little old lady thing. It was a no-holds-barred, cutthroat, winner takes all thing.

And two, Lucas was an old lady magnet. He sat quietly by himself, but as the room filled with patrons, he was virtually surrounded and ooh'd and aah'd over.

"You new, honey?" asked one.

"No worries," cooed another, sitting on his other side. "We'll show you the ropes."

He looked up and met Molly's gaze. She would have said the big, badass Lucas Knight wasn't afraid of anything, but there was a good amount of fear in his eyes at the moment. She sent him a grin and a thumbs-up.

Two seconds later, her phone buzzed with a text.

I will get even . . .

Oh boy. She risked another peek at him, and even surrounded by trembling gray hair buns, he flashed her a look that had her insides quivering.

Why was it getting more difficult to resist him?

"What do you need me to do?" she asked the two green-capped elves at the front who'd introduced themselves as Shirley and Lorraine.

"Well since you look like the hottest elf anyone's ever seen," Shirley said, "you're on numbers. When it pops up on the screen, you call it. Loudly. Most of the payers are deaf so we also flash it on a big screen. Lorraine will do that. Don't forget to flirt with the crowd, wink, stuff like that."

"And shake it," Lorraine said. "Maybe we'll get bigger tips and the boss'll finally be happy and pay it forward and give us a bigger cut of them tonight."

"I didn't get to meet him," Molly said. "Is he . . . unhappy?"

"Shouldn't be," Janet said, coming up to the bingo table. "Sorry I'm late."

Molly looked at her, surprised to see her because the other night at her kitchen table, Janet had mentioned she wouldn't be working again until she got paid what she felt she had coming.

Janet shrugged. "The green-capped elves get better tips," she said. "And I need the money."

"Apparently so does Santa," Shirley said. "He just

built a new home in Napa and bought a brand-new car. And he's started renovations on this hall." She pointed to the back half of the building, which was completely draped from view by tarps.

"*And* he sent his latest wife on a three-month world cruise," Lorraine said. "Don't forget that one. Carol went from a green cap to the Mrs. Santa cap without having to pass Go!"

"Didn't you hear?" Shirley asked. "Carol dumped him last month. Rumor is, he's working on someone new."

"Wait, you guys don't get your cut of the tips either?" Molly asked, trying to keep them on track.

The ladies all looked at each other and suddenly zipped it.

"Look, I don't mean to pry," Molly said. "But you're entitled to your own tips, you know. If you all said something, maybe—"

"Listen," Shirley said, looking around to make sure no one was looking at them. "You're new so you don't know, but it's not healthy to ask a lot of questions around here."

"Not healthy?" Molly asked. "What, are we in a mob movie?"

The ladies didn't crack a smile.

Okaaaaay. "The woman in the office who hired me, Louise, she told me that we all get minimum wages plus a cut of the tips, and then a percentage of the profits."

The elves snorted.

Shirley looked around and then leaned in. "Near

as we can figure out, they're skimming off the top, as if to make sure no one was paying them any attention, stealing all the profits, which leaves us with only bare minimum wage."

"And you're sure there really are profits?" Molly asked.

"Trust me, yes," Shirley said. "You'll see at the end of the night."

They then proceeded to run bingo for three straight hours to a crowd of geriatrics who took the game incredibly seriously.

"I thought older people got tired early," Molly said to Shirley at one point.

Shirley laughed. "Not when bingo's on the table."

By the end of the night, Molly still hadn't seen Santa or his damn brother, and her feet were killing her.

Shirley sent her a sympathetic glance as the crowd finally began to thin out. "The trick is orthopedic shoes." She lifted a foot to show off her black thick-soled shoe, which was possibly the ugliest footwear Molly had ever seen. It actually hurt her to look at it.

"Wear these babies," she said, "and you'll have no problems."

Molly nodded. She didn't have many vices, but shoes were one of them. It was a well-known fact that she spent way too much of her paycheck buying shoes that wouldn't hurt her back, leg, or feet and still looked amazing, and she wasn't about to stop doing that. Not even for her case.

Lorraine came close, eating a big cookie, and Molly's mouth watered.

"Thought you were on a diet," Shirley said to Lorraine.

The elf shoved in the last of her cookie. "If you eat fast enough, your Fitbit thinks you're running."

Shirley rolled her eyes, but Molly thought Lorraine might be onto something.

"We were so busy tonight we didn't even get to chat. New Girl," Lorraine said to Molly, "you did good. When that old geezer asked if you give out happy endings and patted your ass, I started over there to hit him over the head with my tray for you, but you handled yourself like a pro."

Molly smiled. She'd leaned into the guy and asked him if he liked his hand. He'd said he liked it very much. And then she'd suggested in that same polite, conversational tone that if he wanted to keep his hand, he might want to remove it from her hind-end or the six foot plus guy heading toward them with narrowed eyes was going to remove it for him—if she didn't remove it first.

"Oh jeez." The old man had gulped hard, apologized, and tipped her twenty bucks. "Tell your man that I'm farsighted and was trying to grab a drink and not your posterior," he whispered frantically. "Yeah?"

"If you promise not to touch another elf without permission. Or anyone, for that matter, anyone."

He nodded like a bobblehead and she'd moved

on, giving Lucas a long, I've-got-this look. He'd vanished after that, but she'd bet that he'd remained close by, watching her back.

A man dressed in Santa gear minus the hat, wig, and beard strode up the center of the room. He was fiftyish and wearing a grim expression as he grabbed the very large lockbox of cash and tipped it over, dumping it straight into a duffle bag. "How did it go?" he asked Shirley.

"Fantastic. The new girl raked it in for us."

Santa's eyes swept over Molly and narrowed. "Who are you?"

"The new girl," Molly said. "Santa, I presume?"

"Did Louise vet you?"

"Yep," she said with a smile.

It wasn't returned. Without a "nice to meet you" or so much as a "thank you," he hoisted the duffle bag over one shoulder and strode back out of the room without talking to anyone else.

"That is one seriously unmerry Santa," Molly said.

Janet shrugged. "He has his moments."

"And he's the big boss?" Molly asked, fishing.

"Him and his brother," Shirley said. "Though luckily we don't see much of that one. He comes by to pick up Santa late at night after most of us are gone—which is just as well since he's a mean son of a bitch."

"And Santa's not?"

Janet shrugged again. "Not as bad as his brother. His brother makes the Grinch look like a sweetheart."

"To be fair," Shirley said, "the Grinch never really hated Christmas. He hated people, which is fair."

"That was a lot of cash," Molly said. "That huge cash box was jam-packed."

Shirley shoved open a window and stuck her head out to light a cigarette. She inhaled deeply with a look of pure pleasure on her face. When she exhaled, she pulled her head back in and nodded at Molly. "Mostly. We were busy tonight because the seniors all got their social security checks yesterday. They cash 'em out and we're their first stop."

The elves dispersed after that and Molly stepped outside into the dark night to find Lucas leaning against the building, waiting for her.

His gaze slid over her body and went a long way toward warming her up, but what went even further was when he pulled off his windbreaker and wrapped her up in it.

"Thanks," she said, hugging it to herself, soaking in the body heat he'd left for her. Lucas pulled her around the back of the bingo hall and there in the shadows, as everyone else filtered out of the village for the night, she told him everything she'd learned from the ladies.

Lucas nodded. "It's true that Santa's brother comes by at the end of the evening to pick up the dough. I want to stick around and try to get eyes on him. How are you doing, you okay? You've been on your feet—"

"I'm good. How did you find out he'd be here tonight?"

He gave a small smile. "The elf who hired you. Louise. Brought her a laced hot chocolate and she got very talkative."

"Nice," Molly said. "And you didn't even have to shake it all night."

Lucas smiled. "I liked how you shook it."

"How would you know? You were out charming Louise."

"I kept an eye on you."

"Because you thought I needed backup, or because you liked how I shook it?"

"Everyone needs backup, Molly. Including me." He smiled. "But I love how you shake it. I'm going to the offices and watch for Santa and his brother. Would you like to wait in the car?"

"No."

He nodded, not looking surprised. They went through the trees to stay out of sight. It was dark and not easy going for her. Lucas led the way, keeping a tight grip on her hand. The ground was uneven and a wind furled through the trees overhead, brushing over her with icy fingers. She couldn't see a thing. The only thing she could hear was her own accelerated breathing and the occasional hum of an insect, which sure as hell better not be crawling on her. It was hard to believe that they were still smack in the middle of the city of San Francisco.

Then Lucas stopped and she nearly plowed into him. His hands reached out to steady her. "There's still a light on in the office," he murmured against her ear.

"Wait here," she said. "I've got an idea." She started to walk out from the trees, but Lucas caught her.

"No way," he said.

"No, it's okay, trust me. I'll be right back." She strode around to the front of the trailer/office so it wouldn't look like she'd just come from the woods, and headed up the stairs, letting herself in.

Louise and Santa were heads together, going over a ledger. They both looked up when she entered. "Hi," she said cheerfully with a wave.

Louise smiled.

Santa did not.

"I just wanted to say thanks for hiring me," Molly said. "I had a great time tonight and just wanted to know what other nights you need me this week."

Santa rolled his eyes and strode past her without a word. Louise brought up a schedule on her laptop. "I'm good until Friday night. So three nights from now."

"I'll be here," Molly said. "Well, thanks again. Good night." She hustled out the door fast as she dared, heading around the trailer, where she nearly collided with a brick wall. A warm, solid, familiar brick wall.

Lucas easily absorbed the impact, wrapping an arm around her without hesitation, leading her back into the trees.

"If you wanted to get me alone, all you had to do was say so," she said breathlessly, and not all from their fast pace.

"Oh, I want to get you alone." Lucas brushed his mouth up her jaw to speak in a husky low voice right in her ear. "But as previously mentioned, not in the woods—" He broke off when she pulled something from inside her elf costume. A man's wallet.

"Santa's," she said.

He went brows up. "You found Santa's wallet?"

"More like lifted it from his back pocket."

Lucas just stared at her. "Without him knowing?"

"That's sorta the definition of 'lifting it from his back pocket.'"

He shook his head. "I don't know whether to be impressed or . . ."

"—Horrified? I know." She shrugged. "I get that reaction from men a lot." She started to turn away but he caught her.

"—Or amazed," he finished. "I don't know whether to be *impressed* or *amazed*."

"Impressed and amazed are the same thing," she said, hoping he'd ignore the blush of pleasure she could feel creeping up her cheeks.

He flashed a smile that she felt all the way to her toes and everywhere in between. "You're as good as Joe," he said. "But I think I like working with you better."

She squirmed under the high praise. Indeed, she'd learned B&E from way too young of an age, but she and Joe had done what they'd had to and their survival instincts were finely honed. She didn't get to use her skills much anymore, but it was good to know they were still there. "I couldn't get a good snoop on in there," she said. "We're going to have to wait for them to leave and then go back in."

Again his mouth brushed the shell of her ear, giving her another of those full body shivers of the very best kind when he said, "You turn me on when you talk dirty like that."

She snorted, but the feel-good glow was still lighting her up from the inside out. They waited a few minutes. Lights turned off in the trailer and Louise left.

"Was Santa with her?" she whispered.

"I don't think so."

"He had to be. The place is dark. We must've missed him. Let's go."

"No," Lucas said as she ran up the stairs to the trailer door. "Molly, wait—"

Before he could finish the sentence, a car pulled up behind them.

At the same exact moment, the trailer door suddenly opened. Molly froze but Lucas pushed her up against the railing, and with one hand on the back of her neck, began kissing her with the same intensity as he had earlier in the car and then some. She was so shocked, she remained frozen.

Not Lucas. He had one arm low around her back, his other hand slowly fisting in her hair to hold her still for his passionate and demanding mouth, which admittedly left her more than a little weak in the knees. Apparently realizing that, he easily lifted her weight, setting her butt on the railing, pushing his way between her legs to deepen the kiss.

A tingle started at her toes, working its way to her center. From somewhere deep in the recesses of her mind, she knew this was a cover, that it wasn't real, but it was hard to keep that thought. Because if this was the way he solved problems . . . well, she really liked the way he worked.

"Jesus," Santa muttered as he passed through. "Take it to a room."

Molly barely registered the guy clomping down the stairs toward the waiting car carrying his duffle bag bulging with the night's gains before he got into the passenger seat and the car vanished into the night.

Lucas let go of her and turned to get a better look at the car as it drove off.

Both Santa and the driver turned to look at him, and for one heart-stopping beat everyone stared at each other.

Then the car sped up and was gone.

Lucas turned back to Molly, who was still balanced on the railing, dazed. "Did you just . . . put the elf on the shelf?" she asked.

He gave a disbelieving head shake.

She felt a little disbelieving herself. If she closed her eyes, she could still feel his arms wrapped tight around her, holding her safely onto the railing, his mouth sensual and erotic on hers. He'd taken her from chilled to overheated in a blink. In fact, she'd forgotten about the case, about the cold night, about trying to resist him and his insane sexiness for her own sanity. And much as she felt bowled over by their physical attraction, it went far deeper than just physical for her.

She thought *she* was the sneaky queen, but Lucas could teach her a few tricks, making her realize she had a lot to learn. He was badass and sneaky in his own right, and that was a ridiculous turn-on. Dammit.

"There was no license plate on that car," he said. "Did you see the driver?"

She hopped down from the railing. "He had a hat low over his eyes. Looked shady as hell. Also that was cash in that bulging duffle bag and it was full—*also* shady as hell."

"*Everything* about this creepy place is shady as hell," he said.

"I told you they're making bank. Question is, where is it all really going?" She turned to the trailer, but Lucas stopped her.

"Not yet," he said. "We're going to the car to give this place another half hour to empty out."

"Everyone's gone."

He slid her a look. "That's what you thought last time. You've pushed your luck enough tonight."

He was right. "Lucas—"

"Not here."

They walked to the car in silence, where Lucas locked them in. "I asked you to wait before heading into the trailer," he said. "Instead you almost got caught."

"Yeah, but—"

"When I tell you to wait, you need to wait."

She narrowed her eyes. She knew she was in the wrong here, but she couldn't help herself. "Maybe you want to rephrase that."

"I don't."

She crossed her arms, but he didn't back down. "Are you saying that if I'd said '*please* wait,' you would have?" he asked.

Good point. Dammit. She just looked at him.

He looked at her right back. She realized in the year she'd been working at Hunt, she'd never seen him really mad before, but he was close now. She'd missed the signs what with all the adrenaline and lust running through her veins instead of blood. "Okay," she said slowly. "Let's try this again. I'm sorry I didn't wait when you said it. Annnddd . . . *you're* sorry you barked at me like you're my drill sergeant, right?"

"Look," he said, "on the job, I can be . . . focused."

"Wow." She shook her head. "You're really bad at apologies."

"That wasn't an apology. When I apologize you'll know it."

She narrowed her gaze. "Oh, is that right—"

Before she could finish that sentence, he hauled her up and over the console and then his mouth came down on hers in a long, slow, deep kiss. After a long, breathless moment, he pulled back a fraction, eyes dark, voice low. "I'm sorry I told instead of asking all pretty, but in the field things happen fast, and in the case of life and death, I'm *always* going to put your life ahead of mine. So keep that in mind next time you act without thinking."

The magnitude of that, the meaning behind the words slowly sank in and she softened. "Lucas—"

He kissed her again, whispered "sorry" again, taking his time too, and he'd been right, she realized, when he did apologize, she most definitely knew it. And he went on to apologize quite thoroughly too, until she couldn't even remember what he was sorry for.

Or her own name.

Chapter 12

#ShelfTheElf

Lucas had lost his damn mind. Molly wasn't for him, and yet the memo had clearly not made it from his brain to his hands. Or his tongue.

Or to any other essential body parts . . .

He tried to shake off the sensual, erotic haze that always came over him when he was close to her like this, but realized the haze was actually real. They'd fogged up the windows. "Not smart," he said. "Steaming up the windows on a stakeout."

Her short, tight green elf dress had risen high on her creamy thighs, and far before he was done soaking up the sight, she attempted to smooth it down with shaking fingers. "It's the oddest thing," she whispered, straightening her elf cap.

"What?"

"I *really* don't want to want you, but I do." She stared at him contemplatively. "I mean *what is that*?"

He felt his lips curve. He could have said *right back attcha, babe*, but instead he said, "It's because I'm irresistible."

"Keep telling yourself that. And I'll keep reminding *myself* that I'm not attracted to guys like you."

"Guys like me?" he asked. "What does that mean?"

"Big. Badass. Doggedly aggressive . . ." She used her arm to swipe at the steamed-up passenger window. "Annoyingly high-sexualized chemistry," she said to the glass.

He was glad she wasn't looking at him right then because his triumphant smile would've made her mad. He really was trying not to be all in with her, and not just because of Joe and the job but because he hadn't planned on being "all in" with anyone ever again. But she sat there looking so sexy and adorable at the same time in that costume, all pissy and grumpy because she wanted him. It would take a far better man than him to resist that.

"*Very* annoying," she muttered to herself, crossing her arms over her chest.

"You didn't feel all that annoyed a minute ago."

"Hmph."

Her bad 'tude and reluctance to accept their attraction amused him. Which spoke volumes on his mental maturity. But he had to find the humor in this to keep everything—including her—compartmentalized.

And it wasn't as if she was going to go all in with him either. She kept herself closed off to him in most ways, but ever since she'd slept in his bed, their physical chemistry refused to be ignored.

"This is all your fault," she said. "You shouldn't have kissed me again."

He stared at her in disbelief. "It was you nearly getting caught that led to that kiss. And while we're on that, you're welcome for saving your very sexy, impulsive ass."

"So you're telling me that kiss was simply a diversion tactic?" she asked. "All the tongue, the hand on my ass, all of it just for the job?"

Their gazes locked. "That's not what you asked," he said.

"I'm asking now."

There was the simple answer, which was that's what he *wanted* the kiss to have been. A diversion tactic, nothing more. But the more complicated answer was that the kiss had only started out that way and had quickly proven to him that *nothing* was simple between the two of them. Not a single thing, including the emotions she stirred up from deep inside him, emotions he'd long ago buried.

Emotions he couldn't afford. "The kiss started out a diversion," he admitted. "But ended up something else entirely." And every single word of that sentence was 100 percent true. He looked over at her, and in the ambient lighting of the car's interior, waited for a response.

But fascinatingly enough, it was her turn to do a tap dance around the truth. "I was doing fine," she said.

"Sure you were," he said. "You were doing fine at getting caught. You know, I thought your brother was the most stubborn person I've ever met, but he's got nothing on you."

She shrugged, clearly taking that as a compliment. "I could've handled myself."

"I have no doubt," he said. "But you're not an 'I.' You're a 'we.' If any of us at Hunt had pulled that stunt tonight, Archer would have had our ass in a sling." He opened his car door. "Let's go get the rest of this over with."

The village was lights out, locked down. Molly nodded to the now locked gate. "How long would it take you to break in?"

They both knew B&E was Joe's specialty, but Lucas was no slouch. "Two minutes. Ish."

"Move," she said, nudging him aside. "I can do it in one."

And she did. And though it should have annoyed the shit out of him, it had the opposite effect. Watching her work the lock on that gate in the promised sixty seconds dressed as an elf turned him on even more than the costume.

They walked quietly and quickly through the dark village to the trailer office. Also locked.

Molly looked up at him with hope and excitement and he gestured for her to have at it.

Again, she got them inside in less than a minute. She beamed up at him, eyes shining with adrenaline and pride, and he had no idea what came over him. He slid his hand around the nape of her neck, pulled her to him, and kissed her. It was unsatisfyingly short, but no less potent for it, and when he pulled away, he had a surge of male satisfaction at seeing her eyes now slightly dazed.

"What was that for?" she asked.

"I don't know. You drive me crazy."

She nodded. "I get that a lot."

"I meant crazy in a really great way."

She stared up at him, nibbling her bottom lip, appearing to be struck mute by this confession. She didn't know what to make of him.

Which made two of them.

She turned from him and eyed the office. Typical rectangle shape, stuffed with a shabby couch, three seen-better-days desks, and a filing cabinet. "What do you think?" she asked.

What did he think? He wanted to sprawl the elf out on one of the desks and taste every inch of her. That's what he thought.

She looked up, caught his expression, and paused. "Do I want to know?"

"If you knew, you'd be running for the hills."

She paused, as if she was debating pushing him on the issue.

Do it, he thought.

But she shrugged it off and pulled open a drawer. "Oh boy."

He moved to her side in time to see that every drawer she pulled out was empty, including the cabinet file.

"Think he cleans out every night?" Molly asked. "Or was that for our benefit?"

"I don't know. But we're going to find out."

She nodded and did a slow circle, her eyes running over the entire place.

No paper trail. No computer.

Nothing.

"What now?" she asked softly.

"We come back," Lucas said. "Your next shift. There's got to be some point in the evening where this office is left unattended. Maybe during bingo. I'll get in then."

She looked over him. "Sounds dangerous."

He shrugged. He'd been in far worse circumstances.

She just looked at him.

"What?" he asked.

"I don't like the feeling that I'm putting you into a dangerous situation."

He let out a low laugh. "You know the nature of some of the jobs we take on. This is nothing."

"You'd better not get hurt. Not on my watch."

He was torn between laughing again and fighting a sensation he didn't quite recognize, but whatever it was, it sent a warmth through his chest. Been a long time since someone had worried about him. Well, okay, his family worried about him, but he did his best to keep them in the dark on the actual danger level of his job.

Molly knew. And she understood.

And she worried about him.

And it wasn't just tonight either. Four nights ago, she'd caught on to the fact that he'd been out of commission after stupidly mixing pain meds and alcohol, and she'd personally taken on the matter of his safety by getting him home.

That was new for him. And not entirely unwelcome. He'd been feeling off since getting shot. Off and alone. But actually, if he was being honest, it'd been longer than that, a lot longer. He'd cut himself off from feeling too much after losing Carrie and then a few years later, his brother, Josh in an arson fire.

But he was feeling again now and he knew that was Molly.

What he didn't know was what to do about it.

Back at the car, Molly closed her eyes with a tired sigh. "You're staring," she murmured.

When she'd climbed into the passenger seat, the little elf costume had crept up her thighs again. A very nice view, but mostly he was hoping she wasn't in pain. She was, though, he could see it in the tightness around her mouth and eyes, but God forbid he reveal an ounce of empathy; she'd likely kill him. "Does it make me an asshole to tell you that I like the way you look in that costume?" he asked.

She let out a low laugh. "Well you're honest at least."

He started to ask what the "at least" meant but her phone rang. She answered and listened a moment. "Joe, I can't take tomorrow night for you. I told you that already, I'm working on something—" She paused and sighed. "So let me get this straight. You've got a really great girlfriend and she's taking you on some fantastic mystery surprise date tomorrow night with the promise of God knows what afterward and you figured what the hell, Molly doesn't have a life, I'll get her to take my night. Is that it?"

Lucas winced for Joe.

"No, really," Molly said in that same conversational voice. "By all means, let me help you make your already awesome, amazing life even better. I'll handle it." She disconnected and leaned her head back, closing her eyes. "Don't," she said quietly.

"Don't what?" Lucas asked.

"Tell me I'm not nice. I already know it."

"I wasn't going to say that."

"Because I *am* nice?" she asked dryly.

"Because you already know you're not nice."

At that, she snorted.

"And Molly? You do so have a life."

She opened her eyes and met his. "You think so, huh?"

"Yes. You have a lot of good friends, and you're always doing things like girls' night out and shopping and spa stuff. And you have a good job that keeps you busy, and a family you care about."

"I do have good friends," she agreed. "But I don't let any of them too close because I'm bad at that. And my job isn't fulfilling me, which has me chasing down a bad Santa that no one but me thinks is bad."

"I think he's bad," he said.

She sighed. "Thanks." And then she closed her eyes again.

"And your family," he said carefully.

"What about them?"

He didn't know much and he wanted to know more. In fact he was surprised by how badly he wanted that. But prying with Molly had never worked. She didn't like questions. "You say you don't let anyone too close. But you're close with Joe, even when you're yelling at him."

"We're close because we've had to be, you know?"

"Actually, no," he said. "I don't. The only person more closed-mouthed about yours and Joe's past is Joe."

She let out a low laugh and shrugged. "It's a life-long habit," she admitted. "Mostly because there's not all that much to say. We're really not all that different from anyone else."

He glanced over at her dryly.

"Okay," she said on a low laugh. "So we're a little closed off and maybe kinda hard to get to know, and not always . . . welcoming. But until Joe fell in love with Kylie a few months ago, it's been just him and me against the world, sharing custody of our dad."

"Don't you have that backwards? You mean your dad had custody of you guys?"

"No." She turned and looked out the window, giving him the back of her head. "We take care of him, always have."

He resisted the urge to run a hand down her hair because she would take that as pity when what he really wanted to give was comfort. "How long ago did you lose your mom?"

"She died when I was a few years old. My dad was in the military. He came back from the gulf war to be with us. Only he wasn't . . . the same. He had PTSD, though no one really knew it back then. He could manage to hold it together for a while, but then he'd lose it."

"Did you have other family to help?"

"No, but we did okay. It wasn't until I was around ten that he stopped being able to work entirely. And he needed caring for. So that's what Joe and I did."

Lucas tried to imagine this. He'd had a mom and a dad, both extremely active in all their kids' lives. He'd had his siblings and cousins to keep him in line. He hadn't lost Josh until four years ago. So he had absolutely zero experience to compare Molly's childhood to. "Must've been rough, growing up like that."

She shrugged. "I didn't know any different."

That she didn't appear to know about his brother's death meant she hadn't made use of Hunt's computer programs to look him up. If she'd wanted to, she could discover how many fillings he'd had when he was eight. Or that in eleventh grade he'd gotten caught with the vice principal's daughter in the janitor's closet. Or that when he was twenty-four, his fiancée, Carrie, had died in a car accident and he'd missed her funeral because he'd been so deep undercover for the DEA at the time no one could reach him.

Or that when he'd lost his firefighter brother a few years later to an arson fire, he'd checked out of life for a good year, losing his job at the DEA while he was at it. Not that he'd cared much at the time. The memories of those gut-wrenching days always threatened to send him back to the deep, dark pit of hell he'd landed in. It was getting slightly easier to remember, but only slightly, and that in itself caused a setback because forgetting the pain meant he was forgetting Josh and he didn't want to ever forget.

Molly put her hand on his arm and it was the oddest thing, but even though she didn't know what she'd stirred up inside him, her touch settled him.

The drive home was quiet after that. Usual for him. Extremely unusual for Molly, who normally couldn't do quiet to save her own life. He glanced over at her several times, but she seemed quite content to let the silence keep them company. "You good?" he asked.

She nodded.

He'd grown up with a nosy older sister and an even nosier mom. He knew when a woman was full of shit, but he also knew better than to call her out on it. "Hold up," he said, reaching for her hand and holding onto it when he stopped in front of her place and she tried to hop out.

"No need. 'Night," she said, looking to suddenly be in a hurry to escape him. That, or she didn't trust herself—most likely wishful thinking on his part.

"I'm walking you up," he said.

"Not necessary."

"Molly, you just ruffled a whole bunch of feathers of a guy I don't trust, not to mention his brother

Tommy Thumbs. I don't know about you, but I'm fond of your thumbs."

"I thought you weren't sure the Tommy Thumbs part was real."

"Let's just say that I'm keeping all our options open," he said and got out of the car, coming around in time to catch her struggling to get in the little elf uniform without flashing her goodies to the world.

Reaching in, he easily hauled her up, blocking the money shot from anyone who might be around.

He kept his gaze on hers as she thanked him a bit breathlessly and yanked at the hem of the dress. Apparently, she hadn't figured out that when she did that, the top of the stretchy sparkling elf green dress pulled taut across her breasts, both of which threatened to break free with each tug.

Around them, the night was near silent. Her neighborhood skewed older and quiet. It was nearing midnight. All the seniors were probably tucked into bed, hearing aids off, lights off.

"Dammit," she murmured.

Already on high alert, he scanned their surroundings. "What?"

"I left my porch light on so I wouldn't come home to complete darkness, but it's off now. Which means my electricity's out again."

He reached for her hand, slowing her down so that he was slightly ahead of her. Letting her realize he was actively protecting her was always a gamble against the house, but she just shook her head. "It's not Tommy looking to chop off my thumbs," she said. "It's my neighbor's doing. Wait here." Breaking free, she crossed the narrow common grass area to pound on the door next to hers. "Mrs. Berkowitz!" she called. "You've got to stop using your, um"— she glanced over at Lucas with an odd expression he couldn't quite place—"*massager* while you're waiting for your clothes to dry. You blew out the electricity again!"

A woman's voice sounded from inside. "I'm sorry, honey, but a woman's got needs!"

Molly sighed and headed back to her porch where Lucas stood, unable to keep from grinning.

"It's not funny," she said. "It could be tomorrow before the power company gets us sorted."

He could hear the oddest sound coming from the region of their feet. Pulling out his phone, he thumbed on his flashlight and found the biggest, blackest cat he'd ever seen winding around Molly's legs.

"TC," she said in a warm, fond voice that Lucas had never heard from her before.

"Meow," the cat answered.

"Aw, poor baby's hungry," Molly murmured to the cat who could probably eat them both whole if he wanted. She scooped a cup of food from a bin beneath her porch chair and filled an empty bowl. "There you go, pretty baby. Who's a good kitty?"

The cat didn't answer. He was head deep in the bowl, his purring turned up another notch as he inhaled his food.

"TC?" Lucas asked, putting his phone back in his pocket.

"Short for Tom Cat," she said. "He's a stray. I've tried to adopt him, but he won't come inside. So I feed and love up on him whenever he shows up. It's all he'll allow."

"He doesn't look like he's having trouble getting enough food," he said diplomatically.

Molly laughed. "I think everyone on the block feeds him. He's got a good gig. When I'm not quick enough to fill his bowl, he hangs off the front door screen and stares at me until I come outside." She fumbled through her purse for her keys, which Lucas took from her.

He unlocked the door. She moved inside the dark place without hesitation, having the benefit of knowing the layout. He followed and when he heard her drop her keys, he bent to grab them—at the same time she did the same thing.

They bumped into each other and cracked heads. Hard. He saw stars, but reached for her, knowing she'd gotten it worse. "*Shit*. Sorry. You okay?"

"No! You've got the hardest head on the planet!"

"Are you sure?" he asked, gently running his hand over her head. "Because I'm thinking we're probably tied in that category."

They were face-to-face, plastered up against each other. The air seemed to crackle and they stared at each other for a long beat. Finally, he felt Molly take a deep breath. "You know," she said softly, "Sadie's pretty invested in me letting you be The One for a night."

He felt a surprised smile curve his lips. "Is that right?"

"Yeah."

"And how about you?"

"I didn't want to admit it, but I'm starting to re-think things."

Lucas was pretty sure his mind was playing tricks on him. But the truth was, he wanted her more than he'd wanted anyone in a long time, maybe ever, and that was saying something. He ran his hands up and down her arms and could feel goose bumps covering her skin.

And it wasn't from being cold.

She was still leaning into him. He was six feet. Molly was five foot two in her bare feet, but she had a love affair for sexy-as-hell shoes, the higher the better, which he suspected played a role in her leg and back problems. At the moment she wore boots with at least three inches on them, though they were covered with the green elf shoe covers. Still, they put her at a convenient height that could make them both very, very happy.

"Rethink away," he murmured. "Let me know what you decide."

Chapter 13

#Scrooge

Molly's heart was pounding and she had no idea what she thought she was doing, rethinking anything to do with Lucas Knight.

Oh wait, she did know what she was doing.

She needed this. Needed *him*. It used to scare her how much she *wanted* him as well, but realism was her friend. They were both adults. They could do this and move on because, one, Lucas didn't intend to get any more attached than she did, and two, it was pitch-dark and he wouldn't be able to see a damn thing.

But even as she thought it, the electricity flickered back on and the porch light shone in through the window.

She blinked up as Lucas whispered her name, and then his lips met hers in what started out as a light, questing connection but quickly turned hot and insistent.

She looked up when she felt his arms tighten on her, finding his gaze dark and intense on hers. "You finished rethinking things?" he asked. "Because—"

He broke off whatever he'd planned on saying when she slid her hands beneath his shirt to touch . . . yum . . . hot, smooth skin and the tough lean muscles that flexed as he tightened his grip on her.

"Molly," he said, his voice a rough timbre. "I'm going to need the words."

"I'm done rethinking," she admitted.

"And?"

"And I want you. For tonight."

The jacket that was his, the one that he'd wrapped around her shoulders, was removed in the next breath, his own shirt next. Then he nudged her a few feet until the backs of her legs hit her couch. His mouth still on hers, he lowered them both to the cushions, settling his weight carefully over her. "Where's the light?" he asked, voice husky thick.

"No light."

He paused for the slightest of beats but then carried on, kissing across her jaw to her neck and down, whispering inaudibles all soft and sexy-like. She couldn't concentrate enough to soak in the actual words, but the erotic intent reached her just fine.

Then he moved further south, his quick, talented fingers tugging the dress off her shoulders, along with the straps of her bra. When he captured a bare nipple in his mouth, the heat alone bowed her back and had her crying out. She tried biting her tongue to keep the helpless and revealing desperate sounds to herself, but she couldn't shut herself up. Not then, and not when he smoothly divested her of the rest of her clothes.

And then his.

And then he was sliding off the couch, kneeling on the floor, nudging her legs open with his big, warm, callused hands as he headed southbound again, nibbling his way down her belly. A minute later he unerringly found the homeland, and in a shockingly short amount of time, her hands were fisted helplessly in his hair as she hovered on the verge of release.

And forget being quiet. She'd lost the ability to temper herself the minute he'd put his mouth on her. He worked her over using lips and teeth, and when he added his tongue into the mix, she burst with a shudder and a gasp that she couldn't have held back if she'd tried.

He made a sound of deep, male satisfaction while she continued to attempt to suck more air into her lungs, gently kissing the inside of one thigh and then the other before shifting away for a second. She heard the crinkle of a condom packet and then he was back, sliding deep inside her in one slow, controlled push.

She'd forgotten how incredible it felt to be filled and stretched and taken with such carefully controlled power. Long, slow strokes, nearly all the way out and then back in deep and hard. It was more than she could take, and yet she wanted even more, show-

ing him so by digging her fingers into the tense, flu-
idly shifting muscles of his back.

Lucas caught her wrists and pulled them away,
linking his fingers with hers above her head as he
rose over her, lifting his weight a little to better control his thrusts.

And for the first time, she wished the house electricity was back on. She couldn't see much, a few
flashes of his warrior's body as he moved in the
ambient porch light that slashed in from the gap in
her shades. The sheen of his skin and the flex of the
sinew moving beneath it, all the way down his chest
and correlated abs to where they were joined. She
watched, helplessly fascinated as his body surged
into hers again and again. Unable to tear her gaze
off him, she soaked him in, the way his neck was
corded, his head thrown back in pleasure.

And then he dipped his head and caught her
staring.

"Molly." That was all he said, just her name in
a low, strained voice, his expression caught between
rapture and affection, and it might have been that
completely unexpected emotion to send her spiraling
over the edge again.

With a groan, he shifted, lowering his weight to
his elbows, one hand sliding beneath her, arching her
up to take him deeper. Now his entire body caressed
hers with each movement and yet another wave began to build. Panting, she slid her hands into his hair
and whispered his name as she continued to tremble.

She could feel his mouth at her throat, feel the shudders of his own body as he let go of all that delicious control and gave into the erotic sensations.

When she came back to herself, they were on the floor in front of the couch and he was cradling her into the warmth of his body, holding her close. Curled against him, she could feel his heart beating beneath her ear in tune with hers.

She let out one last shaky breath and lay there quietly, unable to talk. Hell, she could hardly think. Had they really just completely taken each other apart?

"Pretty much," he said in a rough voice, making her realize that she'd spoken out loud.

Oh boy.

He had one hand tangled in her hair and the other low on her bare ass holding her snugged up against him. They were both overheated and damp with sweat and yet she couldn't muster up anything but bliss.

His big palm slid off her butt and down the back of her leg. "You okay?"

Was she? She took quick stock. They were on her floor, which she couldn't remember if she'd vacuumed this week. Still, she'd never been more comfortable—or sated—in her entire life. She didn't even try to move because she was pretty sure she *couldn't* move. Her muscles seemed to have completely shorted out. All she could do was lie there with her face pressed into the crook of his neck, but she did manage a nod, too relaxed to get defensive about the question. Somehow he still smelled delicious, and utterly without thought, she rubbed her lips over his skin in a soft kiss before lightly licking him.

Yep. He tasted as good as he smelled.

"Did you just lick me like a lollipop?" he asked, voice low and lazy and laced with humor.

Instead of answering, she sank her teeth into him.

Hissing in a breath, he rolled her beneath him, slid a hand into her hair and tugged lightly to bare her neck. Then he returned the favor, lowering his head to take a nibble of her throat, the curve of her shoulder . . .

And when he continued his way down her body, alternating teasing and nibbling, she arched into him. "Again?" she murmured, her fingers tightening in his hair.

"Oh yeah, again." But then he surprised her by lifting her into his arms and getting to his feet in one easy, athletic movement. "This time," he said, "we make it to your bed. Where's the closest light?"

The question was a bucket of ice water over the top of her head. "Why?" she managed to ask.

"I want to see you."

Yeah. Not happening. She squirmed out of his arms and blindly searched for her clothes. When she touched cotton, she grabbed it and pulled it over her head.

It fell to her thighs. It was Lucas's T-shirt.

"Molly?"

Dammit. She stepped back from his outstretched

arms. "Don't move, you'll trip over something and hurt yourself." She backed to the wall and hit the switch, blinking like an owl in the sudden light as her eyes tried to adjust.

Lucas stood in the center of the living room, gloriously, unabashedly butt-ass naked, looking already perfectly adjusted to the light—and also perfectly at home. As he should, since he was incredibly built.

But it was the look on his face that nearly stopped her heart. Easy affection. Light concern.

He liked her.

And she liked him. Way too much. She was feeling so much more than she thought she could, and that was terrifying. It also didn't make any sense to her. She'd always needed to feel comfortable and cozy and safe to fall in love.

She didn't feel comfortable *or* cozy.

As for safe . . . she wasn't talking about her body. Her body felt safe with Lucas. In his hands, her body was putty.

But her brain . . . her brain didn't see this working out, and therefore she *wasn't* safe.

"I like the look," he said of the sight of her in his shirt. He stepped toward her. "But there's a look I'd like even better—"

Again she backed away from his reach and he stopped. Cocked his head. "Do we have a problem?" he asked.

"*We* don't have a problem," she said and then sighed. "*I* have a problem."

"And that is . . . ?"

She looked everywhere but right at him. The ceiling. The floor. The couch that they'd just done the deed on . . . Man. She was never going to look at that couch in quite the same way again—

"Molly."

She scrunched her eyes closed and then jumped when she heard her phone vibrating. She pounced on her phone, grateful for the interruption.

It was her dad.

"Sharon didn't show," he said.

Sharon was his part-time home care nurse. She showed up two afternoons a week and stayed through dinner, which she either cooked for him or brought him. Tonight had been Sharon's night and Molly looked at the time. Nearly midnight. He'd been alone way too long. "I'll bring you dinner," she said.

"Did I wake you?"

She resisted looking over at Lucas. "No."

"You sure?" her dad asked. "You sound breathless. Everything okay?"

That depended on what part of her they were talking about. Her body, specifically certain parts of it, were more than okay. It'd just sung the "Hallelujah Chorus" and wasn't opposed to another round. But her brain . . . her brain wasn't sure if she was okay. Or if she'd ever be okay again. "I'm fine, Dad. What do you want to eat?"

"A Big Mac."

"You can't have those anymore. Your doctor says your cholesterol is still too high."

"You're both fun suckers."

Yep. That was her mission in life. To be a fun sucker. "I'll be there in thirty." She disconnected and turned to Lucas. "I've got to go." She rifled through her backpack for the pants she'd taken off at the village in order to change into her elf costume.

"Commando," Lucas murmured in an approving voice as she yanked up the pants without searching for her undies.

She looked over at him and he smiled at her. "That alone is going to give me good dreams for the foreseeable future."

Ditto for her with nothing more than that sex-roughened voice of his. She grabbed a boot and hopped into it, toppling over. He winced for her and took a step toward her, but she gestured him away. "I'm fine!" Staying seated on the ground for the second boot, she got to her feet and blew the hair from her sweaty face. She turned in a circle and found the jacket he'd put on her shoulders earlier, which she put on over his T-shirt. She grabbed her purse and turned to the door.

"Molly."

"Lock up when you go," she said and, without looking back, ran off into the night like the chicken she was.

Chapter 14

#ElfingAround

Back at the Pacific Pier Building twenty minutes later, Lucas walked through the cobblestone courtyard, freezing his ass off, every exhale making a little white cloud in front of his face. Old Man Eddie looked up from where he was warming his hands over the fire pit and stilled. "You get mugged?"

Lucas, no shirt, no jacket, both thanks to Molly, shook his head. He didn't speak because his tongue was cold and his nipples were about to fall off.

Eddie's frown turned into a slow smile. "Nice, man."

Avoiding the pub and the certain ridicule of his friends, Lucas strode past the fountain, purposely not looking at it, afraid he might turn into a sappy romantic and make a wish.

The tattoo parlor was open late. Sadie was in there, leaning over a woman, working on her shoulder. She looked up at Lucas, the small smile on her lips going a bit bigger when she took him in.

With a sigh, he took the stairs and let himself into his quiet, dark apartment, stripping on the way to a very hot shower to see if he could save his extremities. Afterwards, he stretched out on his bed, tucking his hands behind his head, staring up at the ceiling to contemplate his current problems.

One, he'd let himself crumble his own walls.

Two, Molly had gotten inside those crumbled walls and made herself right at home.

Three, and this was the biggee, she'd run off on him tonight like her ass was on fire.

And he still wanted her. *What was that?* She should be out of his system now, but if anything she'd only wormed in even deeper. He didn't know if it was the way she'd held onto him, her fingers digging in as if she didn't quite trust him not to pull away too soon. Or maybe it was how she'd kissed him with her entire heart and soul, even though he was quite certain she had no idea how she'd given of herself. Or maybe it'd been those sweet, sexy sounds she'd made when he'd had his mouth on her, or when he'd been buried deep, so deep he'd completely lost himself in her . . .

Yeah, sleep wasn't going to happen. He got out of bed and bent to pull something from the pocket of his pants.

Santa's wallet.

Molly was good. But so was he.

You sure about that? a voice inside his head asked.

*Because she'd managed to pick your heart without
you feeling a damn thing . . .*

Lucas had a doctor's appointment the next morning
and by some miracle was finally cleared for full duty.
Relieved, he went to work but found concentration
difficult. He couldn't stop thinking of Molly and what
had happened. He'd promised himself not to take it
there and yet he'd done exactly that. On her living
room floor of all places, like they'd been stupid, horny
seventeen-year-olds who couldn't control themselves.

He'd always been able to control himself. Always.

Okay, not always. After Carrie had died, he'd lost
control. And then again when he'd lost Josh. But he'd
found his way back to feeling human. The trick?

To not love quite so hard.

Or at all.

"Yeah, he's definitely on another planet."

Lucas blinked and refocused in on the meeting he
was in with Archer and Caleb regarding one of Caleb's
companies that was having some security problems.
"I'm not on another planet," Lucas said. "I'm right
here."

Ignoring him, Caleb turned to Archer. "Think it's
about a woman?"

"Nah," Archer said. "He doesn't tend to let any
women get to him. Kind of like you."

Caleb gave a small smile. "Look at the pot talking
to the kettle."

"I'm with Elle, aren't I?" Archer asked.

"Sure, *now*," Caleb said. "But there for a very long time you treated relationships like they were the plague."

Lucas rolled his eyes. "Is this a meeting to discuss our feelings or are we working?"

Caleb slid him a look. "You tell me."

"Whatever, man, my mind slipped for a minute. I'm back now."

"It's the brunette from the bar the other night, right?" Caleb asked. "She was hot."

"Her fingernails were painted red and green," Archer said. "And they lit up. Never seen that before."

"You can tell a lot about a woman from her hands," Caleb said. "For instance, if they're wrapped around your neck, she's probably pissed off at you."

"It's not that brunette from the bar!" Lucas exclaimed. "Why is everyone so interested in my love life?"

"He said love life," Caleb said to Archer.

"I heard it. *Fascinating*."

Lucas shook his head. "You're both crazy. I'm not seeing the brunette." At least not that one . . .

After that meeting, things exploded. Hunt Investigations worked on a variety of cases at any one time and for whatever reason, three of them came to a head at once, requiring the whole team to put in forty-eight straight hours without a break.

When the dust cleared, they'd cracked a cold case and gotten a man arrested for murdering his wife four years earlier. They'd proven a guy running for

political office on the city senate was not only having multiple affairs, he was not living in the district
he was running in, resulting in him dropping from
the race. They'd provided evidence of corporate fraud
to a huge beer manufacturer in the area, resulting in
seventeen arrests, saving the company millions of
dollars.

On the third day, they'd landed back at the offices
at the crack of dawn after a very long night. Hunter
had instructed them all to go home and sleep it off,
which Lucas had gladly done.

He woke up to someone knocking on his door.
Actually, pounding was more apt. He glanced at the
time. Six-thirty p.m. Groggy, wondering who he'd
have to kill for waking him up, he pulled open the
door and stared blearily at Molly. He hadn't seen her
since she'd walked out on him, leaving him half naked in her apartment.

She was still dressed for work in one of his favor-
ites, a midnight blue wraparound dress with a tie on
one hip. He had no idea what the material was, but
it always messed with his mind because the cut said
business and yet the material looked soft to the touch,
clung very slightly to all those curves, and screamed
sex. Her shiny heels matched and had a strap across
her arch and around her ankle, and all he could think
about was tugging on that bow tied at her hip. Would
the dress glide to the floor and leave her in nothing
but those heels?

She was holding several bags from a retail shop

nearby and a half-eaten pretzel. "I want the wallet," she said.

"Are you going to eat that pretzel?"

"Are you going to answer my question?"

"I'm too hungry," he said and rubbed his belly. "Famished, actually."

She rolled her eyes and handed him the pretzel.

He moaned as he took his first bite. "Would've been better with mustard. Were you shopping?"

"With Elle," she said. "I was trying to Christmas shop but ended up with new shoes and a pretzel."

"Worth it," he said, shoving in the last bite.

"Santa's wallet," she repeated and put her hands on his chest and shoved him back, following him in. "I know you took it that night at my place. And you've been gone working ever since, but I want it, Lucas. I want to see what name he's going by and if there's anything else of use in there before I slip it back to him."

"You're going to give it back?"

"I'm not a thief," she said. "I didn't mean to keep it from him for this long. Now where is it?" She looked around at his place.

He knew what she saw. A guy's place with a big couch and coffee table that doubled as a kitchen table and shit collector, an even bigger TV, several pairs of running shoes near the door along with an empty pizza box he hadn't taken out to the trash yet.

Elle had someone on staff who was in charge of keeping the building clean and neat. Lucas paid her to keep his apartment clean and neat as well, but she only came every two weeks, and in between those two-week visits, he wasn't especially good at doing it for himself.

"Where is it?" Molly asked, walking to the center of his living room and turning to him, hands on hips.

The skirt on her dress flared out before settling against her thighs. "I've gotta admit," he said. "I'm surprised at your restraint. It's been three days. I thought you'd have cornered me by now." He paused, curious as to whether she'd be honest or not. "Or at the very least, broken in and searched the place yourself."

She bit her lower lip and appeared to have an internal discussion with herself. Then she blew out a sigh. "I already did that."

"Excuse me?" he asked.

"I broke in to search your apartment," she admitted, but didn't look happy about it.

And he knew why. "And . . . ?"

She tossed up her hands. "The minute I did it, I turned to leave. I couldn't do it, okay? I couldn't snoop through your things. It felt . . . wrong." She rolled her eyes. "And also I realized you had a security cam, so don't play surprised with me. You knew what I did and you knew what I didn't do."

"Yeah," he said, letting his smile escape. "Watching you spend that ten seconds wrestling with your conscience was the most fun I had all week."

"You're an ass. Where's the wallet?"

"I still have it. I haven't had time to dig in."

"I have time. Hand it over."

"You don't have time," he said. "I know Archer loaded you down hard with that new project we're doing in conjunction with the local FBI."

She sighed and nodded.

"Give me one more day with it," he said. "I promise I'll get to it."

"And you'll tell me everything you find."

"Everything," he vowed, holding up three fingers like the Boy Scout oath.

She rolled her eyes. "You were never a Boy Scout."

True. Very true.

She shook her head and moved to the door.

"Where are you going?"

"Personal business."

"Is that a euphemism for another shift at the bingo hall?"

"No, I'm on dad-duty tonight. Turns out, the Christmas Village doesn't need me again until two nights from now. But Mrs. Berkowitz stopped by today to talk about my progress and I didn't have much to tell her. I need progress, Lucas."

"You're making progress."

"It doesn't feel like it."

"You're doing the due diligence," he said. "You're asking the right questions and following all your leads. Sometimes these things take time."

"Not when you guys do it," she said.

Mostly because they were willing to go the unconventional route when needed. At Hunt, they always worked for the morally right side. But that didn't mean they always followed the letter of the law to the last crossing of the t's. Sometimes there were . . . gray areas. He was comfortable working in those gray areas. He wasn't comfortable with Molly doing it, which he realized made him a caveman.

She rolled her eyes at him and turned to leave. He snagged her hand. "I'd like to go with you," he said. "But I need five minutes."

"Why?"

"Because I'd like to. Is that okay?"

She just looked at him, clearly not sure if it was okay or not, so he did his best to look like something she couldn't live without.

"Fine," she finally said.

He gently squeezed her hand in thanks, pulling her in so that her body just brushed his. He had no idea if she felt the bolt of awareness. Hell, maybe he felt it enough for the both of them, but he waited until she met his gaze. "You'll wait?" he asked quietly.

She was a little breathless. Yeah, she felt it too.

And yeah, she'd wait.

He took a two-minute hot shower, grabbed fresh clothes and wished for caffeine. Since he'd yet to make it to a store, he was still going without. In the promised five minutes, he came back to the living room to find Molly thumbing through a stack of photos his mom had recently sent him.

She flipped a pic in his direction, revealing his

five-year-old self and his dad, both on skis, flashing toothy grins at the camera. The background was a formidable looking ski run.

"Squaw Valley," he said. "I'd just followed my dad down my first black diamond ski run. My aunt lives in the Sierras. We spent a lot of time in the mountains over the holidays. This year will be no different, though my dad's teaching in England until January. He's a college professor and he's on loan to Oxford. But everyone else will be there."

"Sounds nice," she said a little wistfully. "I've never been on skis."

"I'll take you," he said without thinking. And he meant it. He'd love to teach her how to ski.

But she shook her head and gestured vaguely to her leg, making him feel like a first-class asshole for forgetting.

"I'm sorry," he said quietly. "I wasn't thinking."

She sent him a smile that didn't quite reach her eyes. "Don't worry about it, it's easy to forget."

He cupped her face up to his. "Nothing about you is easy to forget," he said. "I want you to remember that."

She stared up at him for a long, vibrating beat and then stepped free. "Time to go."

She had a bag of food in her backseat that smelled amazing and his stomach growled.

Molly's mouth tipped up slightly. "He might share. If you ask real nice."

He had no idea if she was kidding or not. Fifteen

minutes later they pulled up to a duplex in Inner Sunset. "Joe's place?" he asked.

"Joe owns the building," Molly said. "He bought it for me and dad. But I needed to have more independence than that, so I live where I live and they live here. Not together, though—they'd kill each other. My dad lives on one side and Joe on the other. You didn't know?"

Lucas glanced over at her. He and Joe were close as far as partners went, same for being friends, but they spent so much time together at work, as in almost *all* their time, they rarely saw each other off the job.

Which was just as well at the moment since Lucas happened to be lusting after the guy's sister. Not to mention getting naked with her, to a very mutually satisfying conclusion if he said so himself. "Joe's pretty private."

"Yeah, where do you think I learned it from?" she said on a rough laugh.

The neighborhood was blue collar and hardworking. Not all the homes had been shown any love, but this duplex most definitely had. New paint, grass trimmed and mowed, and flowers thriving in the flower pots on both sides of the duplex.

Lucas started to get out of the car, but Molly put a hand on his arm. "Wait here."

He arched a brow. "Like you did at my mom's house?"

She grimaced. "Okay, so I was nosy and curious

and you're the same. I get it. But your mom and your sisters, they're . . ."

"We've already had this conversation," he said. "They're crazy. Nosy. Busybodies—"

"—And wonderful. But this isn't a joke to me," she said. "It's my life."

And she was actually letting him see some of that life, which she didn't do as a rule. For anyone. Knowing how private she was, he felt . . . honored, and let his smile fade. "Okay, you're right. I'm sorry. If you really want me to wait here, I will. But I'd really like to meet your dad."

She stared at him.

He smiled charmingly.

She didn't return it, but he could tell she wanted to. "Okay," she said, caving. "But only because I could use some help carrying the fifty-pound bag of dog food in the trunk."

Lucas didn't ask questions, just got out of the car and went to the trunk, hoisting the huge bag of food onto a shoulder.

She stared at him again.

"What?" he asked.

"Nothing. Except it's annoying how easy that was for you to lift."

"Annoying aaaaannnnnd . . ." he asked in a teasing voice.

"And irritating."

"I think you mean sexy, right?"

She rolled her eyes and made him laugh. At least

she wasn't looking hollow and haunted anymore. They headed up the walkway to the right side of the duplex.

The front door had a sign that read:

WARNING: No Soliciting, No Trespassing
I don't like you
I'm not voting for you
I'm not buying from you
I don't need a vacuum
I'm armed and not tired
of hiding the bodies

Lucas smiled.

Molly sighed and turned to him, pulling him aside, gesturing for him to set the big bag of dog food down. "Listen," she said. "There're a few things you really should know—"

She was interrupted by the sound of a shotgun ratcheting.

In one move, Lucas pushed her behind him and pulled his gun.

"No," Molly gasped, tugging loose and slipping between him and the front door to face him. "Stop. You'll only make it worse. It's just my dad. It's sort of . . . his greeting. *Dad*," she yelled, turning to the front door. "It's me."

"You're late," came a cranky male voice.

"I know."

"It's dark."

"I know that too," she said. "But work took a lot longer today than I thought it would. You should've turned on the holiday lights that Joe strung for you out here. You'd be able to see better."

"What's the code?"

Molly knocked four times on the door, paused, then added a fifth.

Suddenly the outside of the house lit up with icicle lights in white, red, and green.

"See?" Molly said through the door. "Festive, right?"

"Stupid waste of electricity."

Molly sighed. "Let us in, Dad."

"Who's the guy with the gun?"

Molly craned her neck and glanced back at Lucas, her eyes going wide when she saw he was still holding his gun. She waved her hand at him, gesturing that he should put it away. It went against every fiber of his being, what with there being a gun trained on him, but he holstered it.

"I brought . . . a coworker," Molly told her dad.

"Why?"

Molly sighed. "Because he's helping me work on something. He's Joe's partner, Lucas Knight. Dad, it's cold. Let us in."

There came the sound of four locks being unlocked. And then a pause. And then one more bolt shifting.

Molly waited until that last bolt clicked before opening the door and poking her head into the house.

She looked around and then looked back at Lucas with an expression he couldn't quite place. Not fear, but . . . unease.

He gave her what he hoped was a reassuring smile and then she led him inside. The duplex was small but neat. The only holiday decorations in here were some garland on the mantel, and a two-foot tall live potted Christmas tree on the coffee table. Wood floors, no throw rugs, wide open spaces between the sparsely furnished living room.

He got the reason for that when he caught sight of the man in a wheelchair in the doorway to the kitchen wearing an army T-shirt, black boxers, and a rifle across his thighs.

"Dad," Molly said, walking to him, then leaning in and kissing his jaw. "We talked about this. You're supposed to wear pants during the day."

"It's not day, it's night," he said, his gaze never leaving Lucas.

A huge yellow Labrador retriever rose from his bed in the corner. He stretched and yawned.

"Nice job on the watchdog thing, Buddy," the man said.

"Dad, Buddy's your emotional support dog, not a watchdog." Molly dropped to her knees and held out her arms, and the dog walked right into them, snuggling in close for a hug and a few kisses. "How's my good boy?" she asked softly, ruffling his fur. "How's my very good boy?"

Buddy burrowed in closer, a smile on his face.

Lucas loved dogs and dogs loved him, but he'd never actually been jealous of one before.

"Dad, this is Lucas," Molly said. "Lucas, this is my dad, Alan. And this big guy here is Buddy. He also goes by No-no-no, Stop-It, Don't-You-Dare-Do-It, or Get-Down."

Lucas nodded at Molly's dad in greeting and held out his hand.

The man looked at Lucas's outstretched hand, then turned his wheelchair, giving him his back as he looked at Molly. "What's for dinner?"

Okay, then. Lucas crouched down before Buddy, who had a much more enthusiastic greeting for him. A big drooly kiss. When Lucas started petting him, the dog belly flopped at his feet for a belly rub. Yep, a real killer, this one.

"*Nothing's* for dinner unless you're nice," Molly told her dad.

Her dad snorted, but he did turn back to face Lucas and thrust his hand out in a way that wasn't overly friendly, but, hey, at least he hadn't picked up the shotgun.

Lucas shook the proffered hand. "Nice to meet you," he said, which garnered another snort.

"*Dad,*" Molly said.

"Fine. And I suppose he gets points for not running scared like the last one."

"Not fair," Molly said. "When I brought Tim over, you were on the porch cleaning your shotgun. You kept lifting it up to check the site and posturing. I'd have run too."

"Tim was a pansy-ass."

Lucas wanted to know who the hell Tim was, but Molly moved to the kitchen and started to pull out the food she'd brought. "You take your meds today?" she called out.

Her dad shrugged and she stopped what she was doing to go hands on hips for a beat before turning to a drawer and opening it. "Where's your weekly pill box?"

"Bathroom."

"Go get it."

Her dad rolled out of the room.

Molly looked at Lucas. "Thanks for not freaking out."

"Who's Tim?" he asked.

She rolled her eyes. "No one."

"He was her pansy-ass boyfriend," her dad said, wheeling back into the room. Lucas was happy to see he'd put his gun away. "She eventually got smart and dumped him."

"Not true," Molly said, her back to the both of them as she set the table. "*He* got smart and dumped *me*."

Lucas slid his gaze to Alan, who had the good grace to look abashed, but he recovered quickly. "Any man who isn't man enough to look his woman's father in the eyes isn't man enough to miss."

"Well, much as I'd like to blame it on your child-ish behavior," Molly said, still not facing them. "He dumped me because of *me*, not you."

There was remembered pain in her voice and her body language was off, as if maybe she was ashamed.

Lucas started toward her, but her dad put out a hand to stop him. "That just makes him a fucker on top of being a pansy-ass," he said to Molly's back. "Want me to end him for you?"

She laughed. "Dad, it was years ago now, you know that."

Her dad relaxed when she laughed. "Well, the offer still stands," he said. "You just let me know. And same goes for this one too," he said with a chin jerk in Lucas's direction.

"I told you, he's just a coworker."

Her dad looked Lucas right in the eyes. "Gonna call bullshit on that one, sweetheart."

Molly ignored them both, sitting down at the table to dig in. "I'm hungry enough to eat all of this on my own, so I'd get to it if I were you."

That got her dad's attention. He pulled up to the table and dropped his phone in Molly's lap before starting to load up a plate for himself. "The thing's broken," he said. "It says I'm out of memory."

"How is that even possible?" Molly picked up the phone and began to thumb through it. "Ah. Found the problem."

"Knew you would." Her dad glanced at Lucas. "She's the smartest person in our whole family."

Lucas smiled. The guy was badass and as tough as they came, but he clearly had a soft spot for his daughter.

And as it turned out, so did Lucas.

Molly held up the phone, opened to photos. "You've got like thirteen thousand pics of Buddy in here."

"He likes having his picture taken."

"Dad, you don't need thirteen thousand pics of your dog. Delete all but a few hundred."

Her dad grumbled and slid Buddy a few scraps under the table.

Molly sighed. "And you're not supposed to feed him like that either."

"What, he likes takeout. Hey, can Buddy travel? Like on a plane?"

"Why?" Molly asked suspiciously. "You hate airplanes, and as far as I know you've not been on one since you got home from your last tour of duty."

Her dad shrugged. "It's too cold here right now. I was thinking of going somewhere warm."

"Like?"

"Like a deserted island."

"But then who would you yell at?" Molly asked.

Her dad barked out a low laugh. "Good point. How about just a regular island then, with unlimited dogs and pizza. Come on, name something better than that. I'll wait."

Molly shook her head, but her eyes were soft and her mouth was curved. She clearly loved him very much, a feeling that was just as clearly mutual. She didn't appear to mind taking care of him either, which Lucas knew she'd been doing for a very long time, back to when she should have had someone taking care of her.

When they'd finished eating, Lucas helped Molly clean up and then she grabbed her purse. "It's getting late and it's a work night."

"Uh-huh. Thought he wasn't your boyfriend," her father said, eyes back on Lucas in a way that said he wished he still had his rifle.

"He's not," Molly said. "We're working a job together—which you can't tell Joe about."

"Why not?"

"Because I asked real nice."

Her dad narrowed his gaze.

"If you tell," Molly told him, "I'll stop bringing you those Cuban cigars you're not supposed to have."

"You were never even here," Alan said.

She hugged and kissed him goodbye. "You're my favorite," she whispered.

"And you're mine," Alan whispered back so easily that Lucas knew it was part of their routine.

Molly laughed, lightening the moment. "You say the same to Joe, right?"

Her dad just smiled.

When they were on the road again, Molly glanced over at Lucas. "You're quiet. You okay?"

He was lost in thought. And guilt. He hated that he was with her on the pretense of the job because Archer and Joe had asked him to be. Because the truth was, he was in regardless, and now there was a new element too. He wanted her to solve this case and prove herself to her boss and brother so they'd let her be who she was meant to be. She was smart and fun and sexy and easy to talk to, and he enjoyed the hell out of her.

And when that had sneaked up on him, he had no clue.

Half an hour later, they were back at the Pacific Pier Building. "Come up," he said and she looked across the console at him, silent. Contemplating.

To sway the vote in his favor, he leaned in, palmed the back of her head and kissed her.

When she pulled back, she was looking dazed and breathless. He was no better. "Come up," he said again.

"Maybe." She pointed at him. "But no overthinking things."

"Molly," he said on a rough laugh. "When I've got you in my arms, I can't think at all."

She stared at him some more. "And no lights."

He hesitated at that and she pulled back. "I mean it," she said.

He reached out and wove his fingers through hers. "How about you give me ten minutes to show you how amazingly beautiful I think you are, and if you still want the lights out—"

"I still want the lights out."

"Okay," he said easily. "By Braille it is."

"And one more thing. No talking."

"How about dirty talk?" he asked. "That doesn't count, right?"

She surprised him by laughing and lightened his heart.

"Dirty talk is allowed," she decided, and right then and there, he fell in love.

Chapter 15

#ImFine

The next morning, Lucas woke up alone. Not a surprise. Molly didn't seem fond of morning-afters.

Something they shared.

She'd been in a meeting with Archer when he arrived at the office. At his desk, he eyed the wallet sitting next to his laptop. He'd done a thorough search of the ID in the wallet. Santa's given name was Nick Russolini but he was going by Nicolas King—which they already knew. The only things in the wallet had been sixty bucks' cash, a driver's license, and a Domino's pizza card.

No signed confession that he was stealing from old ladies.

But digging deeper, Lucas discovered the guy had enough identities to give even the FBI a run for its money. Shaking his head, he brought up a new search screen, planning on running the aliases all together to see if there was any crossover. But his fingers did something he'd avoided doing for a long time now. He typed in Molly Malone instead.

If he hit the enter key, he knew he'd get a crash course in all things Molly. He wanted to know more than what she was willing to tell him, such as what had happened to her, for one.

His mind flashed back to last night, lying in his bed holding a sleeping Molly, her body sated and still against his. He'd been able to feel the soft heat of her breast against his chest, the gentle touch of her hand on the stubble of his cheek . . . There weren't a lot of things he cherished more than the memory of being with her like that, and how she'd touched him, body and soul.

He was still staring at her name on the screen, his finger hovering over enter when she walked by his office and met his gaze, her own both warm and extremely wary, which tugged at his heart. She wasn't okay with this, not yet, not even close.

Holding her gaze, he knew. He would never hit enter. Whatever she'd faced, she'd tell him when she was good and ready.

And he was willing to wait for that.

She opened her mouth, but Joe walked into the room and grabbed the file he'd left on the table, and whatever she'd been about to say, she kept to herself.

Joe glanced over at the two of them, narrowing his eyes at Molly. "Something's different. You do your hair?"

She put a hand to her head and scowled at him. "No."

Joe cocked his head. "New dress?"

"No!" She tossed up her hands. "I'm just feeling . . . good. Is that so out of the ordinary?"

"Yes," both Lucas and Joe said at the same time.

She rolled her eyes and tried to walk by Joe, who stopped her and dipped down a little to stare into her face. His smile faded. "Who is he?"

"Excuse me?"

"You clearly . . ." He grimaced. "Got some. Who the hell is he?"

Molly gave him a shove. "You're kidding me, right?"

"Did you vet him?" Joe asked.

Molly shook her head. "We are so not having this conversation."

"You didn't," Joe said, sounding shocked. "Who the hell is he?"

Lucas stood up to try and save her from answering that one. "We've got to get going," he said to Joe. "Meeting with our new clients this morning, right? Archer said they were expecting us this morning at their offices. I'll drive while you read us the file."

Joe didn't budge or take his gaze off Molly. "You're not on one of those dating apps again, are you? The guys you dated from there were all tools."

Molly turned to the door. "The only tool in my life is you, Joe."

"Oh, *real* mature," her brother said but Molly had shut the door behind her.

Joe looked over at Lucas. "What's her problem?"

"She was online dating?"

Joe shook his head. "Not anymore. I went in and changed her profile to make her seventy-five years old, using a picture of one of the Golden Girls. I edited it to say she likes slow rides on her motorized scooter and drinking Metamucil while watching the sunrise, since sleeping gave her indigestion. I'm pretty sure that fixed things."

Lucas didn't like the thought of Molly online dating any more than Joe did. But the truth was, he didn't like the idea of her dating at all. He was just beginning coming to terms with that, the fact that *he* wanted to be her one and only.

Not that he was ready to admit it out loud to Molly, much less to her brother and his own partner. But mostly he didn't like that Joe had taken her options away from her. No one should do that. "She can handle herself," he said. "You know that, right?"

"I do, but . . ." Joe blew out a breath, looking torn. "She's my baby sister. I've always looked out for her. It's not an easy habit to break."

"She's smart and she's strong, not to mention levelheaded. Give her a break, man. Trust her instead of playing stupid games with her online profiles."

Joe gave that a moment's thought. "Yes, you're right. Forget the profiles. I could just figure out who she's seeing and run them through our programs to check him out."

"Bad idea," Lucas said. "Real bad."

"Why?"

"Because she'll kill you if she finds out." Although maybe she'd kill her brother before he could kill Lucas . . .

Joe blew out a breath. "Damn. You're probably right. Why are you probably right?"

"Because I'm smarter than you."

Joe gave him a playful shove. When Lucas hit the wall, Molly yelled at them from her desk down the hall. "Stop acting like you're in the MMA! Last time you put a hole in my wall, Archer made you pay for the fix-it bill. Why can't you just pummel each other instead?"

Lucas straightened and wrapped an arm around Joe's neck to give him a hard noogie. "Tell her you're sorry."

"No."

Lucas tightened his grip and Joe yelled, "Sorry!" Then he shoved free, glaring at him. "What's your problem?"

"Nothing."

"Bullshit," Joe said. "You've been quiet, on another planet. And now, you allowed me to nearly put you through the wall. You're . . . distracted."

"I'm fine."

Joe looked at him with an undercurrent of worry and Lucas sighed. "I am," he said.

Joe wasn't buying it, but at least he knew better than to push.

More than Lucas could say for himself. He was feeling more than a little uneasy for not telling Joe how he felt about Molly. But hell, he could barely explain it to himself. After Carrie died, he'd never have become involved with someone as vulnerable as Molly on any level, and he did not mean that as a commentary on her abilities. He meant emotionally vulnerable, which he actually considered a positive attribute. It was just that he himself had been so emotionally bankrupt for so long that he'd have steered clear in order not to hurt her. Maybe a few years ago, he might have slept with her once or twice, no regrets. More recently, he might've slept with her until she realized it was going nowhere and kicked him to the curb.

So what the hell did he think he was doing now?

He was taking a chance.

On purpose.

He was putting himself out there and it was fucking terrifying. He'd accepted that personal goals could change as life went on, but he was still cynical to the bone and wasn't sure he believed people themselves could actually change. He'd been a lot of things. A punkass kid, a bored student, a brother, a son, a boyfriend, a fiancé, a DEA agent, an investigator. He'd been good at all but two.

He'd made a crappy boyfriend and an even worse fiancé.

But had he changed? He'd like to think so. And yet there was no telling for sure until he dove into a relationship with Molly with both feet, eyes wide open—something he wasn't sure how to do, not to mention, he was completely unsure of how she felt about it.

What did she see in him? What did she expect of him? He supposed he needed to ask her, which he wasn't looking forward to. As for what *he* wanted from *her* . . . he wanted to say it was her body's unconditional acceptance for as long as he could get it. But he suspected he was looking for much more. His heart was asking for something his brain kept telling him he shouldn't want.

A soul mate.

And . . . now he was sweating. But he'd already gone through the denial stage of this game with Molly, keeping his emotional distance. Even he knew when to grudgingly accept defeat. She mattered to him, more than anyone ever had.

Joe was staring at him, not looking overly thrilled. "You'd tell me if you weren't okay, right? If something was wrong?"

"Sure," Lucas lied. Because no way was he going to try to explain his feels to anyone but Molly. And even then, the thought was daunting. A part of him knew he'd eventually have to tell Joe too. He knew this.

He hated this.

The next few hours were passed meeting with

their clients and then working on dreaded reports. Finally, starving, he went to the employee room.

One of Caleb's assistants had just dropped off Thai takeout as a thank-you gift. Hunt Investigations did a lot of work for Caleb's conglomerate, and was in fact on retainer. Last week, they'd discovered a subcontractor on one of Caleb's new buildings was taking kickbacks. They'd provided the evidence needed to proceed in court.

Caleb was clearly feeling grateful.

And Lucas was feeling grateful for food. He'd gotten there just in time, too. The masses were huddled in close, piling Thai on their plates. By the time he got his own filled, the only seat left was right next to Molly. She looked up at him as he sat next to her. He smiled.

She didn't.

Okay then. They'd shared orgasms, but they still weren't quite friends. Good to know.

Archer strode in and proceeded to start the meeting without preamble, pointing at various members of the team when it was their turn to run through their current case. When Lucas was up, he opened his laptop and froze. The open tab was on one of their special search programs and Molly's name was still typed in. He smoothly and quickly shifted the screen aside and presented his current case to the room, not looking over at Molly.

Shortly thereafter, the meeting was adjourned and everyone filed out. Molly stood and turned to him, hands on hips. She didn't speak. She didn't have to; steam was coming out her ears.

"Okay," he said. "I get that it looks bad, but I didn't hit enter."

"And I'm supposed to believe you?"

He stood and met her gaze straight-on. "Yes." He waited for her reaction, but she wasn't giving him much of anything. She was just looking at him, eyes intense as if trying to measure his ability for honesty.

Fair enough. "I found something on St. Nick," he said quietly. "I've emailed you the file."

"Did you?" she asked with a surprise that bothered him.

"Yeah. I did. Partners, remember? He's got a lot of aliases to comb through."

They were toe to toe now and the air in the conference room seemed to crackle around them. He didn't know about her, but all he could think about was last night when they'd been this close and what they'd been doing to each other. Was she thinking about it too? How they'd stripped each other in the dark and spent the long hours of the night locked in erotic sensations. And she'd come through on the dirty talk too, big-time. At the memory, he smiled.

Her gaze dropped to his mouth and he knew, oh yeah, he damn well knew that she was thinking about it too. She wet her lips and gave a small little sigh that warmed him in places that had no business being warmed in a damn conference room at work. "Molly."

She closed her eyes and tipped her face up, like she wanted him to kiss her—which he wanted more than his next breath. He put a hand on her hip and leaned in and . . .

Joe walked into the room.

Molly jumped back a few feet and whirled on her brother. "Why are you *always* sneaking up on me? Jeez, wear a damn bell, would you?"

Joe gave her an odd look and pointed to his cell phone still lying on the large conference table. "Forgot that." He gave a half smile to his sister. "I know, I know, I'd forget my head if it wasn't attached to my neck, right?" His smile faded and he divided a glance between Lucas and Molly. "What's going on?"

"Nothing," Molly said quickly.

Lucas shook his head. Nope, nothing wrong here, nothing to see . . .

Archer came back in to grab a doughnut out of the opened box. "Almost left dessert." He stared at Lucas and then Molly. "What's up?"

"Nothing," Molly repeated.

Lucas pleaded the fifth.

Archer didn't look any more convinced than Joe, which meant it was time to get the hell out of Dodge. Lucas grabbed his laptop and nodded to Joe. "Hand me a kiss." Shit. Fuck. Damn. Hell. "I mean a doughnut." God, he was so stupid. "Hand me a *doughnut*."

Joe just stared at him as if one of them had lost their mind.

Not Archer. There was no bemusement in his gaze

at all. Just a blank, deadpanned stare that probably would've had most people running for the hills.

Lucas wasn't most people and he wasn't easily intimidated or scared. But he could admit that his balls tightened slightly and not in a good way. Ignoring everyone but Molly, whom he sent a quick glance to and found her cheeks flushed, he grabbed a doughnut for himself, and then on second thought, took a second. Because this was definitely going to be a two doughnut sort of day. Then he turned his back—a risk with both Archer and Joe being excellent marksmen—and walked out of the room.

By the time Molly lifted her head from her laptop at the end of the day, most everyone else had left work. She'd switched over from Hunt work to the file Lucas had sent her. Back aching, she stood and stretched, giving her leg a moment to get under her. When she could straighten it all the way, she went around closing up for the night and found Lucas in his office on his laptop.

"Oh," she said in surprise, standing in his opened doorway. "I was just about to turn off all the lights on you. What are you still doing here? You came in at five this morning."

"I could ask the same of you," he said and rose, stretching as she just had, rolling his broad shoulders. His T-shirt rose a little, giving her a quick peek at some serious rock-hard abs. She had to force her eyes off him because she knew herself. Knew the danger signs. Her entire body softened when she got too close to him now, and she . . . tingled.

It was the memories of their nights together. She kept replaying the sound of his low timbered rough voice in her ear when he'd been over her, deep inside her, taking her to places she hadn't been in far too long. And then the sound of his sexy triumphant laugh when he'd taken her over the edge for the second time.

And then a third.

If she was being honest, it was about more than just the physical intimacy they'd shared. It was the look in his eyes when he got concerned about her safety—and yet he still let her do what she wanted to do.

Yeah, there was no doubt. She was deep, *deep* in the danger zone with him. "I had a bunch of work piled up," she said.

"And not all of it for Hunt Investigations," he said.

She gave a single nod of agreement.

"Find anything?" he asked.

"I'm working on getting access to financial information on Nick and all his various aliases, along with his brother. And also the workings of the charities that the village supposedly supports. Did you know that there's a handful of people who win bingo? A lot?"

"What's a lot?" he asked.

"Just about weekly, near as I can tell. Almost as if they have a deal with the person in charge of bingo."

He nodded. "So assuming that's true and that Nick has people planted in bingo, the winners probably get to keep part of the winnings, but have to hand the rest back to him."

"Bad Santa."

"Very bad," he agreed in that voice that never failed to rev her engines. Before she could do something stupid, she looked at the time. "Oops. Gotta go," she said.

"Hold up."

"No time," she said and walked down the hallway, grabbing her purse and laptop. At the front door of the offices, she was halted when a long arm reached past her and held the door closed.

He was right behind her, as in so close she could feel the heat of him through her clothes, seeping into her back. She closed her eyes to take it in as he lowered his head and rubbed his jaw to hers.

"Molly," he murmured, his mouth at the sweet spot beneath her ear, making her quiver on the inside. On the outside, she locked her knees.

"Hmm?" she managed, her body moving of its own accord, dammit, tipping her head to the side to give him more room in order to drive her crazy with his mouth now at her throat.

"Where are you running off to?" he asked. His breath was warm, the day-old stubble on his jaw prickling her skin in the very best way.

"Home," she managed. "I've got to rest up for tomorrow night's elf shift. Mrs. Berkowitz and Mrs.

White heard rumors that something's going down tomorrow night." Dammit! Her eyes flashed open and
she whirled to face him, poking her finger in his stupid hard chest. "Stop doing that!"

He lifted his hands, showing her that they weren't
on her in any way. "Doing what?"

"You know what!"

"Breathing?"

"Yes! Especially on my neck."

"You liked it."

Way too much . . .

Clearly able to read her mind, he smiled. "Are you
going to invite your partner along tomorrow night?"

"No," she said.

"Why not?"

"Because I'm just going to work a shift and you
stick out in all your big, alpha, silent badassery. And
plus, there's no way you'd actually wear an elf costume, so . . ."

He'd gone brows up at the badassery comment. "I
can't wear an elf costume," he said. "No place to put
my gun."

She snorted and wriggled her butt against his "gun."

He whipped her around to face him and pressed
her up against the wall with six feet plus of solid
muscle, and her eyes started to drift closed of their
own doing. "That's a pretty big gun," she said breathlessly.

Laughing, he dropped his forehead to hers. "You've
been ignoring me since the meeting. You okay?"

"Sure. Why wouldn't I be?"

His brown eyes met hers and held.

"Because of last night? Lucas, I think we both know exactly how okay I am after that." She gave him a small smile. "Nothing's changed."

He ran his fingers along her jaw, letting them sink into her hair. "Good. But I'm going with you tomorrow night. Tomorrow night and always."

"You'll wear an elf costume?" she asked, teasingly hopeful.

A light of amusement came into his eyes. "In bed I'll wear whatever you want me to. But out of bed, I'm staying dressed as is—including weapons."

She ran her gaze over his leanly muscled body. "Exactly how many weapons are you packing anyway?"

A very wicked smile crossed his mouth. "Unless you're prepared to search me and find out yourself, none of your business."

This caused a rush of heat to go right through her, but she lifted her chin and gave him a light shove.

He let her have her space, but didn't go far. "I'm still coming with," he said.

"Because you think I need backup?"

"Because we're partners. And if you're free right now, I could actually use your help with something."

"Like what?" she asked, eyes narrowed.

He smiled. "Suspicious much?"

"With you, yes."

"Have I ever steered you wrong or left you hanging?"

"No," she had to admit. He'd never done anything but be brutally honest, have her back on this case, and respect her abilities.

As for the leaving her hanging thing . . . he'd never left her hanging at all. In fact, he'd refused to leave her behind.

So she supposed it wouldn't be fair to leave him behind now.

Chapter 16

#AreYouElfingKiddinMe

Lucas couldn't help but smile at the look on Molly's face. At the moment she was utterly transparent, and he liked where her thoughts had gone. A lot. "My aunt's having a holiday party," he said. "And I promised I'd show up."

"Oh, no." She shook her head. "No, no, no."

"And there's an additional problem," he went on as if she hadn't spoken. "I have to bring a date to save me from all the dates my family will have planted at this party for me if I show up single. The fear is real, Molly."

She was still shaking her head.

He blew out a breath. "Please?"

She looked boggled at that, and he got it. It wasn't often he asked for help. "You're not afraid of anything," she said. "I've seen you jump off a fifty-foot bridge to go after a suspect. And only three weeks ago, you threw yourself in front of a bullet to save a client. You're fearless."

"Not entirely. Turns out I'm terrified of the meddling, nosy women in my family."

"Wow."

"Wow in a good way, right?" he asked.

"No."

He had to laugh. She was seriously the only woman he'd ever met who could push all his buttons and yet still make him want her. Which solved it. He'd lost his mind. "You going to help me or not?"

"By pretending to be your date?" she asked.

"Yes."

"Okay, whatever. Sure, I'll save your ass," she said with a martyr-like sigh. "But it's going to cost you. Big-time."

"What's your price?" he asked as they took the stairs down to the courtyard.

"Oh no, you're not getting off that easy. The price is a favor, to be named at a later date. And you can't say no."

"I don't think so," he said.

"Okay then." She shrugged and shifted, reversing directions. "Have a good night—"

He caught her arm. Damn. She was both terrifying and incredibly impressive. If the guys could see him now, they'd be laughing their asses off. "Fine," he said. "We've got a deal. A favor for a favor. But you have to *really* sell being my date."

Her eyes narrowed suspiciously. "Sell? Sell how exactly?"

"Well . . ." He thought about that. "You could brag about me a little bit." He smiled. "Or a lot. And rub up against me and look at me like I'm a sex god. The whole nine yards."

She shook her head. "I'm seeing a whole new side of you here, Lucas."

"A side you like, though, right?"

"Whatever gets you through the day," she said.

He drove. They were out of the city and on the highway before she straightened and took a good look around, which was a testament to just how exhausted she was, working both her regular day job and moonlighting on the Bad Santa case.

"Where are we going?" she asked.

"I told you. My aunt's holiday party." He paused and glanced over at her, hoping she wasn't armed. He was pretty sure she wasn't, but Joe was always armed to the teeth so he couldn't be positive without a pat down—and the likelihood of her allowing that was slim to never. "I told you that she lives in the Sierras. At the base, before the summit."

Molly gaped at him. "As in Donner Summit? Near Tahoe?"

"Well, not quite that far, but yeah."

"You didn't say it was outside the city!"

He shrugged. "You didn't ask."

"Oh my God." But she didn't say anything else, or demand he take her home, both good signs. It was snowing lightly, casting the night in a soft, white glow as they began the climb up the mountains.

"I love the mountains and especially snow," she admitted softly, staring out the window. "It's calm and quiet and . . ."

"And . . ."

She didn't answer.

Romantic. He'd bet that's what she'd been about to say and he agreed. The snow was deceptively romantic.

All of which added up to nothing but trouble.

"Do you come up here often?" she asked.

"My family loves Tahoe and spends a lot of time up here. We gather at the cabin as often as possible. Less now, though."

"People too busy?" she asked.

He shook his head. "Josh, my brother, used to handle most of the planning of these trips. He was the perennial middle kid, the peacemaker, the gatherer. The rest of us try, but we're no match for him."

He had her attention now; he could feel her gaze on him. Around them, the night was so quiet. The gently falling snow was an insulator, making things very close and intimate.

"Will he be there tonight?" she asked.

"No." He gave a small smile. "We were a pair growing up, though. A pair of instigators. If there was trouble, we managed to find it. Gave my mom gray hair early."

She let out a small smile. "I don't remember

much about my mom, but Joe and I were a pair of troublemakers too, though Joe tried to keep me out of it and safe. Only problem was, I was good at being stealth and following him. Used to piss him off big-time."

He let out a low laugh. "If half the things I've heard about Joe's misspent youth are true, then I can see why he wouldn't want you tagging along after him."

Her smile congealed a little bit and he cocked his head. "What?"

"Nothing."

"I know you now, Molly," he said. "I know your tells. Plus you're a shitty liar."

She shrugged. "You're right about Joe not wanting me to tag along after him. He hated it and worried about it, for reasons I didn't understand at the time or I might've gotten smarter a lot faster."

"Something's happened," he guessed quietly.

She hesitated. "Remember when I told you I was hurt because of my own stupidity?" she finally asked.

Oh shit. He had a bad feeling about this story. "Yeah."

"Well, I wasn't kidding. I was fourteen to Joe's seventeen when I developed a crush on someone in his crowd, someone I thought was a friend—but wasn't." She paused, her breath quickening a little. "I didn't know, but this guy and a few others were trying to convince Joe to join their gang because he had some pretty impressive . . . skills. Skills he'd been using to keep food on our table and a roof over our head." She grimaced. "Okay, now I'm making Joe seem like a juvenile delinquent—"

"Hey, no judgment from me," Lucas said, reaching across the console to take her hand. "I've seen Joe's skills firsthand, and he's saved my ass on the job more times than I can count. I'm grateful for him, and grateful for you that he could provide for you when you needed it. I'm just sorry it was like that for you guys."

"My dad really did the best he could," she said. "He just couldn't always keep a job. People don't understand him."

Lucas nodded, not saying anything else, knowing that by holding his tongue she might keep talking and tell him the part of the story she was stalling with, and he very much wanted, *needed*, to hear it.

"Joe didn't want to join the gang," she said. She paused and then cleared her throat. "Sorry. I'm sorry. I'm sweating. Can you turn down the heat?"

He quickly did so and then handed her one of the bottles of water he had stashed in the driver door pocket.

She cracked it open and drank deeply.

"Better?" he asked.

"Yeah. Thanks."

"So . . . Joe didn't want to join the gang," he said casually, hoping she'd continue.

"No. Or do any of the things they wanted him to. He kept refusing, but I didn't know any of those things. All I knew was that he got to go out whenever he wanted and not be accountable to anyone for his comings and goings, and it seemed so . . . exciting." She sighed. "So when one of the guys started paying attention to me, I was flattered." She closed her eyes.

Yeah, he'd been right. He was really going to hate this story. He pulled into his aunt's driveway and parked. Leaving the engine on for the defrost, he turned to her. "Can you tell me what happened?"

She put her free hand low on her belly, as if it hurt. The memories appeared to have her every muscle tense and she was indeed clammy. He cracked her window an inch to get her some air and she sent him a grateful look before closing her eyes again.

"They used me to try to make Joe steal a car," she said.

His hand, still holding hers, squeezed reflexively. "Used you how, Molly?" he asked, still speaking very low, very calm, but he was just about as far from calm as he could get.

She opened her eyes and met his gaze. "They kidnapped me. Hell," she said bitterly. "The truth is that I went along willingly, thinking Darius wanted to be with me. But it wasn't like that. They held me in an abandoned building, waiting for Joe to do as they demanded."

She wasn't the only one sweating now. He was as well. He'd worked enough abduction cases to know all the things that had likely happened to her. No way had she come out of that situation the same person as she'd gone in. And she'd been only fourteen. Just a kid, one who'd already had a rough enough life without this having happened to her. "Did Joe steal the car to get you back?"

"No. Instead, he tore apart the city looking for me. And he found me too, but it took three days."

"Jesus." Lucas brought their joined hands up to his chest, which was so tight now it was possible he was going to stroke out. "They hurt you."

"Yes, but not in the way you think." She swallowed hard and rolled her window all the way down, sticking her head out and gulping in some air. "Sorry," she said when she'd rolled the window back up. "Thinking about those days makes me feel like throwing up."

He understood. He felt a little bit like throwing up himself, imagining her as a young, defenseless teen facing down a gang of thugs on her own. For three fucking days.

"Honestly," she said squeezing his hand. "It's not as bad as you're imagining."

She was trying to comfort him. At just the thought, his throat burned with emotion, and his eyes did too. "You don't have to tell me—"

"I think I should," she murmured, searching his face. "I wasn't—They didn't touch me. Darius kept me separated in a room away from the rest of the guys. He told me that as long as I stayed quiet and didn't cause any trouble, I wouldn't be hurt."

With every fiber of his being, Lucas wanted her to tell him that the asshole punk had kept his word.

"But the problem was," she said, "I wasn't exactly born with the sit down and shut up gene." She shook her head. "I tried, but I just couldn't do it."

No matter how long ago this had been, if she told him that they'd laid a finger on her, he'd single-handedly hunt every one of them down and break every bone in their bodies without remorse.

"I knew Joe would be looking for me," she said, "and that he'd find me. But on the third day, I couldn't wait any more. When Darius came in and tossed me a bottle of water, I picked it up and chucked it at his head. It knocked him over and he hit his head on the way down and was out cold. I stole the handcuff keys from his pocket, unlocked my cuffs and went out the third story window, intending to climb down one of the two trees that were nearly up against the building."

Lucas felt his chest nearly burst with pride and a nameless emotion, both of which threatened to overcome him. The contrast of Molly's tough-girl strength and her not completely hidden vulnerability called to something deep inside him. "Nicely done."

A small smile of pride curved her lips. "Problem was, I was a little weak and off my game, and when I jumped for one of the branches, I missed." She paused. "I fell about twenty-five feet and broke my back in two places, amongst other things."

The air slipped right out of his lungs. "Jesus, Molly."

"Yeah. And I hit the ground right at Joe's feet. He'd finally narrowed down the location I'd been held. If I'd just stayed quiet and pliant as Darius had asked, Joe would've gotten to me."

Lucas felt sick all the way to his gut on how she'd suffered. And he was certain there was more to this horrific tale, that she'd left out a lot of details. Reaching out, he cupped her face. "Don't you dare blame yourself. Joe would hate that."

"Right, because he already blames himself enough," she said. "We're really quite the pair." She stared at him. "Stop."

"Stop what?"

"Stop looking at me like I'm still broken. I'm not. I've had three surgeries, and even though the nerves in my right leg are still damaged, almost everything else is relatively fixed."

He let out a low laugh. "Molly, I'm not looking at you like you're broken. I'm looking at you like you're the most amazing woman I've ever met."

She sent him a look of disbelief.

"Amazing and strong and resilient and . . . *amazing.*"

"You already said that," she whispered.

"It bears repeating," he whispered back and then started to lean in, intent on kissing her.

Just as the front door of the cabin opened.

In all their perfection of timing, his family spilled out, because apparently there was some sort of radar in the Knight gene that let them know when the prodigal son returned.

"Oh boy," Molly whispered. "There's a lot of them."

"Yeah."

"You're really going to owe me big for this one," she said, sounding like herself again.

In that moment, Lucas knew he'd do whatever she wanted, whenever she wanted, wherever she wanted. Because in spite of his determination to hold back from the smartest, most resilient, most resourceful, most incredible woman he'd ever been with, he was in. *All in.*

Chapter 17

#PassTheEggnog

Realizing Lucas's family was watching her and Lucas from the well-lit cabin porch, Molly felt the first licks of panic. She knew this was just paying back a favor, that it wasn't real, but still. If telling him about her past had been an eight on the one-to-ten scale of difficulty, meeting his family was a twelve. Twelve *hundred*. She drew a deep breath and concentrated on the gently falling snow and the incredible beauty of the flakes floating out of the sky seemingly one by one.

Lucas turned her to face him. "Problem?"

"You guys all spend a lot of time together, right?"

"*They* spend a lot of time together. I'm not around nearly as much." He held her gaze. "I'm going to ask you again. Do we have a problem?"

She bit her lower lip. "So I'm pretending to be

what exactly, an online hookup? A friend? I want to
be prepared for any questions."

He laughed. "An online hookup?"

She shrugged, fighting an odd defensive feeling
deep in her gut, one she didn't want to examine too
closely. "Figured that's more believable than a date
or girlfriend. So which is it going to be?"

"Since they've already met you, I think it's safe to
leave the online hookup off the table," he said dryly.
"And if I say girlfriend, you'll run for the hills. Let's
just go with a date."

Would she run for the hills? She tried it out in her
head, the word *girlfriend*, and felt a genuine panic
ball bounced around in her gut to go with the annoying defensiveness.

Dammit. She hated when he was right.

"Molly." He cupped her face, his amusement fad-
ing. "What's going on?"

Lie. "I don't like lying to your family. They're
nice." And actually, nothing about that was a lie after all.

"They're also insane," he said. "Listen to me,
okay? This has nothing to do with our reality and
everything to do with just keeping my family happy
and off my back. And like on any covert op that re-
quires a fabricated backstory, you go with the easiest,
most natural thing you can come up with. Something
close enough to the truth that it rolls off the tongue.
We work at the same place and we're on a date. Just
a simple date. Period."

Yeah. That made the most sense, of course. But she couldn't deny that a small part of her, a *very* small part, actually might've liked to try *girlfriend* on for size regardless, just to see how it fit on her.

"Molly?" He let his thumb slightly glide along her jaw.

"Yeah. Got it." She pulled back. "A simple date. Like our second or third?"

"Sure," he said.

She nodded. "Fine. But there's something you should know."

"What's that?"

"I don't put out on a second date. Or a third."

He flashed her a panty-melting smile. "Bet I could change your mind," he said in a voice that matched his smile.

"Nope," she said, shaking her head. "Once I make up my mind, I can't be budged. I'm like the Rock of Gibraltar, I—"

He kissed her. Quick, no tongue, just the appetizer on the menu of Lucas Knight's variety of kisses, but quite effective all the same. When he pulled back, she opened her eyes, dazed, and asked, "What were we talking about?"

With a grin, he got out of the car and came around for her. They headed up the walk and Molly watched as Lucas's mom broke from the pack and went straight for her son, wrapping her arms around him and hugging him tight, whispering something in his ear.

He hugged her back just as tight, closing his eyes for a beat as he nodded, a look of such love and acceptance on his face that Molly just stared. She'd never seen that expression on him before. It softened him, made him seem young and more carefree.

When his mom pulled back, she turned to Molly and gave her the same sort of hug, and it felt so genuine that she found herself returning the hug in kind. Then Laura and Sami did the same before introducing her to a gaggle of others who all seemed to enjoy each other's company. Aunts. More cousins. Laura's husband, Will, was there with what looked like a two-ish-year-old in a backpack on his shoulders, and more—although not Lucas's dad, who apparently had gotten held up in London. And crowded as it was, it was also . . . lovely. And foreign. For as long as she could remember, it'd been just her and Joe and her dad, just the three of them. Yes, supposedly they had some distant relatives back East. Her mom's cousins. Her dad's family. But her dad hadn't liked any of them and had scared them off a long time ago. Joe had brought Kylie into their small fold and that was great. But their little family unit still had nothing on this huge one.

Dinner had been held for their arrival, which consisted of more food than Molly had ever seen. Mindful of the fact that her clothes were already feeling a little too snug thanks to Joe bringing doughnuts into the office too many times last week, she held back, taking one small piece of honey baked ham and a few green beans baked with bacon because, well, bacon. She managed to refrain from what looked like the most perfectly browned cheesy bread she'd ever seen, but then had immediate regret when the bread vanished in two seconds.

Someone asked her about her job at Hunt and she explained she was the office manager, while wishing she could say she worked investigations. She began to eat, but found herself glancing over at Lucas's plate. He'd snagged *three* pieces of that cheesy bread. He with the perfectly ridged abs and zero percent body fat. Where did he put it all anyway? She tried to forget about it, tried to let it go, but lunch seemed like so long ago, and suddenly all she could think about was how the bread would melt in her mouth.

She waited until Lucas turned to say something to his sister on his other side before stealing one of his pieces of cheesy bread. She was on the last bite when he glanced down at his plate and then at her.

Mouth full, she gave her best innocent smile, turned her head away from him, and . . . came gaze to gaze with his mom.

She was grinning.

At the tap on her shoulder, she turned back to Lucas.

"Something you want to tell me?" he asked.

"Well, I was going to wait until we were alone," she said. "But you've got a little something . . ." She pointed to the corner of her mouth.

Lucas brought his fingers up to the same spot on his own mouth and then looked down at them. "Lip gloss." He smiled at her. "Strawberry, right?"

She flushed. He'd turned that right back on her. *Note to self: you can't outplay a player.*

"I think you took something of mine," he said.

"I don't know what you're talking about."

He touched the corner of *her* mouth this time, coming away with a crumb from the bread she'd stolen off his plate.

She tried to blink innocently, but the feel of his finger on her mouth had set her knees wobbling. Good thing she was sitting down.

"Got a question for you, Molly," Laura said. "Does Lucas still snore like a buzz saw? Because when we were little and we'd come up here, we had to share a room. He'd snore so loud that we'd all want to snuff him out with a pillow."

"Hey," Lucas said. "That was after Sami broke my nose with her baseball bat and before my surgery to fix the deviated septum. I haven't snored since."

"You sure about that?" Laura asked.

Everyone looked at Molly, including Lucas, who seemed to be trying to remind her telepathically about their deal. She was his date. His *romantic* date. Deciding some payback was necessary, she lifted a shoulder. "You know, I almost don't hear it anymore. I guess you get used to it."

Everyone laughed, but Lucas just gave her a slow, devastatingly mischievous smile. "So you want to play it like that, do you?" he murmured.

Conflicting emotions danced through her. The thrill and excitement of what he might do to her in retribution . . . and the *worry* of what he might do to her in retribution. Not that she was afraid of him. More like she was afraid of how much she might like it.

The conversation shifted, ebbed and flowed, and through it all Molly was incredibly, annoyingly aware of Lucas at her side, his arm brushing hers, the way he dipped his head close when she spoke to him, like whatever she might say was the most important thing to him in that moment, and how his unique, sexy scent teased her every time he did.

He lifted his glass for a drink and caught her staring at him. "You okay?" he asked.

Was she? She wasn't quite certain . . .

"Honey," Lucas's mom said to him. "We've been having trouble with the internet connection today. I thought maybe after you finish—"

"No problem," he said. "I'm finished." He reached for Molly's hand. "I'll just take an assistant—"

Molly choked on her water because in the office, *she* was the internet wizard. No one but her could ever get their systems running smoothly, including Lucas.

"I mean partner," Lucas quickly corrected, but by the look on his face he knew he was too late.

Molly smiled at his mom. "I could take a look for you. I'm sure I won't need an assistant, but Lucas could come along and watch and learn if he'd like."

His mom laughed in sheer delight and looked at Lucas. "I love this girl." She stood up, drawing Molly along with her toward the den. "You just stay seated, son, and eat your bread. We've got this."

"Idiot," Sami said fondly to Lucas, who blew out a breath.

A minute later, Molly was unplugging the router and rebooting their system. "This almost always works."

"I know," Lucas's mom said. "And there's nothing wrong with our internet. I just wanted to talk to you alone without my nosy son."

Sami came into the den and shut the door behind her. "He's doing dishes," Sami told her mom.

Molly took in the women's expectant expressions and thought *uh-oh* . . .

"Oh, don't be scared," his mom said. "We're not looking for you to betray Lucas's confidence or anything like that."

"Okay, so what are you looking for?"

The two women looked at each other and then back at Molly. Sami spoke first. "To be honest, we're just so excited to see him in a relationship at all. What can you tell us?"

"Well, first of all, this is just a date, so—"

His mom and Sami looked at each other and laughed.

"What?" Molly asked.

"Nothing," Sami said, still smiling. "It's just nice to see him so comfortable with you. And . . . happy. For so long he's been totally closed off. You know? And yeah, he'd show up to these family things if we bugged him enough, but he always came alone. The hard part is that he refuses to talk about himself at all, so we have no way of knowing how he's really doing, how he's been coping. Recovering." Her smile faded, to be replaced by worry and concern as she leaned in closer and lowered her voice. "So can you help us by telling us how he's doing?"

"Coping and recovering?" Molly asked. "Are you referring to when he was shot last month or—"

They all gasped in horrified unison. Okay, so it wasn't that—

"He was shot?" his mom asked in a small voice.

"In the side, a through and through," Molly quickly said. "Full recovery."

His mom let out a shaky breath. "Dear God."

Sami reached for her aunt's hand but looked at Molly. "He's really okay?"

"Yes," Molly said firmly and apologetically. "I'm sorry, I—"

"Don't you dare be sorry," his mom said. "Not for being there for him and not for being so honest." She swallowed hard. "For a while now, Lucas has pulled inward. Hasn't let anyone in. Works all the time. But since you've been around, we've seen him twice in a week. And he's calling more, checking in. He's smiling too and he does look happy. We all figured that was your doing."

Molly shook her head. "I honestly can't take credit for any of that."

His mom's face softened. "Are you sure? Because love's pretty damn powerful."

"We're really not—" Molly shook her head, unable

to put words to all she was feeling. "We're just not," she finished lamely, and unable to lie to them, this family who loved Lucas so much, she sighed. "Okay, full disclosure. This isn't really even a date. It's a favor. We work together and sometimes we help each other out with stuff . . ."

"Like tonight," Sami said.

"Yes, like tonight," she said, but instead of looking disappointed, the Knight women all exchanged another long look.

"That's a pretty big favor," Sami finally said. "Walking into a family gathering like this can be pretty intimidating, and it suggests a big step."

"He's done the same for me," Molly said, remembering the way he'd dealt with her dad, with a kindness and understanding she hadn't expected. "And mine was worse. Way worse," she added, thinking of her dad's rifle. "Uh, not to say this was bad or anything."

His mom helped her out by laughing, not offended in the least. "Sweet of you to say. And equally sweet of you to try to protect my son—and me—by letting me know you're not together. But I see something between you two, Molly, something I'm guessing you just don't yet see." She smiled. "I used to think that love was all about red roses and expensive dinners. But the truth is, love is letting your mate steal a piece of bread off your plate. It's being awoken by snoring and refraining from shoving him out of bed. It's talking in code and trying to embarrass one another in public. It's going on adventures and making fun of each other. It's stupid fights and memorable make-ups." She squeezed Molly's hand. "Love isn't pretty and romantic. You know that, right? Love is just stumbling through life with your best friend."

Molly's heart was thumping hard in her chest. Because if she was in love, no good could come of it. So thoroughly convinced of that, she shook her head. "I care about Lucas very much. Maybe even too much. But it's really not what you think, it's not what you want it to be."

"There you are," Lucas said from the doorway, making Molly's heart go from pounding to frozen in place. Had he heard what she'd said?

I care about Lucas very much. Maybe even too much . . .

His expression wasn't giving anything away so she had no idea of knowing. Damn. When would she learn to keep her mouth shut? Before she could obsess over what he'd heard, he took her hand and pulled her to his side. His expression was easy and his usual lighthearted as he smiled at her. "I've come to save you from the evil inquisition. Can I interest you in a few s'mores before we make the trip back?"

"Yes," she said gratefully, and if for a beat she could see his smile didn't quite meet his eyes, she told herself that undoubtedly, hers didn't either.

Chapter 18

#SmoresAreLife

"The fire pit's down this incline a bit," Lucas said. He was just in front of Molly, carrying a bag of supplies in one hand and holding onto one of her hands with the other.

She couldn't see a damn thing. The cabin and its lights were behind them. All she could see was Lucas and a vast black night all around them. It'd stopped snowing, but the frozen ground crunched beneath her feet. And truth be told, she was having some trouble on the uneven trail. Her leg was hurting, but hell if she'd admit it.

For the tenth time, Lucas stopped and turned to her.

"Don't," she warned.

He didn't sigh, but he gave her a look that spoke volumes. He wanted to help her.

"I said I've got this," she said. A few minutes ago

she'd shooed off Laura's offer of helping hands. She shooed off Sami's offer of helping hands. They'd reluctantly gone ahead.

But apparently Lucas couldn't be shooed.

"Here," he said and, turning his back to her, hunkered down and reached for her. "Hop up."

"No way."

But apparently he didn't need her to hop up at all because he simply hoisted her up onto his back. "Piggyback race to the pit," he called out as he passed his family, and then proceeded to beat them all down the hill with Molly and her weight of one hundred and thirty-five pounds not slowing him down one bit.

She felt dizzy at his speed. Actually, that wasn't true. She was dizzy from the feel of being plastered against his back, at the feel of his forearms hooked around her thighs to hold her to him. Unable to help herself, she pressed her lips to the nape of his neck and smiled when she felt the rumble of a rough groan/growl go through him.

"No fair," he said.

Maybe not, but she took a little nibble out of him just because she could and there didn't seem to be anything he could do about it.

At the campfire, he controlled her slow slide down his body and then turned to face her before she could swipe the sheer lust from her face.

She expected him to grin at her. Instead, he let her see that heat and hunger in his face too. It reached her in a place that his sexy humor couldn't have gotten to.

Her damn heart.

Yes, she really was feeling things for him, no matter what she wanted to believe, no matter what she'd tried to tell his family. Big, scary things.

"Hey," Laura called out. "We could use Lucas's superior fire-starting skills before Sami tries to blow us all up again."

"Jeez, a girl uses lighter fluid one time and she's never allowed to forget it," Sami grumbled.

"It took a year for your eyebrows to grow back," Laura said.

Ignoring them entirely, Lucas didn't move, just stood there looking deep into Molly's eyes while his sister and cousin continued to lightly bicker in the background.

Hell, the woods could have been on fire for all Molly would've noticed. She couldn't see, hear, or think about anything other than the look in Lucas's eyes as her earlier words seemed to echo between them.

I care about Lucas, very much. Maybe even too much.

Then suddenly he flashed her a wicked just-for-her smile that promised all sorts of things before taking her hand and leading her to the fire pit. Crouching in front of it, he began to build a fire, the muscles in his shoulders and back shifting as he worked. By the time he had flames flickering, Molly had answering flames flickering inside her belly.

And lower.

Lucas opened the big brown bag with the chocolate, graham crackers, and marshmallows, and everyone pounced on it all like they hadn't just stuffed their faces with more food than she'd ever seen.

"So how long have you and Lucas been knocking boots?" one of Lucas's aunts asked.

Molly jumped and her marshmallows fell off her stick and into the fire.

Lucas arched a brow at her and . . . slid two fresh marshmallows on her stick for her. "Aunt Jeanie," he said. "Just because you turned seventy-five last month doesn't mean you get to turn off your inner editor."

"Actually," she said, "it does. I don't have a lot of years left, you know. And the only benefit of being this ancient is that I get to say whatever I want." Then she looked expectantly at Molly.

"Don't answer her," Lucas said. "She'll just send out a letter to everyone in the family. And I do mean a letter because she refuses to use that new iPhone in her purse for anything other than taking pictures of her eight cats."

"Ten," Aunt Jeanie said.

Lucas's mom put her hand over Jeanie's. "I love you," she said to the older woman. "But the only person who gets to grill my son on his love life is me. I pushed for twelve long, brutal hours to bring his big, fat head into this world. I earned that right."

Lucas blew out a breath and dropped said big,

fat head, muttering something about why he'd ever thought this was a good idea.

"Remember when we'd come here when we were kids?" Laura asked, clearly trying to help out her brother. "Lucas would tell us scary campfire stories until Sami peed her pants."

"Hey," Sami said. "I was *way* too young for the Lizzy Borden stories!"

"And then he'd try to crawl into one of *our* sleeping bags in the middle of the night because he'd terrified himself," Laura said to her mom. "Remember?"

"Oh good," Lucas muttered. "Childhood stories."

"How about the time he blew up the shed?" Sami asked. "He'd secretly stored some fireworks there. The fire department came, and the police too. Who peed their pants then, huh?" she asked Lucas.

Lucas ignored her, calmly pulling two perfectly toasted marshmallows from off the fire and fitting them between his two waiting graham crackers.

"How did you get ahold of fireworks?" Molly asked. "You save up your allowance?"

"I didn't pay my kids any allowance," Lucas's mom said proudly.

Lucas met Molly's gaze, his own ironic. "Our allowance was being allowed to live at home."

"How about the time you blew up mom's mailbox with that cherry bomb," Laura said helpfully. "The police came that time too, remember?"

"Which turned out to be a felony," his mom said helpfully. "Who knew?"

"I was twelve," Lucas said, looking pained. "And I wasn't *all* hoodlum. I did some good stuff too. How about when I pretended to be Santa Claus for Sami?" He pointed to his cousin. "I climbed onto your roof and made reindeer noises and everything. You bought it hook, line, and sinker."

"Yep, right up until you fell off and past my window, breaking your arm. For years I thought I'd killed Santa. It was traumatizing."

Molly gasped in horror, reminded of her own fall and the damage it'd done.

Lucas's gaze met hers. "It was only one level, I didn't fall far," he said quickly, clearly knowing where her mind had gone. He looked at Sami again. "And now surely you can remember *something* from my past that doesn't involve trauma, cops, and ERs," Lucas said.

Everyone gave that some thought and came up empty.

"Thanks," he said dryly. "Thanks for helping me impress Molly."

Molly laughed. "Don't worry. I already knew you were a trouble causer." Truth was, she enjoyed the stories of his wild youth, and the way his family clearly loved and adored him. Looking around at the group, she felt her heart warm. Lucas had no idea how lucky he was with this big, open, warm family who hadn't faced anything as devastating as what her own had—several times over now.

Lucas's mom pulled out a large thermos and began pouring everyone eggnog into little cups, which they all lifted in toast to each other. "To Josh," his mom said softly and lifted her cup.

"To Josh," everyone repeated just as softly and they all lifted their cups and drank.

Molly looked at Lucas, her heart sinking.

"My brother died four years ago," Lucas said quietly to her unspoken questions. "Today would've been his thirty-fifth birthday."

Molly felt her heart catch with emotion. Okay, so this family had experienced loss, shattering loss, just like her. They got it, knew the life-changing devastation of losing someone so close to you. She reached for Lucas's hand and squeezed.

He lifted his head and met her gaze, his own filled with more emotion than he'd allowed her to see before. Then, surprising her, he pressed their joined hands to his chest, leaned in and brushed a kiss along her temple. "Time for another round of s'mores," he said.

So they opened another bag of marshmallows and hit round two of the eggnog. Because Great Aunt Jeanie was having trouble with her marshmallow technique, Lucas got up and went over to help her.

Laura scooted in closer to Molly. "Thanks for bringing him here tonight," she said quietly.

"He brought me."

Laura stared at her for a beat. "You really didn't make him come?"

Molly let out a small laugh. "You seem to know

your brother pretty well. Have you ever known him
to do something that someone made him do?"

"You're right." Laura smiled too and startled
Molly by giving her a huge, tight bear hug. "Then
thanks for being the catalyst that brought him back to
us." She pulled back to look into Molly's eyes. "We
lost him for a while, you know. First when Carrie
died and then again after we lost Josh. He didn't like
to come around. I think at first he was worried our
brimming emotions were contagious, but then it was
easier for him to stay away."

"Is Carrie the woman who died in a car accident?"

"Yes, but it wasn't that simple. They were high
school sweethearts, and planned on getting married
at some point." Laura tossed back her eggnog. "I'm
going to blame my big mouth on this, if anyone asks."
She drew a deep breath. "When she died, Lucas was
undercover with the DEA. Deep undercover. It took
his handlers a while to get him the message and get
him out, and by that time, she'd been buried for three
weeks."

"Oh my God," Molly murmured, feeling horrified for all he'd been through. How selfish and self-
centered had she been to not have seen that he'd been
hurt even worse than she had?

"That's why he's so . . . bruised by life," Laura
said.

"I'm not some fragile little peach, Laura."

At Lucas's mild but clearly annoyed voice behind
them, Laura jumped as they both turned to face him.

"Thin walls," he said. "Remember, we learned that when we were little and Aunt Karen and Uncle Steve used to go to bed right at dark and proceed to make noises for hours that Mom tried to tell us meant they were practicing their wrestling moves?"

"I wasn't gossiping," Laura said.

"You sure?" Lucas asked.

Laura had the good grace to look slightly ashamed. "Okay, fine, you caught me. But I'm not going to apologize for loving you so much that I want to see you happy."

"I *am* happy," Lucas said. "I'm here with you guys."

"Oh," his sister breathed, her eyes going suspiciously shiny as she sniffed. "Oh, that's so sweet."

"No, no stop. I didn't mean to make you cry," Lucas said, sounding pained.

"It's not you." She put her hands to her flat belly and smiled across the campfire at Will, who'd passed off their kid to grandma and was adding logs to the flames. "We're going to have another baby and babies make me cry."

"Did my super-powered grandma hearing serve me right?" The grandma to be stood up and clapped her hands together. "I'm getting another grandbaby?"

"Yes!" Laura said with a big smile.

This led to a bunch of happy squeals and whoops and another round of eggnog. Snowflakes began to float gently from the sky, and mesmerized, Molly stared up, watching flakes the size of dinner plates drift slowly down. Everyone moved inside, but Molly just kept staring upward, loving the iciness on her overheated face as the snowflakes touched down on her skin.

"Come on," Lucas said, moving in close, tipping her face to his. "You're chilled."

"It's snowing," she said in wonder.

"Haven't you ever seen it snow?"

"Not before tonight."

He smiled and cupped her face, lowering his head for a delicious kiss that ended all too soon. Wrapping his arms around her, he held on tight as behind them the fire crackled and above them the snow continued to fall. They swayed together in their own slow dance for a few long moments until she shivered.

"Come on," he murmured. "Time to go inside and get warm."

They all crowded into the kitchen for late night snacks. Will put pizza rolls into the oven and Molly's mouth watered.

"Make sure to marry a man who puts his pizza rolls into the oven, not the microwave," Laura told her, smiling at Will. "He knows good things take a little more time."

Her husband winked at her and then moved in close for a kiss while the rest of them drank some more eggnog and nibbled on everything that wasn't tied down. But soon the kitchen felt too warm and crowded, and Molly made her way down the hall, looking for the bathroom.

Lucas and his mom were ahead, just around a

corner, talking. To give them some privacy, Molly turned to try another way back to the kitchen, but then realized they were talking about her and she stilled. Maybe a better person would've still managed to walk away but she couldn't; her feet were frozen in place.

"I adore her, Lucas," his mom said.

"Me too," he responded, stunning Molly. "And keep your voice down. Thin walls, remember?"

"All too well." His mom smiled at him. "Please stay the night. It's snowing good now and the roads are slick. Besides, since you were shot and didn't tell your own family, we need more time to be with you."

He grimaced. "I'm fine, I didn't want to worry you. And we both have to work in the morning. I've got all-wheel drive and great tires, we'll be fine."

"But the eggnog—"

"I didn't drink any."

"How about I call your boss and tell him we have an emergency?" she asked him. "You could stay then, right?"

Lucas laughed. "Mom, Archer's got an ingrained bullshit detector. And Molly won't want to stay. I know you don't want to hear this, but it's really not what you think."

"That's what she tried to tell me too."

"She was telling you the truth," he said. "I had fantasies of pulling this off, letting you think we were on a date so you'd feel good about that, but it was a mistake."

"Lucas. You tried to lie to me?"

"Yes," he said. "And also, I tried to lie to Molly by letting her think the lie was for you, when it was really for her. She's not into me that way, Mom. And if I have to accept that, then so do you."

Molly's mouth fell open at this.

But his mom shook her head. "No way, baby. There's more. Yes, the chemistry, which is obvious to anyone with two eyes, but Lucas, there's *more.*"

"There could be," he agreed. "But she's not going to let it happen."

Molly stopped breathing.

"Lucas—"

"Mom, please. Just trust me, okay? I know a dead-end road when I see it."

"But you care about her very much."

"Sometimes, that's not enough," he said. "And life's too damn short to keep bashing my head up against resistance."

"Oh, honey," his mom whispered. "I don't want you to get hurt."

"I won't."

"How? How can you avoid it?"

"I'm not going to let it go there anymore," he said. "It was a mistake."

Feeling sick, Molly backed away, moving down the other end of the hallway. She ended up in a den with a sliding glass door, which she opened to step outside. Feeling like a first-class asshole, she walked to the edge of the deck and stared up at the still falling snow. It was stunning, but she barely saw it because all she could concentrate on was the ache in her heart.

This was all her doing. Not allowing any sort of real relationship with Lucas. Tonight being "just a date." All of it, *her* fault. And now it was over anyway, deemed a "mistake" by Lucas himself, which was 100 percent for the best.

Probably.

Realizing it was very cold out here without a crackling fire and Lucas's arms around her, she turned back to the sliding door.

It'd locked behind her.

Great. She knocked, but no one came. And given how many Knights were in the house, a good many of them more than a little tipsy, no one was going to do a head count and figure out she was missing—including the man who'd brought her here because after all, it was a mistake. She was a mistake.

Wow. Look at her rock the pity party for one.

The snow began to fall harder, no longer quite as charming as it was stinging her face now. And it was absolutely the snow and *not* a few pity tears. Swiping at her face, she pulled her phone from her pocket and did the first thing that came to mind.

She texted Sadie and Ivy, because they were single too and would understand. Then she added Elle because even though she wasn't single now that she was with Archer, Elle would still understand:

Men suck. They suck worse than root canals. They suck worse than when you get one of those hair

> balls stuck in your shower and it won't drain. They
> suck worse than . . .

She had to actually pause here in her texting. Damn eggnog brain. Come on, Molly, you're on a roll . . .

> They suck worse than getting your period in the
> middle of a staff meeting with a bunch of alpha
> men who've seen and done it all, but look faint if
> you mention the words menstrual cramps. And you
> know what else sucks? Love. Love sucks golf balls
> and I'm never ever going to allow it in my life.

She hit send so hard she broke a nail. Not five seconds later someone came out the slider behind her and she went still, knowing by the state of her traitorous nipples who it was.

A jacket was set on her shoulders and an unbearably familiar masculine scent wrapped around her like a hug.

"I got locked out," she said into the silence.

"Yeah, I figured that out when I got your text."

She froze and then whirled to face him, horrified. "What text?"

"The one about never ever loving someone. Which, by the way, is not only a long time, it also sounds like a Taylor Swift song."

"Oh my God." She whipped out her phone and stared at the text she'd sent to Sadie, Elle, and Ivy . . .

And Lucas.

It was a damn group message, probably leftover from when they'd been sending jokes back and forth about a week earlier. "Oh my God," she said again on a moan and smacked her own stupid forehead just as a few texts came in.

> IVY: Dear Train Wreck, this isn't your station, please get off at the next stop . . .

> SADIE: **On a scale of 1 to Nature Valley granola bars, how much is your life falling apart right now?**

> ELLE: Rookie mistake, babe . . .

Molly groaned. "Oh my God."

A touch of a smile curved Lucas's lips as he eyed the texts he also accessed, but it didn't quite reach his eyes. "I'm guessing it's been one of those days for you."

"It's been 'one of those days' for years now," she said.

"So definitely an accident then on the text."

She stared up at him. "Do you really think I'd say all that to you *on purpose*?"

He shrugged. "You should've been able to say anything to me."

Should have. Past tense. A reminder that this, whatever "this" was, was over. She should've been relieved at that, but the truth was she was hurt. And yet, looking up into his face, she knew he'd been hurt worse. Far worse. He'd lost the woman he'd loved. A brother he'd loved. To him, love meant a possible loss.

And yet he'd still put himself out there, willing to get hurt again. She admired that. She envied that. Maybe even dreamed of it for herself. Of course when she'd secretly dreamed of such a thing, she'd pictured a softer, gentler man than Lucas. One who wasn't quite as . . . well, everything that encompassed and screamed alpha male like Lucas did.

But sometimes the heart wanted what it wanted, and if hers could speak, it'd say it wanted the man standing right in front of her, bigger than life, stoic and silent. His hair was dusted with snowflakes, as were his shoulders, and when he met her gaze, his inky black lashes had flakes on them as well.

"I think it's time to go," he said.

No. Tell him you were wrong. But instead, she played the coward. She nodded and they left.

Chapter 19

#WhyIsTheRumGone

Lucas was no closer to understanding exactly what had happened between him and Molly when he woke up the next morning. For the first time in a very long time, he didn't have a plan on how to proceed on a problem. Not a clue. Because no matter what he wanted to tell himself, this thing between them wasn't over just because he wanted it to be. It didn't work like that because this wasn't just a physical attraction. It was far more and he knew it. And, yeah, he'd gone in reluctantly, and not just because he was friends with Molly's brother, or that he and Joe were in fact partners. Or that Archer might kill him in his sleep if he found out Lucas had touched her.

It was the fact that more than anyone he knew, Molly deserved love.

But love hadn't ever worked out for him. Not once. And he wouldn't hurt her, not for anything.

And yet even knowing all that, he was *still* in. All in.

But she wasn't.

And that meant that his feelings were his own issues, and he'd figure out how to deal with them.

When he got to work, Molly's desk was vacant. He moved past it and into the employee room and found her doling out doughnuts and coffee. Ignoring him completely, she served everyone before turning to him.

He managed a small smile.

She didn't manage any smile at all.

He peered into the doughnut box. Empty. Damn. He lifted his gaze. "We need to talk."

"When hell freezes over."

He blinked and she rolled her eyes and held up a finger in his face. "Let me repeat. When. Hell. Freezes. Over."

That was when he realized she had on a headset and was speaking into her microphone. She was on the phone. Her gaze was on him, though, and he knew from experience that she got pissy when she was uncomfortable.

Well, he was uncomfortable too, dammit. And worse, he missed her already even though she was standing right there in front of him.

Still talking on the phone, she turned from him and left the room.

"Ouch, man," Joe said, munching on a doughnut and sipping coffee. "What did you do to piss her off?"

"Good question," Archer said, his sharp gaze steady on Lucas. "Is there something we need to know?"

"Other than this plan of yours for me to be her secret backup while at the same time being your spy is ruining my life?" he asked. "No, there's nothing you need to know, except you're both on my shit list." And with that, he snatched the rest of Joe's doughnut and—taking his own life into his hands—Archer's coffee, and took off for his own office.

Joe showed up a few minutes later. "How's it really going?" he asked Lucas.

"It's . . . going."

"I mean with the *project*," Joe said, putting the word *project* in finger quotes.

Lucas leaned back and looked at his partner, well aware of what he was asking, but feeling just peeved off enough about *the project* to make him say it out loud. "Which one?"

Joe looked behind him to make sure they were alone. "Molly and the old lady elves. What's really going on with that?"

"Have you tried asking her yourself?"

Joe grimaced. "Look, she doesn't belong out there doing what we do, okay? She's . . . amazing, but too soft to do it." He shook his head. "She's always been that way, far too tenderhearted for her own good, dragging home strays, wanting to save the world. She'll believe any sob story given to her. She loves too hard. She'll get taken advantage of doing what we do—"

"Don't," Lucas said. "Don't do that."

"Do what?"

"Don't belittle her. She's not a little kid anymore, Joe. Nor is she incompetent. Far from it. In fact, she's smart as hell. Look, a lot of bad shit happens to all of us, and our experiences have made us hard. Cold. But not her. She's special, and stronger than both of us put together."

This got a moment of surprised silence from Joe. And since Lucas didn't want to fight with him, he rose and grabbed his laptop for their meeting.

"What's going on between the two of you?" Joe asked.

Lucas turned back. "You asked me to get involved. I'm involved. And you know what? Out of all the things she loves, she loves you the most. Instead of trying to hold her back, do you know what you should be doing? *You* should be doing the job you asked me to do. *You* should be training her, letting her fly, and stand at her back while she does."

Joe was stunned. "This is all just a phase for her. Why would I do that?"

"It's not a phase. And you should do it because she would do it for you," Lucas said. He then walked out of his own office, doing his best to shrug off his irritation at Joe.

If this is how Molly felt all the time, he didn't know how she dealt with it.

The rest of the day went on in much the same vein. He and the team had been working a corporate investigation case. An HR director at a large attorney firm had heard rumors that the president was known to be having an affair with a subordinate. Notwithstanding the fact that the executive was married to someone else, company policy expressly prohibited such office relationships. The affair put the firm at significant risk of legal action by the female against the company and the executive if the relationship became public, or worse, failed in a bad way. Unfortunately the HR director needed hard evidence to support the termination of the employees for violating company policy.

Enter Hunt Investigation. Today was day five of surveillance and Lucas and Joe were up.

Lucas drove, feeling Joe's eyes on him. "Something on your mind?"

"I feel out of the loop."

"On what?" he asked, and watched Joe struggle to maintain the guy code that said they couldn't discuss emotional issues for too long. That was the real five second rule. He sighed. "I feel out of the loop on you and Molly."

"There's no loop," Lucas said and wished that it wasn't true.

Joe took a deep breath. "You were right before," he said quietly. "About me being overprotective of her. It's a lifelong habit, one I don't know how to break."

"You need to learn before you lose her." *Like I did . . .*

They fell silent after that, each lost in his own

thoughts. Fifteen minutes later, they were in an up-scale restaurant not far from the law firm's offices, watching the illicit couple in question order and toast themselves with a very expensive champagne.

"He's telling her he got her a little something special," Lucas said behind his water glass.

"If it's his dick, I hope it's more spectacular than his hairpiece and beer belly stressing the buttons on his shirt," Joe said.

"It's probably jewelry."

"Bet?"

"Yeah," Lucas said. "Today's lunch."

"You're on. But if you lose, I'm ordering the most expensive dessert on the menu."

Lucas watched the woman give her lover a secret smile and cock her head toward the back hallway where the restrooms were. Then she got up from their table and sauntered down the hallway and out of sight.

Shit. It *was* going to be his dick.

Joe shook his head in disbelief as the man waited a minute and then followed her. "Going to need some audio for evidence," he said. "Your area of expertise."

"Since when?"

"Since I want dessert," Joe said, raising a hand to their waitress.

"What about backing me up?" Lucas asked.

Joe tapped the comm he had in his ear. "I've got your six, man. Tiramisu, please," he said to the waitress.

Lucas shook his head and moved down the hallway. The men's room was empty, even the stalls. He waited a minute outside the women's room, not wanting to surprise any patrons, but when no one came out, he slipped inside.

One of the stalls was closed. He could see a pair of men's dress shoes facing out, trousers pooled around the guy's ankles. It was that along with the rhythmic pounding against the door, accompanied by a male voice that was moaning and panting out, "Bill's doing a great job, a really great job! Watch Bill do it, tell Bill he's doing great!"

"Wow," Joe said in Lucas's ear. "Sounds like he's giving himself his own evaluation. Wonder if he's going to get a raise."

There weren't many days where Lucas missed working for the DEA, but this was definitely one of them. Several hours later, they'd delivered the needed evidence to the HR director, closed up the case, and were back at the office.

Molly had locked up and was gone.

Shit, Lucas thought. She was working the Christmas Village tonight. Not bothering to change, he left again, calling her on her cell as he strode across the courtyard. "Come on," he muttered, listening to her phone ring in his ear. "Pick up."

She didn't. Shaking his head, he stopped and texted her:

Where are you?

He could see that she was responding to the text, so he stopped walking to wait. She took her sweet ass time, too. It was three full minutes later when he saw that she'd stopped texting.

And yet nothing came through. Shaking his head, he tried her again.

LUCAS: Tell me you're not heading to the Christmas Village alone.

MOLLY: Going through a tunnel, bad connection.

"Dammit," he muttered.

"Problem?"

Lucas turned and found Old Man Eddie sitting on a bench in front of the fountain, tossing a coin up and down in his hand. "Women are insane."

"Son," Eddie said on a laugh. "Tell me something I don't know." He tossed the coin to Lucas, who caught it automatically, reflexively.

"What's this for?" Lucas asked.

"To make a wish."

He laughed and shook his head. "You've been eating your homemade brownies again if you think I'm going to bet on this fountain. I know what it does. Look what it did to your own grandson Spence."

"Hey, I haven't made any brownies in a while now," Eddie said. "Archer went directly to my . . . er, um . . . supplier and told him if he delivered to me again, Archer would relocate him. Permanently. So

I'm annoyingly sober, which means you can take it to the bank when I tell you that what this fountain did for Spence was bring him Colbie and give him a life he'd never dared dreamed of."

"You're going to feed me a line like that and seriously expect me to believe you're sober?"

Eddie smiled. "You're scared. I get it. I'd be scared too. Wishing for love on this fountain has been wiping out the single community here one unsuspecting lonely soul at a time. Might as well stop fighting it and toss in the coin and wish."

"Not going to happen," Lucas said, knowing that Molly wasn't going to fall in love with him. She wasn't going to let herself.

"If you're so sure it's dumb," Old Man Eddie said, "then why not just give it a try?"

Lucas rolled his eyes, a gesture he was aware he'd picked up from Molly. Which made it all the more ironic when he held his closed fist above the water and closed his eyes.

And wished . . .

He let the coin fall from his hand into the water, where it hit with a very small splash. He stared at it as it sank to the bottom and wished . . . wished he believed in the fountain.

Eddie just smiled. "It works in mysterious ways, you know. Going to be exciting to see what happens."

"Yeah." Not willing to believe, Lucas went through the pub intending to grab an order of something to satisfy his gnawing belly before hunting down

Molly, but he found her at the bar paying for an order to go.

Some of her friends were there eating and talking, and when he moved closer, he heard Sadie say, "They really should put prizes in our tampon boxes, like 'hey, your period sucks, but here's a fifty percent off ice cream coupon, you cranky bitch.'"

The girls all laughed and Molly spotted him. She grabbed her bag of food and headed over.

"Going through a tunnel, huh?" he asked.

She shrugged.

He grabbed her free hand when she went to walk away. "Talk to me, Molly."

"Okay," she said. "I'd never go to the village alone. I'm not completely stupid, you know." She paused. "But I do have a shift there tonight that I promised to take, so if you're ready, I'm driving."

"Not necessary. I'm parked closer."

She craned her neck, eyes narrowed at him. "Let me guess. Women can drive in your bed but not on the job?"

He found a smile in the shitty day after all. "You've driven me before. When we first went to your dad's house."

"We weren't on the job that night."

"Okay, first, let me just say that you're welcome to drive in my bed any night of the week," he said. "But when we're on the job and you're the one going undercover, that makes me the getaway man. Makes more sense for me to be behind the wheel."

"Fine," she said.

"To which? In bed or on the road?"

"Keep dreaming," she said.

Yeah, he had no doubt he'd have to make due with just that, dreams. He eyed the bag of food in her hands. "Bringing your dad dinner first?"

"Yes. But not you."

"Liar," he said on another smile. "You won't be able to help yourself. You're a caretaker."

She slid him a look. "Guess it takes one to know one." She paused and took in his surprise. "Come on," she said. "You already know this about yourself. You take care of your family. You take care of the guys at work. You're every bit as much of a caretaker-slash-worrywart as I am."

He thought this over and then shook his head. Damn, she just might be right. "If you tell anyone, I'll deny it."

"Don't worry," she said dryly. "Your secret's safe with me."

A few minutes later, Lucas pulled up to her dad's duplex. He eyed the building. "Joe home?"

"No, he's staying with Kylie tonight. They're marathoning some show they've been saving up. It's their only night off together this week."

Lucas snorted.

"What," she said. "Did he lie to me? That son of a bitch. What are they doing instead?"

"If I had to guess? They're not watching TV, they're having wild gorilla sex."

She thought about that and sighed, sounding a little wistful.

Lucas took the bag of food from her hands and set it on the car. Then against his better judgment, he nudged her up against it. "Say the word and you could have the same thing for dinner."

"I thought you were . . . done," she said.

He met her gaze. "I thought so too, but apparently my brain and body aren't in accord."

The sound of someone ratcheting up a shotgun stopped him in his tracks. They both turned to the porch and, yep, there he was, Alan Malone sitting in his wheelchair on the porch. "How sure are you that thing isn't ever loaded?" Lucas asked Molly.

"One hundred percent. But that isn't a comfort if he decides you're a threat because the military trained him how to kill a person with his bare hands without breaking a sweat."

"Right. Something to remember," Lucas murmured and lifted his hands off the man's daughter and sent what he hoped was a reassuring smile as they walked up the path to the duplex.

"Hey, Dad," Molly said in greeting.

"Baby," he said, eyes never leaving Lucas.

"You remember Lucas?"

"Uh-huh." Her dad casually lifted his gun and checked the site.

"Dad, stop that. He knows there aren't any bullets in this house. You can't intimidate him. And we aren't staying. I'm going to put the food inside for you. *Behave.*"

Her dad didn't answer, but she went inside anyway.

"So," Alan said to Lucas.

"So." Lucas mentally cracked his knuckles. It'd been a damn long time since he'd tried to impress a dad of any kind. "Nice evening, huh?"

"You going to do right by my daughter?"

Oh boy. He let out a breath and eyed the gun. "It's not like that between us, sir."

"Soldier, it's *always* like that."

"I like your daughter," Lucas said carefully.

"Yes, I believe I heard just how much you like her when you offered her . . . what was it? . . . gorilla sex?"

Lucas grimaced. "It's not like that either." At least not anymore.

"So what *is* it like?"

Lucas drew a deep breath, because he was still coming to terms with the answer to that question. "I care about her very much."

"*Everyone* cares about Molly. The question is, will you protect her?"

Finally, something he had an answer for. "With my life."

Chapter 20

#LobsterLove

After dropping the bag of food on her dad's table, Molly stepped back outside onto the porch and caught Lucas's answer.

I'd protect her with my life . . .

She stilled as a set of the warm fuzzies went through her, but then ruthlessly shrugged them off. They were done with that. "Let's do this," she said briskly, bending to brush a kiss over her dad's jaw. "Love you, Dad." And then she headed past Lucas, leaving him to catch up with her.

In twenty minutes they pulled into the Christmas Village.

"Close your eyes," she said and pulled her elf costume from her bag. She shook it out. "And you just *know* something's wrong with a costume when it fits into a small purse."

Lucas let out what sounded suspiciously like a snort, but when she glanced over at him, he was blank-faced. "You're still looking," she said.

"I've seen it all already, remember?"

"Actually, no, you haven't. We played assault with your friendly weapon in my dark living room. And then in your dark bedroom. You haven't seen anything."

He turned toward her in the driver seat, brows arched so high, they vanished into his hairline. *"Assault with my friendly weapon?"*

"Just close your damn eyes!"

Shaking his head, a small smile curving his mouth, he closed them. Suspicious, she stared at him for a long beat, and when he cracked one eye open and looked over, she pointed at him and said, "Aha!"

"You weren't moving, I was just checking to make sure you weren't sneaking off without me."

"Maybe I was just being all stealthy and silent."

He gave a soft, amused laugh. "Molly, you're a lot of things, most of them really great, but you've never been stealthy or silent in all the time I've known you. Not even once."

She was all kinds of insulted, but her mouth disconnected from her brain. "I can think of two occasions where I was silent," she said.

Their gazes met and his heated as his mouth curved with a soft, affectionate smile. "Sorry, but you were most definitely not silent on either of those two occasions."

She felt her face flame. "I was too!"

"I'll give you that you didn't exactly scream my name, but you did whimper it, all breathy and short of air. And you begged a little too, very sweetly I might add." He paused and his smile widened. "That was my favorite part."

Her entire body quivered. Stupid body. "Just . . . close your eyes!"

He did as she asked.

"No cheating," she warned.

"I never cheat," he said and she knew that was most certainly true.

He wasn't a man who needed to cheat, at anything. He was honest to the core, almost brutally so. Still, she kept an eye on him as she quickly changed from Business Woman to Bingo Elf. "Okay," she said when she was done imitating a contortionist to get into the costume. "I'll be at bingo. I get a break in two hours. According to Mrs. Berkowitz and Mrs. White, that's the same time that Louise goes on break. She's the one who used to be an elf, but got a promotion and works in the office now. On her break, she walks to the woods and smokes two cigarettes, taking every second of her allotted twenty minutes. That's when I'm going to go back into the office and snoop around while their laptops are in there, hopefully unguarded."

"I'll be with you."

She nodded. This was not a surprise. What *was* a surprise was how much she knew she could count on him and how good that felt.

Dammit.

Lucas got out of the car and watched as Molly entered through the front gates, being waved through thanks to the costume.

He paid the entrance fee for himself and made sure Molly got into the bingo hall safely before he went wandering. He made his way through the grounds including all the booths, noting who was working where. The booths were run almost entirely by female elves, although there were a handful of male elves as well. Their costumes were shorts instead of a dress, and they were just as unfortunately snug in all the *very* wrong places.

There was a new addition since they'd last been here. A Christmas tree lot, worked by two teenage kids. All transactions seemed to be cash. In between the booths and the tree lot was another new area—a Santa photo booth. It sat empty. The sign said Santa would show at eight p.m.

The same time as Molly's break.

Lucas circled around to the office trailer and spent some time staking it out. He could see through the two lit windows that the only people inside were Louise and Santa. At five to eight, Santa stood up and pulled on a red coat and wig and exited the trailer, stomping down the stairs and past Lucas in the bushes.

At two minutes to eight, he heard Molly come up from behind him to stand at his side.

"Caught you," she whispered.

"I heard you coming."

"Okay, Mr. Never Screws Anything Up."

He slid her a look. "If that were true, you'd still be sleeping with me."

"We're not . . ." She broke off and shook her head. "Not doing this now." She pulled her phone from her bra and looked at the time. "It's time to go in."

He handed her a blank flash drive. "Copy whatever you find onto this if you can."

She slipped it into her bra.

"Interesting hiding place," he said.

"Look at me." She held out her arms. "You see anywhere else to hide anything?"

Nope. He saw nothing but warm, soft, perfect curves. "I'm giving you two minutes."

"Seven," she said. "Louise won't be back for ten."

"Make it five."

"Fine," she said so easily he knew he'd been had and she'd planned on five all along. "Wait here."

"Like hell." He took her hand and led her up the stairs, trying not to notice how incredibly long her legs seemed in that short dress and booties. Long enough to be wrapped around his waist while he—

"It's open," she whispered of the office door and slid inside, putting a hand on his chest when he went to follow. "It makes much more sense for you to wait outside. It's far easier to explain me being in there than you, if it comes to that."

He didn't give a shit about explanations. He gave a shit about keeping her safe. "Understood," he said, putting his hand over hers and giving a squeeze. "But only because this way I can watch your six and the door at the same time." He then gave her a quick kiss that shocked him every bit as much as it shocked her.

"Stay alert," he said.

She saluted him. "Yes, sir."

"I like that," he said, pointing at her. And then he left, vanishing into the surrounding shrubbery.

He hung out in the shadows, counting off the minutes in his head. At the three-minute mark, Louise unexpectedly showed up at the bottom of the stairs to the office.

She was early.

He headed up the walk to stall her. "Hey," he said. "Just who I was looking for. You're in charge of the crafting elves, right?"

Louise looked flustered at the sight of him and put a hand to her chest. "Yes. How did you know—"

"They're having a little tussle at the stockings booth. Someone insulted one of the ladies' goods and you can imagine how that went over."

"I bet it was Eleanor. She's such a bitch."

Lucas nodded. "Anyway, it escalated and I think they need a referee."

"Dammit, I told them the next time they started throwing things at each other that I'd fire their geriatric asses and buy out the dollar store and slap homemade tags on everything." She whirled and stormed back down the path.

Lucas checked his watch.

The five-minute mark.

Just as Lucas got back to the shadows, Santa rounded the corner and jogged up the steps. He entered the trailer yanking off his hat.

Shit. What the hell was with everyone being early tonight?

Lucas took the stairs quickly and silently, plastering himself against the wall to listen. Santa hadn't shut the door all the way so he could both hear the guy clomping to his desk and also see him through a break in the shades.

"What the fuck?" Santa said to Molly.

She'd turned away from his computer and was leaning back casually against his desk as if she'd been waiting for him. She sent an easy smile, but Lucas could practically hear her heart pounding from here.

"I said what. The. Fuck," Santa repeated. "No elves allowed in here."

"Oh." Molly winced, looking apologetic. "Sorry. I didn't know."

"Unless maybe . . ." Santa cocked his head, the anger leaving his voice. "You came to see me for some reason. Maybe you want to sit on my lap and tell Santa what you want."

Lucas shook his head. Christ, women were right. Men were pigs. He started to move inside, but Molly's gaze slid to the window and she gave a subtle shake of her head.

She wanted to handle this on her own.

Santa closed the distance between him and her, trapping her between his desk and a table that held a coffeepot along with cream and sugar and cups, as well as an opened tin of popcorn.

Santa smiled. "I really like it when pretty elves sit on my lap and whisper their fantasies to Santa."

"Oh," Molly said, leaning back as far as she could. "Well, I'm not really much on fantasies."

"Are you sure?" He leaned into her. "Because I'm pretty good at it. Tell me what you want."

Molly's smile congealed. "A little more personal space might be great . . ."

Santa chuckled. "Come on, you can do better than that. Would it help to know that I actually *specialize* in . . . *sexual* fantasies?"

Okay, that was it. Again Lucas started to go in, but Molly spoke first, saying, "And *I* specialize in handling such things on my own."

Shit. She was talking directly to him. She wanted him to stand down. Still at the ready, he paused, willing to give her another minute, *tops*.

Santa laughed. "Feisty," he said. "My very favorite. You're legal, right? Cuz I don't do illegal chicks anymore. Turns out you go to jail for that."

Molly put out a hand to ward him off. "Legal, yes," she said. "But willing? Not so much. Aren't you married? To like your tenth wife?"

"Fifth," he said. "She's brand-new, but no worries, she's the understanding sort."

"Well good for you," Molly said. "But I don't put out on a first date."

Undeterred, Santa slid a hand down her waist and hip and then back up again, beneath the short hem of her dress this time and all bets were off. Fuck her cover because Lucas was about to string the guy up to teach him a lesson in how to treat a woman. He slipped inside the trailer just as an angry roar came from Santa.

His amazing, smart, quick-footed elf had grabbed the coffeepot behind her and poured hot coffee on his crotch.

"Oh!" she gasped, covering her mouth. "I'm so sorry!!!! I don't know how that happened—" She set the coffeepot back onto the counter. "I thought I'd pour us a cup, but you must've jerked my arm! Are you okay?"

"No, I'm not fucking okay!" Santa spit out between gritted teeth. "You burned my dick!"

"No, look, the pot's just on *keep warm*," she said quickly. "See? But I can still 9–1–1 if you'd like?"

"No!" he growled, doubled over, cupping himself.

"Okay, then, well . . . I should go. Break's over and all . . ."

Santa opened his pants and peeked inside, and that's when Molly made her exit. She came out the door at a dead run. Lucas grabbed her hand and they flew down the stairs. She stumbled a little on the last step and he slipped an arm around her, guiding her to his hiding spot in the bushes.

"You okay?" he asked.

"Yep, except for the near heart attack."

"When he touched you?"

"No, he didn't get to cop a good feel. The almost

heart attack came when I thought you were going to come in and kill him." She closed her eyes. "But I dropped your flash drive when he came in. I'd just pulled it from the computer and he startled me. I managed to kick it way under Louise's desk, though."

"Quick thinking," he said.

"It was stupid. I'm going to go back and get it after my shift, at the end of the night after everyone's gone."

"You're not going back to bingo," Lucas said.

"Of course I'm going back. I'm learning all kinds of new stuff."

"Such as?"

"Such as the renovation going on at the bingo hall hasn't made any progress in days, if all week. It's a big enough job to have a full crew on site, but the elves say no one ever sees more than one or two guys working there for maybe an hour or so every few days. And guess what else?"

"Santa owns the construction company," he said.

She gaped at him. "Yes, how did you know?"

"The craft elves love me."

She rolled her eyes.

"I'm going to go out on a limb here," he said. "And guess that Santa's overbidding all of the so-called work and then understaffing it to keep more of the money for himself."

"I heard his fifth wife likes cruises."

"That would've been my second guess," he said. "You realize you just smoked your second job, right?"

"Me coming back won't be any more dangerous than it's been," she said. "He's not onto me."

Lucas sent her a steadying look and she gave him a return gaze that told him she realized he was about to say something she wasn't going to like.

"You just messed with a dangerous guy," he said.

She let out a low laugh. "Yeah. Well in case you haven't noticed, *all* the men in my life are dangerous."

"Look, you don't know this because you'd have no reason to, but if you took twenty to thirty years off of Nick's face, he resembles what Tommy Thumbs looked like back in the day. I happen to know that he's *not* Tommy because he's still got both thumbs and Tommy lost one of his to someone he crossed way back when. It's why he used to go after people's thumbs first. Petty revenge."

"So you believe the driver was Santa's brother then? Tommy?"

He shrugged. "I couldn't see his face and he was wearing gloves. And then there's the fact that everyone, including the authorities, believe him dead."

"But you don't," she said, watching his face.

"That's my point, Molly. I'm not sure what to believe. I need more information. But you're on their radar now."

"Are you mad?" she asked.

"At you? No. But I think there's a really good chance that we're right, that Santa's brother is indeed Tommy Thumbs with a few decades on him, which makes him no less dangerous. He cuts people who cross him up into pieces, Molly. Some of the pieces were never found."

She swallowed hard and nodded. "But he's laid low for a long time. He's going to want to remain low profile."

"True," Lucas said. "He changed his name in the '90s after declaring bankruptcy and walking away from a million bucks of debt and a lot of people who were missing body parts. Lying low has become his MO, but he's wanted in God knows how many states and he's on guard and focused. I just don't want him to focus on you."

"I'm wearing an elf costume," she said. "No one has any reason to suspect me."

"That's not a risk I'm willing to take."

"You won't have to," she said and gave him a small smile. "Since you tend to stick to me like glue out here."

He gave a ghost of a smile. "Just remember, you poured hot coffee into Nick's lap. He's not going to be happy with you."

"*Warm* coffee," she corrected. "And what a big baby. Trust me, I can take him again if I have to."

He knew that. Hell, he was proud of that. She was amazing. But this was more than any of them had thought. "You know we need to bring Archer and the guys in on this," he said.

"Hell no. They didn't want this case."

"It's not about that, or proving you're worthy of the work. It's about your safety."

Her smile was gone. "If you tell them, they'll take over."

"We could use the additional resources."

"Fine. I'll think about it," she said and turned away. "I'm going back to work."

"Molly—"

"Either watch my back or don't," she said without facing him. "Just don't stop me."

So he did the only thing he could do. He watched her back.

Two long hours later, she emerged from the bingo hall looking exhausted. "Did you get the memory stick?" she asked in lieu of a greeting.

"No. Janet got a migraine and is crashed out on the couch in the office. A couple of the elves are sitting with her drinking straight out of a bottle of cheap whiskey. They're not going anywhere tonight."

"Shit," she murmured.

That about summed it up. Unable to do anything else, they headed to the car. Inside the dark interior, he looked over at her. "You were incredible tonight."

"Yeah. So incredible you want to cut me out of this job."

He shook his head. "I'm not going to do that to you. I'd never do that to you."

The wariness vanished from her gaze. "No?"

"No. I just said that it's time to think about backup on this. *Backup*, Molly. No one's going to take this from you."

She sent him a dazzling smile. Losing the battle

to keep his hands off of her, he hauled her in close and kissed her.

"What was that for?" she asked breathlessly when he dropped her back into the passenger seat and drove them out of the lot.

"I have no fucking idea," he said, eyes on the road.

"Maybe it's because I totally handled myself tonight with Santa," she teased.

"You did." He merged them into traffic and slid her a look. "It turned me on."

She smiled smugly.

"*And* terrified me." He shook his head. "Archer and Joe are idiots. If they took you seriously, you'd be our biggest, most impressive asset."

She stared at him. "That's the sexiest thing anyone's ever said to me."

"I'm not kidding. You're terrifyingly good at this. Archer needs to see you in action."

Her eyes were dark and luminous in the ambient lighting as she slowly dragged her teeth over her lower lip. "Now you're just talking dirty to me on purpose. Lucas?"

The husky low whisper of her voice had him already hard. "Yeah?"

"If I say take me home, can we have the same rules as last time?"

"You mean the no talking thing unless it's dirty talk?"

"Yes."

He wanted more, so much more, but he'd take

what he could get from her and deal with the consequences later.

Seeing the answer in her eyes, she gave a small, heated smile. "Take me home, Lucas," she whispered.

She didn't have to say it twice.

Chapter 21

#YouSleighMe

Molly wasn't all that surprised when Lucas brought them to the Pacific Pier Building and his apartment instead of her place.

He had the bigger bed.

It'd started pouring on the way home. He parked and turned to her, his eyes hotter than sin. They sat and stared for a moment, and then by unspoken agreement they twisted toward each other, kept from complete contact by the console between them.

Lucas slid his hand around to the nape of her neck, pulling her in closer, brushing his lips over hers, lightly at first, small, teasing kisses until it wasn't enough. She moaned for more, touching her tongue to his bottom lip until he deepened the kiss.

Closing her eyes, she let herself fall into the sensations. The sound of the rain hitting the roof of the car. The taste of Lucas, the feel of his touch, the scent of him, the heat radiating off his body . . . all of it making her feel like this was all that mattered. Screw thinking. All she wanted to do was feel.

As if he could hear her thoughts and he agreed, he made a low sound deep in his throat, tightening his grip on her as he pulled his mouth back a fraction. "Be sure, Molly. Because after last night I didn't think we'd—"

"Shh." Not wanting to think about last night, or what would happen later, she brushed her mouth up his jaw toward his ear at the same time as she slid her hand beneath his T-shirt to caress his abs. "I'm sure," she whispered and nipped his earlobe.

With a low growl, he hauled her over the console and into his lap. Outside, the icy rain and windstorm continued to beat at the car. They'd heated up the interior and fogged all the windows, so the real world was a complete blur. Inside, things went just as wild, but thankfully without the cold. Just the crazy heat and chemistry between them as he aided the already rising hem of her dress northbound until he had a front row view of her pale blue lace panties.

With a rough sound of pure male pleasure, he ran a finger along the lace, making her fist her hands in his hair to hungrily pull his mouth back to hers. When he slipped past the lace barrier and gently stroked her wet flesh, she arched against his hand and cried out.

She'd only meant to tease him out of his famed control so that he'd feel some of what she did, but she was the one she'd teased out of control. She needed him now, and to that end, she reached for the button on his jeans.

He caught her hand. "Not here."

She rested her forehead against his, her breathing irregular and coming in short gasps. "Why not?"

"Because you deserve a bed."

"I don't need a bed."

"Good to know. But inside at least, where no one can interrupt us, because Molly?"

"Yeah?"

"This is going to take a while."

She gulped and the bones in her legs melted as he came around for her, grabbing her hand, running with her through the cobblestone courtyard up the stairs to his fourth-floor apartment.

They were drenched and dripping all over the hallway as he pulled out his keys. When he turned to the door, Molly took in the way his shirt clung to the muscles of his shoulders and back, and utterly unable to help herself, she ran a hand down his spine.

He dropped his keys and swore.

Smiling as he straightened, she pressed a kiss to his wet biceps.

With a groan, he shoved the door open, curled an arm around her and pulled her inside. Kicking the door closed, he picked her up and headed with fierce intent toward his bedroom. Setting her down by the bed, he stripped before backing up a few steps to hit the light switch with a slap of his hand.

Then he came back to her, dropped to his knees and fisted his hands in the material of her dress to tug off of her.

"Wait," she gasped.

Going still, he met her gaze, his passion in check thanks to his incredible control, but she'd bet by the look in his eyes, he was barely leashed.

She'd felt that way herself only seconds ago, but the light flooding the room had been like a bucket of ice water. "The light . . ."

"Molly." He cupped her face. "I want to see you."

"Yeah . . ." She squeezed her hands together and stared down at her white knuckles. "About that. Um . . ."

He glided his hands up and down her thighs. "You're beautiful, Molly. Let me show you how much."

"See, I was sort of planning to skip the show part."

He took her chilled hands in his warm ones, a question in his eyes, though he didn't say speak.

She blew out a breath. "Okay, so I have a . . . *thing*."

"A thing."

"A hang-up thing," she said.

"Okay, well, that's better than what I thought you were going to say. A hang-up we can work with."

"I—Wait," she said. "What did you think I was going to say?"

"That you didn't want to get me naked again."

She snorted. "Have you seen you naked? I'd have to be dead to not want to get you that way again."

He didn't smile. Instead he pressed her hands to his chest. "Molly."

"Right," she murmured. "You realize I'm trying to scare you off."

"Yes, but I don't scare off easily."

"I'm starting to get that." She blew out a breath. "Okay, it's just that . . . You know what happened to me, about the surgeries."

"Yes, and it sucks you went through that, but they helped, right?"

"Some," she said. "They've gone in from my front, from the back, and in through my side. And there are scars. Ugly ones. And I don't know if you know, but if you're not a size two with zero body fat, and if you have a bunch of scars in some of your . . . problem areas, things don't look quite right once you heal. There are bulges where there shouldn't be bulges and—"

"I've felt your scars," he said. "They don't matter. They're just a road map of your life. I have plenty myself. Nothing changes the fact that I think you're incredibly sexy and absolutely perfect."

"But that's because we were in the dark," she said, "and you were highly motivated to get to the good stuff."

He flashed a smile at that. "Still highly motivated. But, Molly, it's *all* the good stuff."

Damn, he was good. "Okay, so here's the real thing," she said.

"Finally."

"So when I've been in this situation before . . ." God, this was awkward. So awkward. "People sort of freaked out on me and then I couldn't . . . um, *finish*, so to speak, and I ruined everything."

Still on his knees before her, butt-ass naked, he didn't budge. Maybe he didn't even blink. "People?"

"My first boyfriend." She grimaced. "And my second." She'd been nineteen when she'd dated Ben. They'd both been inexperienced and it'd been several times before they'd had sex with enough light for him to really get a look at her. There'd been no missing his reaction—and she'd only had two of the surgeries at that time—but he'd gone from aroused, to horrified, to pity.

Pity was her kryptonite.

And maybe the worst part of it was later, when he'd tried to deny his reaction, they'd petered out before trying again.

Her second boyfriend, Tim, had been four years later. She'd been twenty-three. They'd dated for six months, during which time she'd managed to make it so they'd only had sex in the relative dark. If he ever questioned the feel of her scars, he'd never said a word. She'd liked him. A lot. Probably too much. She'd let her guard down and allowed herself to be talked into going out on his family's boat on Lake Shasta. He'd taken one look at her in her bathing suit and gotten that expression in his eyes.

Horror. And then pity.

It'd been a lot harder to dump Tim than Ben.

And it would be even harder to dump Lucas. She drew a deep breath and told Lucas the bare minimum about both Ben and Tim.

"Dumbasses," Lucas declared. "Anyone else?"

"No. Well . . ." She squirmed a little bit at having to admit this. "I did have a one-night stand once, but we didn't, erm, undress all the way."

He smiled. "Nice."

She had no idea what she'd expected, but it hadn't been this easy acceptance of her choices.

"Show me," he said.

Holding his gaze, she bit her lower lip in indecision.

"Molly, I just saw you single-handedly handle Bad Santa on your own. You're kickass. What are you afraid of?"

Oh so many, *many* things . . .

"Okay," he said. "I'll show you mine first." He pointed to a scar on his left pec. A puckered, half inch divot in his skin. "From a bullet back when I worked at the DEA. I cornered a bad guy. He didn't like it."

It was so close to his heart it nearly stopped hers. Leaning forward, she pressed her lips to the spot.

He made a very low, very male noise and slid a hand up her thigh. "Show me," he repeated softly. "Please?"

She hesitated, but her body wanted his and over-ruled her brain. Her elf costume was snug. Pulling her arms free of the material, she pushed the dress down to her hips, revealing her black strappy sports bra. She pointed to a six-inch long horizontal scar on her side at her waist that had sliced her from front to back. You couldn't miss it as it'd puckered a little bit and cut inward, which made her look like she had a panty line there, even though her panties were far lower. As far as her other scars went, though, it was her most minor. "Surgery on my L2-L4," she said.

His hands went to her hips and he leaned in, his broad shoulders blocking out much of the light as he brushed his mouth over the scar gently. Then he straightened and pointed to a four-inch scar low on his abs. "Knife wound," he said. "Working for Archer. A perp got the jump on me and tried to gut me. He was very nearly successful too."

She ran her fingers along the scar, which due to his extreme fitness level had healed well, no puckering of fat or unevenness for him. Still, it was a visceral reminder of exactly how dangerous his life had been. Still was. He'd nearly lost his life several times over. And he hadn't let it affect him, she thought.

Not like she had.

When her fingers touched his skin, he'd hummed in pleasure and his eyes darkened like they did when he was aroused. She stared at him, awed by how a simple touch from her could render him boneless.

It was exciting.

Empowering.

Eyes maintaining contact with his, she scooted back on the bed and then rolled to lie down on her stomach, cradling her head on her folded arms. She couldn't see him in this position, but heard him rise and set a knee on the bed.

Knowing what he was looking at now, she closed her eyes. A vicious-looking scar ran from the base of her neck all the way down her spine, broken in two spots signaling two different surgeries. With her dress still at her hips, he couldn't see all of it, but he could get the gist.

Along the length of the worst of the scarring was the tattoo Sadie had given her that read:

Pain is inevitable, suffering is optional . . .

She stilled when she felt his lips on the back of her neck, sighing in pleasure as he ran hot, open-mouthed kisses down the length of her spine.

When he started to tug the dress the rest of the way off, she flipped over. "Wait," she said. "It's back to your turn."

"I think that's it," he said.

"No." Sitting up, she put a palm to his heart. "What's wrong here?"

He covered her hand with one of his. "It's been broken," he admitted quietly.

"When you lost Josh."

He nodded.

"And Carrie."

He nodded again.

She nodded too, and then leaned forward and pressed her mouth to the spot right over his heart. He sank his fingers into her hair and gently pulled her away, nudging her down to the bed where he then proceeded to kiss every one of her doubts away.

It'd been a long time since she'd allowed herself

to trust a guy to see past her flaws. But it was as if he didn't even see them at all. He simply saw all of her, as a whole, and that was incredibly freeing.

"You're so beautiful," he murmured against the skin of her hip as he slid her dress the rest of the way off, tossing it over his shoulder. Positioning one knee between her legs, he braced himself over her, dipping his head down to lick the skin of her collarbone.

In reaction, she arched up off the bed, craving more. So much more. Sliding her hands up his back, she urged him closer because she needed this. Needed him. Needed the feel of his skin pressed to hers, radiating all that heat and power of his into her. Feeling the steady beat of his heart against her own, she raised her hips, hungry to have him inside her. "Please, Lucas," she breathed. "Please, now."

With a rough groan, he managed to strip her bra and undies off and to come up with a condom. He buried himself inside her in one perfect thrust. When he began to move, she lost her mind. Wrapping her legs around his hips, she pressed her heels against his lower back. "Faster," she whispered.

He smiled against her lips. "What else. Tell me."

"Harder."

With a rough groan, he gave her what she wanted until she came apart for him, and only when the last of the shudders left her did he lift his face from where he'd had it buried in her hair. Watching her now, he pushed the hair back from her damp forehead.

"Again," he said.

She wasn't much for demands, never had been, but no one had ever demanded anything of her in the bedroom. Apparently that was entirely different because just the sound of his low voice was enough to nearly topple her over again. *Nearly.* Because she was nothing if not stubborn to end.

Undeterred, he simply smiled his badass smile and slowed his motions, taking care to stroke and touch every inch of her that he could, making her muscles clench and tighten around him. She tried to keep her eyes open, but they drifted closed at the myriad sensations—and emotions—washing over and through her from the feel of being with a man again.

This man.

Taking her hands, Lucas linked his fingers with hers and slid them over her head. His body moved slowly over hers, every inch of his skin caressing her, and unbelievably, she felt the ripples of her release twisting and curling deep in her belly.

Lowering his head, he rubbed his jaw along hers like a big cat. A big sexy cat that looked far too in control of himself to suit her. Twisting her hands free, she grabbed his wrists. Mr. Cool's pulse was hammering, and when she rocked up into him, she wrenched a very sexy male sound of hunger from deep in his throat. Egged on by that, she began to twist below him in counterpoint to his thrusts. In response, Lucas threw back his head as her body sought his rhythm, their combined movements taking them *both* over this time.

It took her a while to come back to herself, and when she opened her eyes, she found Lucas, head propped on his hand, watching her with a small but warm smile. "Hey."

"Hey back," she said a little shakily. Because holy cow. She lifted her hands to push her hair back and in doing so realized she was still wearing the elf ears. Or in this case, *one* of the ears, as the other was long gone. And now that she thought about it, she could feel it beneath her. She craned her neck and, yep, found it stuck to her bare ass.

And here she'd been worried about how she'd look to him and she'd been wearing one elf ear . . .

He laughed softly, lazily, and took the ear, tossing it behind him, where it took the same trip through the air that her clothes had. Then he lay back and had her straddle him, gliding his hands reverently up her legs.

"Love having these wrapped around me," he said huskily, tugging her down for a kiss.

Gasping at what she found pressed up against her good parts, she smiled. "Again?" she murmured hopefully.

"If you like."

Oh, she'd like . . .

She awoke some time later. It was still dark and still raining. Her head was on Lucas's chest where she'd fallen asleep, his skin warm beneath her. His breathing was slow and deep and she could feel the steady beat of his heart beneath her face and fingertips. A strong heart, a steady heart.

The air in the room was chilly. The contrast between the heat of where they touched and the cold where they didn't was almost erotic.

She shifted against him and felt him respond in his sleep—a slow contented rumble from deep in his chest. There was just something about him that made her own chest too warm. Warm and . . . tight, the latter having been there since last night when she'd thought they were done.

"Hey," he murmured in a sleepy rough voice, pulling her in closer, wrapping her up in his warmth. "You okay?"

"Very."

Lucas ran a hand up her back and down again until he had a palmful of her ass, pressing her close. "Warm enough?"

"Yes, thanks to my own personal heat source."

He smiled against her neck and then began kissing her there, working his way up to her mouth. The kiss was tender and he cradled her head in his hands.

"Lucas?" she whispered.

"Yeah?"

"I'm in trouble with you."

He lifted his gaze to meet hers. "The way I see it, that's a lot better than being done with me," he said.

She closed her eyes and pressed her forehead to his.

"Hey," he said gently and then waited for her to look at him. "What happens in this apartment stays in this apartment." He paused. "But only if you want it to."

Unbearably touched by that, she stroked the rough stubble of his jaw. "I have no idea what to do with you," she whispered. "You know that, right?"

"Maybe you're thinking too hard. Maybe you just take it one minute at a time." He put his hands over hers. "And I bet you can figure out what to do with me this minute . . . Yes?"

She met his gaze, which had gone from sleepy to sexy hot. "Most definitely yes," she whispered.

Chapter 22

#Balls

The next day, Lucas was in a staff meeting, but his mind was back in bed with Molly. He'd made it a point to never spend the night with a woman, and yet he'd done so a couple of times now with her. True, for one of them he hadn't been sober, but still. He hadn't driven her home last night, not until this morning.

And maybe even more surprisingly, she hadn't asked him to.

They'd woken when his alarm had gone off. Stunned to realize it was morning, he'd reached across a still-dead-to-the-world Molly to turn it off before lying back down. She'd been warm and naked beside him, and far too tempting. So he hadn't even tried to resist pulling her in for a rare cuddle.

Still asleep, she'd turned to him, pressing as close

as she could, her arms around his neck. "Don't go," she'd murmured.

And he'd thought that had sounded like the perfect plan. Not to go anywhere.

But then Archer had called, and within thirty minutes he and the team had been on a job that had involved rappelling down a twenty-story elevator shaft, all in the name of security and investigation.

Now it wasn't quite noon and he was falling asleep in the meeting in spite of the huge cup of coffee he was mainlining. It took him five minutes to realize that all was quiet around him.

The meeting had ended.

"Problem?"

He looked up at the soft sound of Molly's voice. She refilled his coffee while he stared up at her face. "I'm tired," he said.

She looked around to make sure they were alone. "Yeah, well, that's the price you pay when you're a sex fiend."

He snorted and caught her hand before she could turn away, studying her face. She was . . . glowing. And smiling too, eyes bright. She looked positively cheerful, which she absolutely never, ever did, at least not before noon. "How is it that you're not looking like you're about to kill someone?"

Her smiled softened. "I guess having a one-night stand agrees with me. Who knew?"

A one-night stand. Which was right up his alley. So why then did he feel a little insulted? "Technically," he said carefully, "it's been more than one night."

"And technically," she said. "We weren't going to have *any* night stand."

Molly left work at lunch to hit the gym. She needed an hour to get out the kinks in her back and leg. Normally she went before work, but her second job as an elf was taking up too much brain power and she'd been too tired to get up early.

Bad Santa was really cutting into her life.

As were all the orgasms with Lucas . . .

Okay, truth. She needed out of the office and away from Lucas to think. Think about how she kept doing the opposite with Lucas than she planned. Think about the look on his face this morning when she'd said they weren't having *any* night stand.

She made him . . . happy. And hell if he didn't return the favor. He made her *very* happy. Which was terrifying.

In the gym, she wasn't surprised to find Caleb going at a hanging bag, beating the shit out of it with a combination of punches and kicks. And given the look of him, drenched in sweat, face grim, he'd been at it a while.

She didn't disturb him. Instead she warmed up with stretches and then hit the weights. She was at the bench press when two hands caught the bar and adjusted her arms, pushing it up a little higher.

Caleb.

He watched her, nodding in approval as she finished her set.

"Thanks," she said. "You done beating up whoever ruined your day?"

He held her gaze, arms crossed over his chest. "I could ask you the same thing."

She sighed.

"Work?" he asked. "Love life?"

"Both." She gave him a look. "And you?"

He lifted a broad shoulder. "Same."

"So we're both screwed up?"

A very small smile curved his lips. "No doubt."

She went by her place for a shower, her body humming from the workout. She was feeling pretty good, though she wasn't sure if it was from the exercise or how she'd spent last night. She glanced at the time. She never took a long lunch. But she wanted to today. She told herself she could take another thirty minutes or so if she wanted.

And oh, she wanted. She reached for her phone to send a text.

> **MOLLY:** I have some research I could use an assist on. Are you anywhere near my place?

> **LUCAS:** Please tell me that "research" is a euphemism.

> **MOLLY:** Of course not.

It totally was a euphemism.

He got there in ten minutes. She was still in just her towel from her shower. "Oh," she murmured. "I didn't realize you could get here so quickly. I haven't had time to get dressed."

He walked over to her and pulled her up into his arms. His mouth descended on hers, hot and persistent and she felt her nipples bore through the towel into his chest.

He dropped his hands to cup her butt, slipping them beneath the towel to grip bare skin. "Liar," he said with naughty accusation in his voice. "You're lying in wait for me. Hoping to seduce me by wearing only this easy access towel."

She slid her arms around his neck and rocked into his erection with a purr. "Is it working?"

"Molly," he said on a rough laugh. "All you have to do is look at me."

She raised her gaze to his and studied him. "I'm glad you were close by."

"I wasn't. I broke five laws getting here."

She snorted and his hold tightened on her. "You have a power over me," he said. "Use it wisely."

"I intend to." She laid her head on his chest. "Are you going to give me what you came here for?"

Eyes dark, he raised an eyebrow and she tried not to blush as she stared back at him. Nothing in the world was sexier than his eyes when they got like that. Except for maybe his abs when he sat up first thing in the morning. Or his shoulders when he reached above his head to stretch. Or his—

They made it as far as the couch. She felt frantic, dragging him down on top of her, reaching for his zipper. "Condom?" she panted.

Swearing, he dug it out of a pocket and ripped it open. He jammed himself into it and reached for her.

It was the best, more erotic lunch break of her entire life.

It was nearly quitting time when her phone vibrated across her desk. A text from Louise saying her elf services weren't needed tonight. She was still looking at it wondering what that meant when a FaceTime call came in from Mrs. Berkowitz.

Molly swiped to answer and then stared at a pair of crinkled lips painted in matte red.

"Molly?" the lips asked. "Molly, is that you, dear?"

"Yes, it's me. You don't have to hold the phone quite so close to your face," she said. "In fact, I can see you better if you don't."

The screen pulled back a little tiny bit, enough that Mrs. Berkowitz's entire face filled the screen now, not just her lips. She smiled. "There you are, dear. Listen, there's something rotten in Denmark." She paused. "Do young people read anymore? That's a Shakespeare reference, you see, and—"

"I get it," Molly said. "I've read *Hamlet*. You mentioned something was going down last night. I was there, and I agree, the renovation seems off—"

"Santa just put out the word that since it's a weeknight and it'll be slow traffic at the crafts booths, he's sending us elves to Reno, on him. There's some sort of Santa convention up there and he's rented a luxury bus to take us."

"I thought Santa was a cheap bastard."

Mrs. Berkowitz smiled. "I knew you were a smart

cookie. He's *way too* cheap to spend this much money on us. And plus"—she lowered her voice—"I overheard him on the phone telling someone that he was taking care of things tonight and not to worry. That's bad, right?"

Well, it didn't sound like anything *good*.

"Do you think he's going to have the bus run off the narrow curvy summit on the way to Reno?" Mrs. Berkowitz asked. "So he can be rid of us pests once and for all?"

She actually didn't. That would be a lot of counts of murder. But just in case, she asked, "When are you all due to leave?"

"In an hour."

"I'm on my way," Molly said. "Don't let that bus leave before I get there. Stall, distract him, whatever you have to do."

"Wear your elf costume, dear. He still thinks you're just a green-capped elf. He hasn't yet placed you as an investigator."

Molly blinked, a bad feeling going through her. "No one should be able to place me," she said. "I didn't tell anyone from the village that I was there for anything other than work."

"That was very smart of you."

Molly sighed. "Did you?"

"Did I what?"

"Tell anyone I was there for something other than work?" she said, trying to be patient.

"Oh. Well, you know how people talk . . ."

Molly rubbed her temples where she was getting a stress headache. "People like you and Mrs. White?"

The picture on the screen suddenly went sideways and then upside down.

"Sorry!" Mrs. Berkowitz yelled. "Dropped you!" The screen straightened out and Mrs. Berkowitz blinked owlishly at Molly. "There you are again. And your hottie boyfriend's there too."

"What? I don't have a—" Molly turned and found Lucas leaning against the doorjamb, arms crossed over his chest. His biceps and chest strained the material of his black T-shirt. His cargo pants fit him like they'd been made for him and it didn't escape her attention that he was loaded for bear.

And not looking very pleased.

She turned her attention back to her phone. Mrs. Berkowitz had shifted, holding the phone farther away, which allowed Molly to see more of the elf's surroundings for the first time. They were near the offices in Santa's Village. The office trailer was maybe twenty feet back, but the setting sun was just at the right angle to allow Molly a clear view inside the office window.

A woman stood inside, smiling as someone came up behind her. He bent close and kissed her on the neck.

Santa.

Molly tried to focus in on the woman. It wasn't Louise. It was . . . *Janet*, who closed her eyes in what appeared to be bliss before turning to face Santa, who pushed her up against the desk and kissed her. Arms locked around each other, they sank out of view, presumably to the floor to finish what they'd started.

Santa and *Janet*? But the elf was supposedly on Mrs. Berkowitz and Mrs. White's team, trying to catch Santa at being a criminal. "Janet?" she murmured, shocked.

"Janet's not here," Mrs. Berkowitz said. "She left me a text that she's not going with us to Reno. She got a better offer, whatever that means. At our age, we don't get better offers than a free to trip to Reno."

Molly didn't want to have this conversation until she was on the premises to protect her neighbor. "Just don't get on that bus," she said. "Stall if you can. I'll be there as soon as I can get across town." She disconnected.

Lucas held out her jacket for her to slip her arms into. His was already on and he had his keys in his hand. "What's going to be your reason for going in?" he asked.

"I'll say I didn't get the text canceling me for tonight. Did you see inside the office window?" she asked. "Janet and Santa are doing it."

"Doing what?"

"*It.*"

He grimaced.

"If those two are involved—"

"I know," he said grimly. And that was the thing about Lucas. He could be absolutely wild in bed and often was, but give him a mission and he turned into a super sexy bundle of focused intensity. "She's hiding something," he said.

"Yeah, like maybe she was never on Mrs. Berkowitz's side at all."

"Or she's a plant to report back to Nick," Lucas said. "She could be totally out of his loop, just a pawn."

"You really think so?"

"I think I want that memory stick," he said. "And a little chat with Janet."

She nodded. "That's my plan."

"You mean *our* plan," he said. "Partners, remember?"

It was getting hard to forget . . .

Lucas drove to the Christmas Village, doing his best to watch the road and not his partner as she once again managed a full costume change in his passenger seat. Only two wheels went off the road when she gave him an inadvertent peekaboo hint at a midnight blue silky thong. He was proud of himself for that.

"Whoa," she said, sliding up against the door.

He grimaced and righted them, being more careful even though he got enough of a view of her breasts to know her bra was a matched set to the thong, one of those low-cut numbers that nearly revealed her nipples.

"You know it's laundry day when I've reached the thong portion of my undie drawer," Molly muttered, making adjustments. And then she leaned forward to shuck her socks and it happened—

Nipple-gate. Partial left nipple and full right nipple, both puckered tight, begging for his attention.

She was most definitely trying to kill him.

He must've made some inadvertent sound because she glanced over at him, followed his line of sight to her chest and rolled her eyes. "Keep your seats, ladies," she murmured and tucked herself back into the bra. "Sorry."

"Don't be. I've already seen it all." Seen, tasted, licked, nibbled . . .

She slid around in her seat as if antsy. "That's . . . different."

He glanced over curiously. "How?"

"I don't know," she said, still squirming. "It just is."

"You're thinking about it." He smiled. "And getting turned on."

She looked down again, taking in the fact that her nipples were hard, pressing against the fabric of the dress. "Maybe I'm just cold," she said.

"Are you?"

"No."

He laughed softly and she blew out a breath. "It's all your fault, you know," she said. "You've turned me into some kind of a sex fiend."

He opened his mouth to say something entirely inappropriate when her phone buzzed an incoming call.

"It's Mrs. Berkowitz," she said and answered on speaker. "Are you okay?"

"Why does Santa go down the chimney?"

Molly blinked. "What?"

"It's a joke, dear. Why does Santa go down the chimney?"

"Uh . . ." Molly looked at Lucas and then shook her head. "I don't know."

"Because Mrs. Claus said he could never go in the back door!" Mrs. Berkowitz yelled cheerfully.

Lucas choked out a laugh.

"Have you been drinking?" Molly asked Mrs. Berkowitz.

"Yes! There's spiked wine."

Molly looked pained. "Wine is already spiked."

"Well this is the good stuff," Mrs. Berkowitz said. "We were going to dance, but some of the elves are worried about their hip and knee replacements going out, so we're just drinking."

"Switch to water," Molly ordered. "We're nearly there. And don't get on that bus!"

"I won't," she said happily. "Because I'm already on it!"

"Is it moving?" Molly asked.

"I'll take another!" Mrs. Berkowitz yelled to someone. "Make it a double!"

"Mrs. Berkowitz," Molly said. "Talk to me. Is Janet on the bus with you?"

"Told you, she blew us off. Gotta go, dear. The male elves are going to put on a striptease for us." Then she disconnected.

Molly stared at her phone, looking worried. "If something happens to her—"

"We'll make sure it doesn't," Lucas said grimly.

"Hang tight." He accelerated, and five minutes later he pulled them into the lot.

Molly was sitting forward, trying to peer through the dark, foggy night. "I don't see a bus."

Neither did Lucas. He parked and they got out and found the entire village seemingly deserted. Lights off. Dark. Quiet.

Not good.

Molly turned in a slow circle. "I've got a really bad feeling about this." She stopped short. "Whoa, *wha—*"

"Shh." Having already seen what she just saw, Lucas backed her up to the shadows.

The north end of the lot was completely filled with cars, all parked against the very back two rows in the darkest area.

Lucas turned to Molly. "What are the chances you're going to go back to the car and lock yourself in and let me handle this?"

"Zero," she said. "But since I'm not interested in getting either of us hurt, I promise that if it gets dangerous on top of fishy-as-hell, I'll do whatever you say."

He slid her a look. "For the *entire* night?"

"You know what I mean!"

Yeah, he did, but it was fun to watch her mind join his in the gutter. He took her hand and pulled her in closer to his side. "Stay close."

They kept to the shadows, which wasn't hard since the whole place was dark.

"It's creepy," she whispered.

She was definitely right about that. There was something horror-movie-waiting-to-happen about the village being shut down like this. No one was taking tickets and the gate was locked.

And the lot oddly full.

Lucas eyed Molly's short little dress. "I can climb that gate, do what has to be done, and be back in here five minutes."

"I don't hear the 'we' in that statement," she said.

Shit. He gave her a leg up and boosted her over the fence, absolutely taking a good long look at the midnight satin thong wedged up her world-class ass.

"Did you just peek up my costume?" she whispered, climbing down the other side of the fence so slowly that he vaulted it and landed before she did.

"Yes." He put his hands on her waist and lifted her down. "You can yell at me later. I really like those panties. I'm going to take them off with my teeth later."

She wobbled and he righted her. With a smile, he took her hand and headed toward the offices, suddenly distracted by a rhythmic sound of applause that didn't fit in with the deserted grounds.

"What the—" she murmured and in unison they switched directions and headed toward the bingo hall. The shades on the windows were drawn, and from the outside looking in, it appeared to be as dark as the rest of the place.

Except for one of the five windows on the west

wall where they stood showed the slightest sliver of light at the bottom where the shades weren't quite lined up with the windowsill.

The applause had stopped, but a minute later it came again.

"Why are they doing bingo on the sly?" she asked.

Lucas shook his head and then stilled as he heard someone coming, footsteps light. Unafraid.

Two seconds later, an elf came down the path. She was at least seventy, and both smoking and coughing at the same time.

"Shirley," Molly said. "Hey. You're working tonight?"

Shirley stopped and blinked. "Yes. Why aren't you on the bus with the others on your way to Reno?"

"I'm working tonight too," Molly said easily.

"Oh," Shirley said. "I didn't realize. Only the . . . *special* elves are working tonight."

"That's me," Molly said brightly, not missing a beat. "A *special* elf. So the bus . . . with the other elves . . . it's Reno bound?"

"Yes," Shirley said. "It's their bonus for jobs well done."

Molly nodded. "Is Janet around by any chance? I needed to chat with her."

"She's around," Shirley said. "With Santa, last I saw. They're very busy tonight, as you can imagine. I'd steer clear."

"Sure," Molly said. "Steering clear. So where do you want us?"

Lucas wasn't surprised at how well she was handling herself, but he was hugely impressed and wished Archer and Joe could see her in action. They'd stop trying to clip her wings.

"Well, you're both quite late," Shirley said, looking at Lucas. "And you're not in costume."

"Yeah, sorry," Molly said smoothly. "We had a fight."

"Honey, you don't fight with a man who looks like that."

Molly slid Lucas a glance and he went brows up. She narrowed her eyes slightly. "We were fighting over money. I think I should be able to get a wax job whenever I want. He's being tight with the credit card."

"A girl's gotta have her wax jobs," Shirley told Lucas. "I assume you're the muscle the big boss has been bitching about not being at the back door. But you gotta wear the costume. He'll freak if you don't."

"He shrunk it," Molly said, giving Lucas a sideways glance that might've been humor. She was enjoying this. Which meant she was every bit as nuts as him. "Don't get me started with how he does the laundry," she told Shirley. "Do you have a spare? In the offices, right?" She met Lucas's gaze for a moment.

Shirley nodded and jerked a chin for Lucas to follow her. Hating every second of this, he turned and gave Molly a don't-you-dare-get-dead look.

She winked at him.

Damn. He loved her. Hard.

Shirley led him to the offices, which were empty, and went hands on hips. "Wonder where Louise keeps the men's costumes?"

Lucas's gaze locked in on the floor beneath Louise's desk, and the very corner was the flash drive still thankfully resting there. "Uh, maybe in that closet?" he asked pointing toward what he hoped was a storage closet.

Shirley shrugged and headed that way.

Lucas bent down and scooped up the flash drive, shoving it into his pocket just as Shirley turned and looked at him.

Lucas affected a bored look and glanced at his watch.

Shirley tossed him two costumes. One looked to be a child size, the other possibly a man's medium. Great.

"Better hurry," Shirley said. "You're late. Boss hates that." And then she turned her back on him.

He stared at her. "What are you doing?"

"Waiting for you to change. Duh . . ."

He held up the costume but no miracles had occurred in the past thirty seconds. Shit. The male elf costume was the same color and material as the female version, but at least it was shorts instead of a minidress. Short shorts. The top was loose enough and hung just slightly past the waistband of the most ridiculous, asinine shorts he'd ever seen.

They fit him like he was auditioning to be a 1980s wrestling celebrity, and he was not happy as he stuffed his gun in the back of them, which only made the shorts even tighter in the front. But there was no way he was walking about this Stephen King book come to life place without his gun. He was still trying to arrange his junk in the front of the shorts when Shirley turned back around, looking disappointed that he was covered up. "Hmm," she said with an approving nod. "It works on you."

If by working on him she meant clinging to his every inch like Saran Wrap, then she was correct. It worked.

"Let's go before the boss has a coronary," she said. "Where is he?"

She gave him a funny look. "With his brother in the bingo hall, along with everyone else. Someone's got to watch over the elves. He likes to personally check on everyone." She left in front of him.

But something about the way she said *personally* had his instincts screaming, but he nodded noncommittally and followed her out, walking like he'd been riding a horse for twelve hours, thanks to the ridiculously too-tight shorts bunching up his goods.

He had no idea if Nick or his brother Tommy Thumbs suspected Molly of anything, but he wasn't taking any chances. He reached down and searched his pants pockets for his phone to warn her to get the hell out of there, that he had the memory stick, but he had no phone. He'd left it in the car. He looked around. There was a phone and laptop on one of the desks. He didn't know whose it was and didn't care. He was just glad that whoever had left it behind didn't have a security code and he was able to actually use it to call Molly.

Who didn't answer.

Chapter 23

#SubordinateClause

Molly stood in the back of what had formerly been bingo central, staring in shock at the room. The tarps supposedly covering the renovations were down.

It hadn't been renovations going on behind them at all. Instead, the area had been transposed into a gaming area and now looked like a casino, complete with high top tables featuring various ongoing card games.

Serious card games by the look of the players and the people in charge of each table.

There was garland and twinkling strings of lights and mistletoe hanging from the rafters and several decorated trees along the walls. Christmas music was blaring out of hidden speakers. There were several elves circling the room with trays of drinks. The place positively hummed with the sound of voices, laughter, and glasses clinking together.

No one even glanced at Molly.

She searched for a glimpse of Janet or Santa. Or Santa's brother.

Nothing.

From her bra, her phone vibrated an incoming call. She pulled it out and glanced at the screen.

A number she didn't recognize. Ha. Nice try, unknown number, but she didn't even answer to people she knew. So she hit ignore and walked through the room. People were gambling in a very big way tonight. Pulling out her phone again, she texted Lucas.

Bingo hall transformed into an underground and very illegal gambling site. Maybe we really do need backup.

Feeling very proud of herself, and like quite the professional, she slid away her phone just as someone came up behind her. Shirley. "You're not going to make any tips just standing there like that," the elf said. "Get moving. Go to the bar, get your tray, and start serving." She gestured with a jerk of her head to the bar off to the side of the large room. "You want the boss to notice you're not doing your job? Trust me, the answer to that is no."

"Understood." Molly started walking toward the bar, sneaking another quick text to Lucas.

Where are you?

At the bar, she nodded to the bartender. He was in an elf costume and looking pissy about it. "Hey," she said. "How's it going?"

"How's it going? My nuts are caught in these stupid short shorts like a vice and the material's so snug it's going to give me hemorrhoids. Worse, it makes me look all . . . lumpy, so there goes any chance of getting laid tonight. Here," he said, thankfully not requiring a response as he shoved a tray at her. "Right now we're serving free eggnog, heavily spiked. If they want beer or wine, that's five bucks a glass. A cocktail is eight. Cash only. The boss doesn't like it when the girls write down their orders. They want you to memorize them, so go do your thing and don't screw it all up."

Okay then. She took the tray of eggnogs and turned back to the room. The first table waved her over and took all the drinks from her tray, saving her from worrying about what to do with them. She shifted, heading to the back of the room, planning on making her escape to go find Lucas. But just then she caught sight of Santa's brother coming out of a narrow hallway, one she knew from bingo nights led to several small rooms, mostly used for storage.

He never even glanced her way as he headed toward one of the gaming tables. She pretended to be busy until he walked away and then she sneaked her way down the hallway he'd just come from.

Two doors. Both locked. She glanced over her shoulder to make sure no one was watching before pulling two bobby pins from her hair to work the lock.

Sixty seconds later, her tongue between her teeth in concentration, nearly there with the lock, a hand settled on her shoulder. Instinct kicked in, as well as everything Caleb had taught her in the gym, and she whirled and kicked out hard.

Usually, whenever she'd practiced that move on Caleb, he'd let her connect so he could teach her how to not fall into whoever she was fighting.

But she didn't connect. That was because the person standing there ducked and then straightened faster than the speed of light, whipping her around, holding her back to his chest, his arms pinning hers at her sides.

Before she could so much as draw a breath, he breathed her name in her ear, a whisper of surprise and shock in his low voice.

Lucas.

She sagged into him and he immediately loosened his grip, turning her to face him.

She started to say something, but then she got a good look at him and her mouth fell open in utter delight.

He was in an elf costume, and no one in the history of *ever* had filled out an elf costume like Lucas. Words failed her.

"What the hell was that?" he whispered with a good amount of shock. "You know martial arts?"

"A little. Sorry I almost kicked you."

"Are you kidding?" he asked in disbelief. "If this costume wasn't cutting off vital circulation, I'd be hard. With moves like that, why did you pour coffee into Santa's lap rather than kick his ass?"

She shrugged. "Coffee in his crotch seemed more appropriate. Hey, do you know that you make a pretty damn hot elf?"

He grimaced. "I don't want to talk about it. Ever. You didn't answer your phone. I've got the flash drive. Time to get you and this memory stick out of here and call in reinforcements—"

"*Yes* please," she agreed. "Just as soon as I get into this room. I've got a feeling about it."

"Okay," he said and turned his back to her, watching the hallway. "Go."

Not having to be told twice, she went back to the lock. "I thought for sure you'd go all caveman on me and try to carry me out of here."

"You've got a feeling," he said simply and right then she felt her heart roll over and expose its underbelly. "As for the caveman thing," he went on. "We'll play that game later."

She dropped the bobby pin, but she'd gotten the lock open.

"Nice," he said.

"Not my first time."

He snorted and opened the door. Dark room. He gestured her in, shut the door behind them and used her phone as a flashlight, shining the glow around the room, letting out a low whistle.

There were two long tables. One held two large duffle bags, one stuffed, one empty. The other table had some money wraps and a paper register filled with numbers. Lucas flipped through it and shook his head. "Cash entries. *Large* cash entries, by date. There's already one written in here for tonight. Five grand—" Breaking off, he unzipped the full duffle bag and found it filled with cash. He looked at the still empty bag. "Someone's going to be back and soon," he said. "We're out of here."

"Agreed," Molly said, snapping pics with her phone. "Just give me one more minute—"

"What the hell?" asked a woman. *Janet.* Standing in the doorway, she wasn't in her elf costume, but in a Mrs. Claus costume instead, a red-and-white number that made her look like an apple dumpling. She was smiling her usual warm, sweet smile as she pointed a very small but lethal-looking gun at Lucas.

"Criminy," she said, pulling the door shut behind her. "You two are such a pain in my patoot!"

Lucas reached for the gun at his back, but Janet shot him in the leg and what made it all the more shocking was that there was no real sound. She had a silencer on her gun.

Lucas hit the floor. "Molly," he grounded out through his teeth. "Run."

Like hell she was going to leave him. She dropped to her knees at his side and stared up at Janet in shock. *"What are you doing?"* She didn't have to fake the quiver in her voice; it came naturally watching Lucas's pant leg become soaked in blood as she slowly tried to reach beneath Lucas for his gun.

"Dammit to hell, Janet," Santa grumbled as he came into the room, followed by his brother, Tommy Thumbs. "I told you to leave these two alone, that they'd be nothing but trouble."

"And I told you I'd handle it," she snapped.

Tommy sighed and pulled a huge gun from somewhere, pointing it at Molly's face. "Freeze," he ordered.

Molly froze.

Santa's brother glowered at Janet. "Are you shittin' me?" He looked at his brother. "I'm not going back to jail for you two. Why the fuck do you need so many women in your life anyway?"

"No one's going to jail, Tommy," Janet said.

"Really?" he asked. "Because the one you just shot is a cop."

"No, he's a security specialist and an investigator," Janet said.

Molly used this argument between the crazy old people to slowly reach beneath Lucas again, trying to get his gun free. Which was a lot harder than it looked in the damn movies.

"That's even worse!" Tommy yelled at Janet. "We can't let them go now, they're onto you, you crazy old bat. And you'll implicate me."

"No, we're not onto anyone, honest," Molly said, coming up on her knees, holding Lucas's gun behind her. "You can let us go."

Tommy rolled his eyes, reared back and back-handed her with his gun. As she spun with the momentum, stars bursting behind her eyelids, Lucas somehow pushed to his feet. He reached for his gun again, but she'd dropped it at impact. She could see the exact second he realized they were both unarmed, but he changed tactics without blinking and took out Santa with a hard punch to the face.

It all happened in slow motion. Molly hit the floor in tandem with Santa. Darkness crept into the edges of her vision just as Tommy aimed his gun at Lucas and pulled the trigger.

Nothing happened.

They all stared at each other and then Lucas dove for his gun. But Tommy grabbed a hunk of metal pipe from a shelving unit and swung it at Lucas's head before he could reach it.

Molly screamed, the sound echoing in her head as darkness claimed her.

Chapter 24

#BabyItsColdOutside

Molly came to in a dimly lit space with a gasp.

Lucas had been shot.

Trying not to panic, she went to sit up and realized that her hands were bound behind her. At least her feet were unhindered, she thought as she blinked her vision clear. She was still in the storage room. Lucas lay only a few feet away, so terrifyingly still that her heart stopped. Flex-cuffs bound his hands too, and blood pooled beneath both his left leg and his head.

Scrambling to her knees as fast as she could—which wasn't very fast without use of her hands—she scooted over to him. He had a nasty-looking gash at his temple. "Please be okay," she whispered, fighting back an impending meltdown of epic proportions, because it was quite clear that he *wasn't* okay, wasn't even in the vicinity of okay, and in fact might not even be breathing. "Oh God, Lucas, don't be dead." She bent over him and saw that his chest was rising and falling with shallow but steady breaths.

A soft sob of relief escaped her, but she managed to bite back the one right on its heels. *Get it together, and fast,* she ordered herself and nudged Lucas with her shoulder.

He didn't move.

She nudged harder.

Still no response.

"You've got to wake up," she begged him. "I need you. I love you and I need you and I didn't really know either of those things until right this minute, so if you could . . ." She broke off, suddenly realizing that there was a third person in the room.

Santa.

He lay on his back, his hands unrestrained at his side and a large bullet hole between his eyes. A shocked expression remained etched on his face.

She understood the sentiment. Cute, feisty, sweet, warm, little Janet, aka Mrs. Santa Claus, had taken all of them down.

From down the hall came the sound of applause. She could figure out what that meant. The evening was possibly coming to an end, which meant someone would be showing up with the last of the evening's till.

And to finish what they'd started.

This would most likely include getting rid any evidence, of which she and Lucas most definitely were.

Bending over him, she tried to rouse him again. "Please wake up," she murmured, pressing her cheek to his chilly one.

He groaned softly, but didn't come to. He'd lost a lot of blood and needed medical attention, but with her hands behind her back, she couldn't help him. Instead, she gently dropped her forehead to his shoulder and allowed herself one last sob. "Just don't die, okay?"

More applause, louder this time.

Struggling to her feet, she twisted to try the door. Locked or jammed somehow.

There was a window. Unfortunately, it was high up on the wall. Long and shallow, it was meant for letting light in and some ventilation, not for escaping out of. She used her hip to shove one of the tables beneath the window, but the table was heavy and it took her a ridiculous amount of time to get it around Lucas without hurting him further. It also meant getting way too close to Santa, and when his leg jerked, she nearly had heart failure thinking he was still alive—until she realized the table had bumped into him.

When the table finally was up against the wall, she hit another snag. No hands to climb onto it. Turning her back, she attempted to hitch her butt up, but she couldn't quite reach. Facing it again, she tried lifting her leg, but her numb thigh kept her from getting high enough. She tried the other leg and . . . her bad leg collapsed under her full weight and she fell onto the floor.

Hard.

Shaking her head to clear it, aching from the impact, she rolled over to get her legs under and came nose to nose with Bad Santa, now Dead Santa. With a startled squeak, she backed away and swallowed hard, getting over her aches and pains pretty quick because hey, at least she was still alive.

And so help her God, Lucas had better stay that way too.

She staggered upright and with sheer grit, managed to get onto the table. Getting to her feet from there was trickier because her leg was protesting loudly. Ignoring that, she slowly straightened and eyed the window. It was locked. She'd need her hands to get it open.

"Dammit." She dropped to her butt and slid off the table, frantically running her gaze around the room for something sharp. The old, rickety metal shelving unit lining the wall had promise. The corner of it had rivets along the seam, basically just rusty, jagged edges of metal meeting metal.

Tetanus seemed preferable to being shot to death by Mrs. Claus, so she backed up to it and pressed the flex-cuffs against the metal, moving her arms up and down, trying to saw through the plastic. Moving too fast, she slipped and cried out as she sliced her hand open.

Taking a deep breath, she repositioned her hands and went at it again. It took what felt like hours, but was probably only a few minutes before her hands suddenly sprung apart.

Blood dripped down her fingers from a deep cut in her palm. Ignoring this, she ran back to Lucas. Still breathing, and . . . still not responsive. She needed help. She tried to find her cell phone, but it was gone. She looked at Santa. Blowing out a deep breath, she patted him down, looking for his phone. "You were an asshole," she whispered when she found it in a pocket. "But I'm still sorry."

She used the emergency feature on the phone to call 9–1–1. She asked for the cavalry and then wanted to call Joe. Unfortunately, Santa had a passcode, but she had the option of using a thumbprint. Gingerly, she picked up Santa's hand and pressed his thumb to the home key. "Sorry about that too," she murmured and called Joe.

He picked up on the third ring sounding breathless. "Who's this?"

Normally, she'd bug him about his phone manners, but that could wait for later. All she could manage at the moment was his name. Her leg hurt and her hand hurt and her head hurt, and her stomach was thinking about throwing up. "I need you."

His voice went from annoyed to very serious. "Molly? Where are you?"

"At the Christmas Village in Soma. I already called 9–1–1, but I need you."

"Call Archer," he said to someone with him, "tell him to get everyone to the Christmas Village in Soma ASAP."

Molly knew he was probably talking to Kylie and that he'd already be on the move to get to her. That was Joe, that's what he did, he moved heaven and earth to get to her whenever she needed him.

"Molly," Joe said, an engine turning over in the background. "Talk to me."

She opened her mouth, but suddenly she realized she could also hear voices from the main room rising, like the games really were over now and everyone was saying their goodbyes. She managed to roll herself up onto the table again, leaving a gory bloody handprint that made her swallow hard. She looked out the window. The distance to the ground was nothing compared to the three-story distance she'd faced last time she'd been in a similar situation, but the brain was a funny thing. The drop felt like a hundred miles.

It didn't matter, it was hers and Lucas's only exit.

"Molly," Joe said again, tightly. "What's going on?"

"Just hurry," she whispered. "The bingo hall. South window." Again, she jumped down from the table, gritted her teeth against the pain and went to Lucas. Stuffing the phone in her bra with the connection to Joe still open, she hooked her arms under his armpits and pulled. All lean muscle, he weighed a ton. She huffed and puffed, managing to drag him over to the table. "Lucas." She shook him. "Dammit, you've got to wake up. You weigh a freaking ton and—"

He groaned and cracked open an eye. "Did you just call me fat?"

She choked out a laugh that might have been more like a sob of relief.

Lucas blinked and appeared to focus in on the

blood all over her. Suddenly looking far more alert, he struggled against his restraints to sit up. "You're hurt," he said. "The blood—"

"Mostly yours," she said, trying to hold him still. "Santa's dead and Janet's MIA with Tommy, but they're going to come back. We need to go out the window. Now."

"Talk to me, Molly," Joe said from inside her bra. "I'm ten minutes out. What the fuck is happening?"

"Lucas has been shot," she said. "He also took a pipe to the temple and has a head wound. Mrs. Claus lost her shit. *Hurry.*" Then she grabbed a chair— she had no idea why she hadn't thought of it sooner, probably because her brains were scrambled—and shoved it near the table. She turned back to Lucas and pushed him toward the chair. "Get on the table. We're going out the window."

She kept her hands on him to keep him steadied and climbed up beside him. Then she bent for the chair. "Duck," she said to Lucas. And when he did, she threw the chair against the window.

It broke straight through the glass and hit the ground. It didn't sound like too far of a fall, she assured herself.

There were glass shards still in the window. Lucas was leaning heavily against the wall, looking more unconscious than conscious, but he straightened and pulled off his shirt, grimacing as it brushed his head wound. He tossed it to her. She wrapped her already bleeding hand in the material of the shirt and knocked out the rest of the glass, and then tugged Lucas to the window. "You first, big guy."

He resisted, crouching and giving her a push with his shoulder, lifting her with some reserve of strength she hadn't imagined possible.

"No," she gasped. "You first—"

He never slowed, just shoved her through the window opening.

For a single heartbeat she clung to the window ledge, the remnants of glass biting into her hands. She didn't feel it. Her eyes were locked on the ground, only ten feet down or so, her entire body frozen in terror. Well, not exactly frozen since she was shaking like a leaf.

"Molly."

She lifted her head and locked eyes with Lucas's.

"Listen to me," he said, leaning as close as he could without the use of his hands. "You saved us. You did it. You're amazing, but we've got to move. Right now they're overconfident, unsuspecting that we're on the move. They won't stay that way. We have an edge and we need to keep it."

"I can't jump."

"Yes, you can. Loosen your arms and lower yourself until your arms and legs are both fully extended. Then it's only a few feet. I promise, you've got this."

"But you're shot and you don't have use of your hands—"

"I'll be right behind you, don't doubt that for a second."

She stared at him and in spite of the urgency, he nodded patiently, no frustration or irritation showing in his face or body.

"Keep your body loose, not tight," he said. "Don't lock your knees. You've got this," he repeated, his gaze calm on hers. Calm and patient, even with one pupil clearly blown and blood dripping down his jaw and onto his bare chest.

Behind him, she heard the lock rattle, and her fear for him overcame her fear of dropping out another window. "Promise me you're right behind me!"

"I promise you."

So she took a deep breath, relaxed her body and let go.

Chapter 25

#GoElfYourself

Lucas came to lying flat on his back on a stretcher with people hovering over him using medical speak and poking him with what felt like a very large needle. He hated needles. He tried to sit up, but he also had an oxygen mask on his face, which he shoved aside. "Molly."

A hand settled on his chest. Not Molly's. Joe's, and not to comfort, but to restrain him.

"We've got Mrs. Claus and Tommy Thumbs in cuffs," Joe said immediately, knowing that intel was the only way to calm any of them down. "Santa's in a body bag. The elves made it safely to Reno." His voice was tight, his eyes were hot. He was pissed that he'd been left out of the loop, and Lucas knew he had every reason to be.

"Molly," Lucas said again, shoving one of the

EMS's hands aside as he tried to replace the oxygen mask. "Where is she—"

"Also being treated. She's got a few cuts and bruises, but no bullet holes, which I can assume is thanks to you," Joe said. His voice softened. "Thanks, man, for having her back here tonight and saving her ass."

Lucas shook his head. "You've got that backwards. She saved *my* ass. I was out from the moment I got shot. She . . ." He started to shake his head in marvel and pride, but that hurt too much so he closed his eyes. "She fought like pro, and even when she was overpowered, she *still* got herself out of the cuffs. And then she managed to drag my dead weight over to the window, up onto a table, and get us out. You should've seen her." He opened his eyes again and met Joe's. "It wasn't easy for her, but she handled it. She's handled everything on this case from start to finish like one of us would have. Maybe even better than one of us."

Looking troubled, Joe nodded. "They're transporting you to General—"

"No, I don't need a hospital."

"Yeah," Archer said, coming up behind Joe. "You do. You've got a bullet lodged in your thigh and a gash on your head that's going to need like twenty-five staples and maybe a lobotomy while you're at it since you didn't call your team. We're going to circle back to that later when your brains aren't in danger of leaking out, believe me."

Great. He could hardly wait. "Since I didn't call, why are you all here?"

"Molly called. Apparently she's smarter than you. Also, nice look."

Lucas looked down at himself. He was still in the elf costume. Correction: *half* an elf costume, meaning just the short shorts.

Archer slid Joe a look. "Might want to get a pic of that for future leverage."

Joe patted his pocket. "Already did."

"I'm going to release you," the ER doctor told Molly.

She started to get up, but he held out a hand to stop her. "But only," he continued, "if you promise me to take it easy for a few days and let those cuts and bruises heal before going back to work."

"It's okay, my work isn't—" She broke off. She'd been about to say her work wasn't dangerous, that it was desk work, but given the past twenty-four hours, she'd be lying. "I'll rest," she promised. Not a lie since, thanks to a nice, big, fat, pink pill, she was feeling pleasantly numb. "Where's Lucas?"

"Coming out of surgery."

"I want to see him," she said and this time managed to sit up, hiding her wince of pain that the movement caused.

"You need to move slowly," the doctor said. "As for Lucas, someone will let you know when that's possible."

When he was gone, Molly looked at Joe sitting

moodily in the chair in the corner. He hadn't left her side, but nor had he uttered a word.

"I'm going to see him," she said stubbornly.

He ran a hand down his face. "Do you have any idea what went on tonight?"

"Yeah, Joe." She waved her bandaged, stitched-up hand. "I've got a pretty good idea considering I had a front row seat."

He sat back with a heavy sigh. "You took ten years off my life."

"Welcome to the club," she said. "Remember last year when you got hurt on the job and were in the hospital for two days before we knew you were going to be okay? I was sitting right where you were, so I get it. I know. And for the record, what happened tonight doesn't come anywhere close to all the times I've been in your shoes."

Joe grimaced, looking pained. "Look . . . I know, okay? And I'm sorry."

She stared at him, waiting for the rest of that sentence. When Joe held his silence, she shook her head. "Wow. A sorry without a *but* on the end of it. Did it hurt?"

"Okay," he said. "I deserve that. I've . . . been hard on you."

"Not hard," she said. *"Impossible."*

"I'm working on that." He paused when she gave him a disbelieving look. "I am," he said. "I swear. But that's going to lead to an argument I don't want to have with you until you're up to it. Let's try a different conversation. Lucas."

Well, hell. "As it turns out," she said, lifting a shoulder. "I'm not really in a talking mood."

"Too bad. I don't know exactly what's going on with the two of you, but—"

"—What's going on is that he took a bullet meant for me," she said. "And he was hit in the head with a steel pipe—also for me—and I'm not leaving here until I see for myself that he's okay." She slid off the bed, holding onto the railing for support while she got her sea legs.

Joe was there in an instant, having risen out of his chair and putting his hands on her arms. He had brought her cane, which she absolutely did not intend to use.

"I want to know what's going on," Joe said.

"I just told you."

"I don't mean on the case—the one you weren't supposed to take, by the way. I mean between you and my partner and best friend."

The question gave her a flashback to how she'd felt the night before, sleeping in his arms. Contented. Happy.

Fulfilled.

And though he hadn't said as much, she'd seen the look in his eyes that morning. She'd felt the way he touched her. How he said her name.

Things had changed.

She wasn't exactly sure when or how, but she knew they had. He'd fallen for her.

And unbelievably, and against all odds, she'd fallen for him too.

"Molly."

Shaking her head, she yanked the curtain from around her bed and eyed the large ER, decorated with garland and some twinkling lights. She took in all the other curtained beds. Fine. Eeny, meeny, miny, mo it was. "Lucas!" she called out, making a scene and not caring.

"Damn, Molly." Joe grimaced and shoved her cane at her. "At least use this while you're yelling your fool head off."

She snatched the hated cane and leaned on it. *"Lucas!"*

Archer's head appeared from behind one of the curtains across the room and he stared at her.

It used to be that Archer intimidated her. He was an intimidating sort of guy, dark eyes, dark thoughts, and until Elle had bashed through his brick walls, he'd also led a dark life. Joe had gotten Molly the job, but she'd still had to prove herself to Archer. She'd started out as receptionist, only answering phones and keeping the schedule. She'd slowly proven her worth to the company and now he trusted her to run his office and his world completely. It was a compliment of the highest order, and she loved and appreciated both the job and the chance.

But as he knew, she'd wanted more for a while now. She felt as if she'd really proven herself on this Santa case—and he hadn't even known. It was frustrating. And being frustrated, and maybe also a little bit high on pain meds, turned off her inner filter.

"I want to see him," she said.

Archer stepped outside the curtain and held his ground as she stormed toward him.

"Get out of my way," she said.

"Molly—"

She moved around him and whipped open the curtain.

The bed was gone. Her heart stopped. Everything stopped, including her ability to talk. Blood rushed through her ears and she felt her vision start to go.

Archer swore beneath his breath and scooped her up. He set her on the chair in the cubicle and whipped the curtain closed for privacy. "He had surgery to remove the bullet. Now he's having a CT. He'll be back any minute. Alive, I promise. You should be in your bed."

"I've been released."

"Where's your keeper?" Archer asked.

Joe slid into the cubicle. "Here," he said grimly. "She's not real good at staying put."

"No shit," Archer said and both men just stared at her, good and well pissed off because they'd been left out of the loop—which was their own damn fault.

Molly tossed up her hands. Well, her one good hand. "Hey," she said. "I just worked a case from start to finish and got my man. Or in this case, Mr. and Mrs. Claus *and* his felon brother. You should both be patting me on the back and asking if I want to go out for a beer after work, like you do with each other after a job well done."

They both looked at her in shocked disbelief. "Okay," she admitted. "Since you didn't know I was even on a job, I guess that might be taking it a little too far. How about just something along the lines of 'Hey, sounds like you handled yourself, Molly, welcome to the team.'"

Archer let out a breath, an unusual show of frustration from the guy who rarely if ever broadcasted his thoughts. "First of all," he said, "you're right. You didn't tell us you were on a job. You didn't tell us when it started to detonate. Neither did Lucas. Let's start there."

Huh. This wasn't exactly going in the direction she'd hoped. "I tried to bring you in on it," she started but Archer interrupted her.

"And I told you that you weren't ready."

"Well," she said, "I disagreed."

"That's the thing, Molly," he said in that hardass boss tone. "You don't get to disagree with me on the job. I'm the boss. I'm *your* boss."

And he'd given her a job when she'd needed it. He'd done so with her having little to no experience in his world, and he'd never been anything but generous, with both money and his time. She tried to remember that. "I understand all that. And you've been amazing. But you're only in charge of me when I'm on the clock." She paused and then said gently but firmly, "What I choose to do off the clock is none of your business."

Archer slid Joe a look.

Joe tossed up his hands. "Man, if you think I can talk any sense into her, you're sorely mistaken. Why do you think I came up with the idea of putting Lucas on her six?"

"Wait," Molly said slowly. "What?"

Joe's expression went from mildly pissed off to *oh shit*.

Molly pointed at him. "Repeat that."

"Hell," Joe said and scrubbed a hand over his face.

"You asked Lucas to watch over me?" she asked. "When?"

Joe blew out a heavy breath. "Does it matter?"

"Oh my God, Joe," she said, horrified. "From the *beginning*? Are you serious?"

"I was trying to protect you."

Furious, and also more than a little hurt, Molly turned to Archer. "How attached to him are you because I'm thinking of killing him."

Archer looked pained. "This is on me, not him. I'm the one who actually insisted Lucas make sure you turned the elves down. When you didn't, I kept him in place to make sure you stayed safe."

She blinked a few times, but nope, she wasn't sleeping or dreaming, or in fact having a nightmare. This was all real and it was happening. She stood up to leave, realized she was shaking, and sat back down just as Archer got a text.

"He's in recovery, we can go see him now," Archer said and they all paraded through the hospital, where they found Lucas in another cubicle.

He was awake, but just on the wrong side of green. She hardened her heart. "Are you okay?" She needed to know that he was before she killed him too.

He nodded.

Of course. Typical man. He'd say he was fine even if he had body parts literally falling off of him. "Lucas," she breathed. "Are you sure?"

"Quit babying him," Joe said. "He's going to be fine."

Lucas flipped his partner the bird without bothering to look at him. He never took his eyes off Molly. "You saved my ass," he said, sounding just surprised enough to piss her off.

She narrowed her eyes and he smiled. It was a tired, pain-filled smile, but there was also so much more in those dark eyes that she felt her breath catch.

"You were amazing, Molly," he said softly, reaching for her hand. "Kickass."

She felt herself flush with pride, until she remembered and tugged her hand free when what she really wanted to do was stroke the hair from his forehead and lean in and kiss his pain away. "They had you spying on me," she said, jabbing an accusatory finger behind her at Archer and Joe. "A fact you kept to yourself. And you," she said to Joe. "I didn't tell you about the case before tonight because I knew you'd take over and try to keep me out of it. And you and Archer tried to do exactly that."

"Whoa," came a female voice. *"What?"*

Everyone turned and found Elle and Sadie standing there.

Elle crossed her arms and looked at Archer.

Her man wasn't showing much but there did seem to be the slightest twitch in his left eyelid. "What are you two doing here?"

"Making sure my friends are okay." Elle came in and slid her arm around Molly, giving her a hug. Sadie flanked Molly's other side.

"Great," Joe muttered. "Girl power."

Molly drew in a deep breath. She appreciated the backup, but all her cuts and bruises hurt, and so did her head. And her heart. That hurt most of all. She was mad at all three men, and more than anything, she was over having everyone think they had to constantly babysit her. Coddle her. She'd proven herself, dammit.

Lucas locked eyes on Molly. "Out," he said in a soft but deadly voice.

She stopped breathing. She was angry, oh so angry, but he didn't have a single reason to be mad at her, and she opened her mouth to blast him because no man spoke to her like that, not ever, and—

His hand caught hers. "Not you," he said.

Oh. Well, then. She tried to pull free again just on principle, but he wasn't having it this time. He held on, gentle enough to not hurt her, firm enough that she wasn't going anywhere without making a scene.

And she 100 percent intended to make a scene, but it'd be nice not to have an audience for it, so she waited it out impatiently, listening to the rustling behind her indicating that people were leaving the small cubicle.

"We'll be right outside if you need us," Sadie told her.

Her throat tightened, but she didn't take her eyes off Lucas. "Thanks," she managed.

"*Right* outside," Sadie repeated, and then Molly and Lucas were alone.

"Molly," Lucas started. "I—"

"You lied to me."

"No," he said. "I omitted."

"Same thing."

"Not the same thing," he said. "When Archer realized you were going to take this case regardless of what he'd told you, he asked me to keep you safe."

"And you do everything Archer tells you to?"

He grimaced when she tugged free and took a step back.

Archer stuck his head back into the cubicle just then and she pointed at him. Clearly everyone was still eavesdropping, not that she was surprised. "I'm not on the clock," she grated out. "Which means you're not my boss right now, so when I tell you to get the hell out, you can't fire me for it."

"Molly—"

"Get the hell out," she said and then looked at Joe, who'd also stuck his head back in. "You too."

"I've got this," Lucas said to the clearly reluctant men.

Archer ducked out.

Joe held Lucas's gaze. "You sure, man?"

"Oh my God!" Molly yelled.

Joe skedaddled.

Lucas held out a hand for Molly, an unspoken request for her to come closer.

Instead she crossed her arms over her chest, which hurt her hand, not that she intended to admit any such thing.

"Molly."

"You were asked to protect me, which you agreed to," she said. "And then didn't tell me."

"It wasn't exactly like that."

"Okay, then tell me, Lucas. What was it like exactly?" she asked.

"Archer tried to tell you that he didn't want you to take this case."

"Because he thought there was no case."

"Because he's booked up for two straight months," Lucas said. "Whatever he thought of the case, he didn't want to take it on because he didn't have the ability to give it his all, and that's his prerogative."

She looked away.

"And yes," he said quietly. "I agreed to try and dissuade you from taking the case in the first place. But then I met the elves and realized they were right and something was going on. And plus, you were onboard no matter what anyone said."

"So that's when Joe and Archer put you on the case *with* me," she said. "I get that, misguided and stupid as that was. But you . . ." She shook her head, feeling her chest tighten as she realized the horrifying, pathetic truth. "You were working, and I thought we were . . ." She closed her eyes and turned away.

"Molly. We were."

"We weren't." She was proud of one thing, that her voice remained even. No way was he going to know how much that hurt. "We were just coworkers, and you know what? That's what we told everyone anyway, so it's fine. We're all on the same page now."

"It's more than work between us, Molly, and you know it."

"Do I?" she asked.

"You love me."

She stilled and then whipped back to face him.

"Yeah," he said. "I heard you say it, back in that storage room."

From the other side of the curtain came a sudden rush of barely there whispers like a bunch of kids in the back of church.

"She told him she loved him?"

"What the hell's been going on when they were working?"

Molly whipped the curtain open and all the faces that had been up against it pulled back. Everyone bumped into each other and they shifted, trying to look very busy.

"Go away," Molly said.

As a collective whole, they backed up a few feet.

"Further," Molly said, then whipped the curtain closed again and stared at Lucas. "You were unconscious."

"I was in and out. Okay, mostly out, but I definitely heard you say you love me and ask me not to die so sweetly that I told myself I had to make it just so I could say it back to you. I love you too, Molly."

Her heart kicked. "You love me. But you lied to me. Love doesn't lie, Lucas."

He didn't smile, didn't blink, just let his dark eyes lock onto hers. His mouth curved into a soft, remorseful smile that made it difficult to remember to keep her distance. So did the white bandage around his head.

"You know that I'm not good at this," he said, worry in his expression. Or maybe it was regret. "I'm out of practice."

"So am I," she said. "But I didn't lie to you. I wouldn't." She was aware that she was self-destructing this, but couldn't seem to stop herself. Maybe because a little tiny part of her was relieved that there was an out.

"Molly—"

"I've got to go."

"Wait," he said. "What about me—"

"You do what you want."

"No," he said. "Don't go. I can't come after you—"

"I don't need you to." She backed away from him. "Take care of yourself, Lucas."

And then she forced herself to walk away.

Chapter 26

#IOnlyWantYouForChristmas

Lucas watched Molly walk out of the small cubicle and—he was afraid—out of his life. He struggled to sit up and had barely made it upright before everyone except the one person he wanted crowded back in.

"Man," Archer said. "Even I know that when a woman says 'Do what you want,' you don't do what you want."

"What do you do then?" Lucas asked wearily.

"You go perfectly still. You don't blink. You don't even breathe. You just play dead."

Lucas closed his eyes. He felt half dead and wondered if that would count . . .

A harried-looking nurse showed up and gasped at the number of people squeezed into the small space. "Is this a party or a hospital?" she asked tartly.

"It's both," Elle said. "But the party's really just a

pity party for our dumbass friend who just screwed it all up with the love of his life. I know you said only two of us at a time back here, but it's going to take all of us ganging up on him to make him see the light and rectify his dumbassness."

The nurse eyed Lucas. "You screwed up?"

"Yeah."

"Men," she said with a shake of her head, and started checking his vitals. She pulled the stethoscope from around her neck to have a listen and then gave him a long, hard look at whatever she heard.

Probably his heart dying.

"You need to rest," she said and turned to Elle. "I'm sorry to interrupt The Dumbass Intervention, but—"

"Hey," Lucas said, closing his eyes. "Lying right here."

"You'll have to fix his life for him later," the nurse went on. "He really does need some quiet."

When she'd shoved everyone out, Lucas felt relief. Finally, he could hear himself think. But . . . he could hear himself think. Molly was gone, and given the look that had been in her eyes, she was going to stay gone.

Which meant it was official—he really was a dumbass.

He woke to an annoying beeping that told him he was still in the hospital. He sat straight up and then went utterly still, fighting both pain and nausea.

Thanks to an infection in his leg, they'd admitted

him instead of letting him go home. That had been two days ago. Two long, restless days and nights of high fever and barely consciousness. He'd dreamed that Molly had been at his side the whole time, alternately holding his hand or stroking his hair from his eyes. He was certain he'd heard her mutter "dumbass" affectionately as well, but every time he managed to wake himself up and crack open his eyes, the chair by his bed remained empty.

He sat up now, staring at it. Wishful thinking, no doubt.

"Problem?" Joe asked, coming into the room.

"I thought I heard . . ." He shook his head.

"What?"

"Nothing."

Joe tossed a duffle bag to the bed. "Thought you might want some clothes that your ass won't hang out of."

Lucas stripped off the hated hospital gown. "If I don't ever see another of these in my entire life, it'll still be too soon." He gingerly set his feet on the floor. His thigh was healing where the bullet had ripped through, but it still hurt like a sonofabitch. He very carefully slid his legs into the jeans Joe had brought, forgoing underwear since he didn't know if he had enough in him for the extra step. "Tell me what happened with the case."

"Let's start with why you kept it from me. I get why Molly did, but not you, Lucas."

Lucas drew a deep breath, which hurt like hell.

"She's good, man. She deserved a shot at this case. And it wasn't for me to decide to bring you in on it. She's her own person and not only that, she's good at this. You're going to have to come to terms with that. Now tell me what the hell happened when I was passed out."

Joe took in what Lucas said and nodded, not looking happy but resigned. "It turns out that Santa had told the elves the truth on one thing—the Christmas Village itself really wasn't making much money. One to two grand a weekend. But their gambling profits were coming in at ten to twelve grand and they were stupid enough to be claiming the illegal gains in order to wash the money through a legitimate business. They cooked their books, but didn't count on one thing."

"Molly," Lucas guessed.

"Molly," Joe agreed. "Tommy Thumbs and Janet are going away for money laundering, conspiracy to launder illegal gambling profits, racketeering, and lots of other fun stuff including murder one. Santa's already six feet under."

Lucas nodded and reached for a T-shirt. "So," Joe said casually as Lucas pulled it over his head. "You and my sister."

Lucas pushed his arms through the sleeves and shoved the shirt down before looking at Joe. "Yeah. Me and Molly."

"So you freely admit it, that you were fucking around with my sister when you were supposed to be protecting her."

"I *was* protecting her," Lucas said. "And it wasn't fucking around."

Joe raised a doubtful brow.

"It wasn't," Lucas said, closing his eyes. Even though all he'd done for days was sleep, he felt exhausted to the bone. "It's different with her."

"So different that you did your usual be-a-dick until you're dumped move?"

"You want to go there with me?" Lucas asked. "Because whose fault is it that she's mad at me for lying? I fell in love with her, Joe. I didn't mean to, and God knows I didn't want to, but it's the truth. I know she doesn't believe me, but that doesn't make it any less real. And seems to me that only a few months ago you fell for Kylie while protecting and helping her as well, so please, tell me more about this whole thing being so wrong."

Joe sighed. Scrubbed a hand down his face. A rare tell and an admission of guilt. "In case you're confused on the details, she dumped you."

Lucas nodded. "I'm going to fix that."

Joe looked at him for a long moment and Lucas knew this could go one of two ways. Either they were still friends and partners or they weren't.

Joe sighed again. "She was here."

"What?"

"You woke up looking for her, right?" Joe asked. "Because she was here. Pretty much the whole time, actually. Wouldn't leave your side, and believe me, I tried to convince her otherwise, but she refused to go and get the rest she needed until she knew you were out of danger."

Lucas's heart squeezed painfully. "I'm going to make things right, Joe. I'm going to get her back."

Joe snorted. "Good luck with that. Getting Molly to change her mind once she's set it is . . . well, you'd have a better shot at getting hell to freeze over."

Lucas shoved his feet into his beat-up running shoes. "It's going to happen." He straightened. "Are we okay?"

"You really think you can fix it with Molly?"

"I have to believe it."

Joe stared at him for another long beat and then nodded. "Then we're okay."

Two days later Lucas showed up at the office. Once again he wasn't yet cleared for work, but also once again, he was going batshit crazy at home with nothing to do.

Especially when everything he needed was here.

He walked up to Molly's desk. She lifted her head and met his gaze, and for a beat he saw so many emotions there he couldn't breathe. But in the next beat, she shut herself down and gave him a look utterly clear of any emotion.

"You're not cleared for work," she said. "Doctor said you have to stay off your leg."

"I know."

She arched a brow. "And yet you're on your leg. Where're your crutches?"

"Probably wherever your cane is."

She sighed and went back to her keyboard, her fingers moving at the speed of light, but he could tell she wasn't in it. Her attention was still on him.

Good, because he had something to say. "You were looking for an out, and when you found one, you took it. Tell me that's not what you did."

She opened her mouth and then closed it. Her eyes too. Then she drew a deep breath and opened them again. "I can't tell you that," she admitted. "Because that's what I did. But for whatever it's worth, I regret it and I'm sorry."

He nodded, accepting that for gospel, because another thing Molly didn't do was lie. Feeling tentatively hopeful for the first time in days, he set an iPad down in front of her.

"What's this?" she asked warily.

"Why don't you look?"

Instead, she stood and walked around the desk toward him. She was limping pretty badly, more than he'd seen in a long time, and he reached for her.

She let him pull her in and he let out his first real breath since that night in the bingo hall, the one that was haunting him because she'd gotten hurt on his watch.

"You're shaking," she murmured and pulled back an inch to look into his face. "Are you okay?"

His throat went tight. She'd been through hell too, and yet she wanted to know if *he* was okay. He ran his hand up her back and into her hair to palm the back of her head, holding her to him. "Better now," he said, wondering if she'd let him hold her like this for the rest of time. "You turned off your phone. Didn't answer your door. When I went to your dad's, he threatened to shoot my balls off from where he sat."

She gasped. "He did not!"

"He did. And I risked said balls to ask him to get you to call me."

She shifted free of him and looked away. "He told me that part."

"You didn't call."

She bit her lower lip. "I almost did." She turned to her desk and the iPad he'd set on it. "But I needed to think."

"About . . . ?" he asked.

"Relationships. How I self-destruct them when I'm scared." She slid him a look. "You lying to me . . ."

Ah, and now onto the gut-wrenching portion of the day. Reaching for her hand, he tugged her back into him, waiting until she met his gaze. "We already talked about this," he said quietly. "I didn't lie to you. I will never lie to you. I did withhold the truth. I had my reasons at the time, but I regret them too. *Deeply.*"

She stared at him, her thoughts hidden. "Keep going."

"Yes, I was asked to watch after you. I was happy to do so. I didn't consider it a betrayal, I considered it a job—"

She sucked in a breath.

"—Which lasted about two seconds," he said.

"Until I realized that not only did you have a real case, but that you weren't going to let it go until you'd done right for Mrs. Berkowitz and her friends, and that scared me."

"I thought you weren't scared of anything," she said.

"You thought wrong. I'm scared of plenty. One of which is letting you get hurt." He let out a deep breath. He hated facing his fears, much less admitting them. "Another is losing you."

"I understand that," she said quietly, surprising him. "You've had losses, too many. Carrie. And Josh . . . But you need to know, Lucas, I'm not them. I'm . . . me."

"I know." He cupped her face and pressed his forehead to hers. "And I was working through all of that, about how I'd buried my emotions deep, how I'd closed myself off . . . it was all coming to a head for me right about that very first night when I woke up with you in my bed—all over me like white on rice."

She narrowed her eyes. "That did *not* happen."

He lifted his hand as if taking an oath. "*All* over me."

She blushed. "Whatever. You sleep like a furnace and my feet were cold."

He smiled. Her feet hadn't been cold. His smile faded as fast as it'd come. "You have a lot of people who love and care about you very much, Molly."

She rolled her eyes. "Some of them are way too

overprotective. Joe and I are going to work on that together, probably the hard way. Now tell me something I don't know."

"I'm one of those people. It's in my nature to protect and defend. It's ingrained deep, and I won't apologize for it. What I will apologize for is not fully understanding just how strong and capable and amazing you are." He paused to let that sink in. "You don't need someone to stand at your back, Molly. But I'd sure like to stand at your side, if you're done self-destructing us."

She just looked at him. Not angry and closed like before, but not quite on board with him yet either.

"Look at the case file I brought you," he said, nudging his chin toward the iPad.

She swiped the screen active and skimmed the summary sheet. "This is a custody case gone bad. We don't take these kinds of cases."

"No," Archer said, coming into the room from the back. He nodded a greeting at Lucas and they fist-bumped. "But our newest investigator does."

Molly sucked in a breath and lifted her gaze. Not to Archer, but to Lucas, an entire world of hope in her eyes and he felt his heart swell. "New investigator?" she whispered.

"Yeah," Lucas said. "Our resident expert."

"On what?"

"On everything."

Molly glanced at Archer.

He nodded at her and then turned and left them alone.

"You got me a case," she breathed.

Lucas shook his head. "*You* got you a case. You earned it."

"But you went to bat for me with Archer or this wouldn't have happened."

Actually, he'd gone to war with Archer, who didn't doubt Molly's abilities but did have concerns about her being a team player. Same problem he had with Lucas. But in the end, Archer had been willing to give Molly a shot rather than risk losing her, and that was all that mattered.

"You did this for me even though you're worried about me going into the field," she said.

He nodded again.

Her eyes went a little misty and filled with affection and more, much more, and mended his fractured heart.

"Why?" she whispered.

"You know why," he said.

Ignoring that comment for now, Molly thumbed through the case Lucas had fought for her to have.

And she had no doubt that it *had* been a fight.

She could love him for that alone . . . She kept reading and the more she read, the more she could see how bad the case was and the happier she got.

Lucas, clearly seeing that on her face, had to laugh. "You're an evil woman, Molly. I love it. I love you."

She stilled and looked up at him, her heart on high alert. "Say it again," she whispered.

"Molly Michelle Malone, I love you ridiculously."

She gasped. "Joe has a big mouth."

"Yeah, he does."

"Hey!" Joe said behind them.

They both craned their necks and found Joe and the rest of the team all eavesdropping. Reyes was holding up his phone, FaceTiming with the girls, who appeared to be eating tacos from Ivy's taco truck in the courtyard. Reyes shook his head. "I hate it when a couple argues and I missed the beginning and now I don't know whose side I'm on."

"The woman's side," Max said. "Always. It's safer that way."

"I heard from Old Man Eddie that Lucas wished on the fountain," Max said. "I thought that was bullshit because, well hello, it's Lucas, but now I actually think it might have happened."

Lucas turned his back on the circus and faced Molly. "We have dumbass friends."

"No doubt." She was still feeling . . . wary. But other emotions were busting through that. Things like hope. And a tentative excitement. "You wished on the fountain?"

"Yes. Pure desperation."

"Okay," she said on a nod. "Well . . . first of all—"

"Oh shit," Reyes said. "Our boy's toast."

Lucas turned and gave him a look.

"Sorry," Reyes said, "but when a woman says 'first of all,' you should run hard and fast because she's got research, data, charts, and is about to destroy you."

Archer put a hand over Reyes's face and nudged

him to the back of the crowd. He then gave Molly and Lucas a go-ahead gesture.

Molly turned back to Lucas. "First of all . . ." she repeated and then bit her lower lip. "You're really okay with this?" she asked, gesturing to the iPad and the case intel.

"Of course I am."

"Just making sure," she said. "Because it's a part of me. And for me to be with you, I need to know you accept all of my parts." She held her breath on his response.

"I love every single one of your parts." He paused. "You want to be with me?"

His shock brought her a smile. "Very much," she said.

"Holy shit."

This had a low laugh escaping her. "Yeah. That was my initial reaction too. So . . ." Suddenly she felt a little gun-shy. "This would be a really great time for you to tell me you want to be with me too."

He dragged her up against him, wrapping her up in those strong, warm arms she loved so much. "I want to be with you more than I've ever wanted anything in my life," he said and leaned down to kiss her. "Do you have any idea how much I love you?"

Pressed up against him as she was, she had an inkling, but she shook her head. "Maybe you should show me."

He smiled at the challenge and tightened his grip, lowering his head—

"Hey!" her brother called from the hallway. "You've got an audience, you know."

"Archer," Lucas called, never taking his gaze off Molly. "About that time off to fully recover . . ."

"Take it," Archer said. "Both of you. Get out of here. That's a direct order."

"Hear that?" Lucas asked Molly. "A direct order."

She smiled. "Maybe it's one we'll actually follow."

He smiled and kissed her, and *everything* was in that kiss; his promise, his hope, his love. Everything she'd never known how much she wanted.

Epilogue

One year later

Molly waved goodbye to everyone at the pub and made her way through the holiday-decorated court yard up to Lucas's apartment.

Their apartment, as he'd insisted she think of it. They were sharing both of their places and were looking for something to lease together.

She was pleased with herself, having just closed up a missing person case for Archer. She no longer worked the front desk; they'd hired someone new for that. Molly had her own office and worked with the guys, and also on her own.

She'd never been happier.

She set her purse and keys on the sideboard. Had she not been two margaritas in and thinking about when Lucas might get back from the job that had taken him away for three straight days, she might've noticed there was already a set of keys in the tray.

And that the lights were on. She turned to take in their pretty, shining Christmas tree when she was suddenly scooped up and tossed over a shoulder, making her gasp in surprise. "Lucas!" She swatted his delectable ass as he headed toward the bedroom. "You scared me!" Wait a minute . . . he wasn't wearing a shirt and with a hum of approval, she licked along his shoulder blade.

A low, sexy growl sounded from his throat and then she was in the air, being tossed to their huge bed. His body followed her down and then his mouth covered her with a possessive, hungry kiss, making her moan as her arms came up around his bare back. He kissed her until she was breathless and then pulled back with a smile. "You taste like a strawberry margarita," he said. "Girls night?"

"Yep." With a smile, she buried her face in the hollow of his neck. He was fresh out of the shower and his scent made her dizzy with desire.

"That might be the tequila making you dizzy," he said, sounding amused.

Oops. She'd spoken out loud. "I'm not drunk," she said, kissing her way over every inch of his chest and then back up his throat, ending at his mouth.

He smiled his very best badass smile. "Good. Because I want you to remember every second of what I'm going to do to you." He divested her of all her clothes and she lost herself in his caressing hands and demanding kisses.

"I missed you," he whispered and was just about to slide home when someone rang the doorbell.

"No," Molly said, trying to get his mouth back on

hers. "I've been dreaming about this for days. *Days*, Lucas. I need this. *Bad*."

"Mmm," he said, his voice pure sex. "Tell me all about this dream, slowly and in great detail." He bent to kiss her again, but before his mouth touched hers, the doorbell went off several times in quick succession, prompting him to blow out a frustrated breath. "They're not going away."

"Take your gun," she said. "Kill 'em quick and hurry back."

He was laughing as he bent to pull on his pants.

"Don't forget to hurry," she said when he left the room.

She was thinking about all the ways she was going to make him stop laughing and start moaning her name when he came back. He stood at the side of the bed with a bag hanging off one shoulder and a baby on the other.

"That was Finn," he said with a half smile. "Something you forgot to tell me?"

Finn had been behind the bar serving Girls Night, bemoaning that he needed to get Pru away for an overnight all to themselves, and somehow Molly had opened her mouth and promised to babysit for the next twenty-four hours. After all, what could wrong in twenty-four hours? "I'm babysitting tonight! I forgot!" She slapped her forehead. "Shit!"

Baby Penelope focused in on Molly with a toothless grin. A line of drool hit Lucas's shoulder. "Shhhht," the little cutie-pie said and bounced up and down in excitement at the sight of one of her favorite people.

Molly froze in horror. "Did she just—"

"Shhht," the baby said again and laughed her full belly baby laugh.

Fighting a smile, Lucas dropped the bag onto the bed and smiled at Penelope. "Uh-oh. Someone's in trouble . . ."

"This isn't funny!" Molly cried, sitting up. "*Shit* can't be her first word!"

"Shhht!" Penelope cried out again gleefully.

Lucas lost the battle and grinned. He pressed a kiss to Penelope's sweet curls. "Time for a new word, sweetness, or your mommy's going to kill the woman I love."

Penelope tipped her head back and stared up at him in clear adoration as she let out a stream of gibberish syllables.

"That's right," he cooed at her. "Who's my pretty girl?"

Penelope all but melted for him and Molly found her ovaries doing the same. "You look good like that," she said softly.

He met her gaze, caught her serious expression and cocked his head. "Like what?"

"With a baby."

He didn't laugh, didn't make fun. "You want one," he said. Not a question.

She'd honestly never given being a mom much thought. But in that moment, she knew she wanted to try. With Lucas.

With a soft smile, he handed her the baby.

"Where you going?"

"A minute."

He vanished in his closet.

"Lucas?"

"A minute," he repeated.

She sighed at Penelope and tickled her belly. "Men are from Mars."

Penelope giggled.

Then Lucas was back, still in nothing but his cargos. Bare chest, bare feet, expression baring his heart and soul as he sat next to her on the bed and handed her a small black velvet box.

"Merry Christmas, Molly."

She stared at him. "Is this . . ."

On his knees on the mattress before her, he smiled. "I've known you were meant for me since that very first night you slept with me."

She might have rolled her eyes, but her heart was pumping so loud she couldn't concentrate. Penelope, sensing the attention was off of her, patted Molly's cheeks. She took the baby's little hands in hers while continuing to stare at Lucas. "I didn't think we were going to go there—"

"I wanted to give you time," he said. "But I also want you to know that you're my heart. My soul." He shook his head. "My entire life. I tried fighting it, but I lost that battle a long time ago. I love you, Molly. Will you marry me?"

"Are you asking me so that I'll give you a baby as cute as Penelope?"

Penelope smiled at the sound of her name, farted, and then spit up down the front of Molly.

Lucas laughed and easily scooped up the baby, handing Molly a towel sticking out of the baby bag. He was good at this, she thought, and opened the ring box.

And gasped at the beautiful diamond solitaire.

"I'm asking you," Lucas said quietly because Penelope had set her head down on his shoulder and her eyes were drooping, "because I can't imagine you not in my life. With a baby, without a baby . . . I can go either way. What I can't go either way on, Molly, is you."

She felt her eyes go misty and her heart swell at the words as she slid the ring on her finger. "It's a perfect fit," she whispered.

Leaning in, Lucas kissed her over Penelope's head and smiled. "Yes. We are."

Keep reading for a sneak peek
at the next book in Jill Shalvis's
New York Times bestselling Heartbreaker Bay series

PLAYING FOR KEEPS

Coming February 2019
From Avon Books

Chapter 1

Alone per usual, Sadie walked through the day spa, closing up for the night. Her coworkers had left, but even if they hadn't, they'd just be walking around with their ridiculously expensive teas, talking about how hard this job was.

Laughable, but as the lowest person on the totem pole, she'd managed to keep her opinions to herself. Still, if she was being honest, it was only a matter of time before her mouth overtook her good sense.

As she moved around, shutting down the computers and dimming the lights, she dreamed about going home and replacing her daytime yoga pants with her nighttime yoga pants. Unfortunately, even after eight hours on her feet, that wasn't in the cards for her tonight.

When her phone buzzed with an incoming call, she glanced at the screen and felt an eye twitch coming on. "Hey, Mom."

"You always forget to call me back. I've been trying to discuss your sister's wedding details with you for weeks now and . . ."

Sadie listened with half her brain, the other half busy wondering if she had time to grab an order of sliders and crispy fries from O'Rileys, the pub across the courtyard, before heading to her other job. Her mouth watered at the thought. Lunch had been eons ago . . .

"Mercedes Alyssa Lane, are you even listening to me?"

"Of course." She wasn't listening. She was dreaming of what dessert might be. Maybe cookies. Maybe a brownie.

"I'll take that. Honey, you're not feeling . . . *sad* again, are you?" She whispered "sad" like it was a bad word.

And to be fair, it had been for most of Sadie's teenage years. To say she and her mom had a complicated relationship was the understatement of the year.

"Nope," Sadie said automatically because she didn't want to hear the "*all you have to do to get over the blues is think positively*" speech again, wellmeaning as it was. But her mom was winding up for the big finish and once that happened, there was no stopping her, so Sadie braced herself because in three, two, one—

"Because remember what Dr. Evans always said. To get over the blues, all you have to do is think positively."

Resisting the urge to smack her phone into her own forehead, Sadie drew a deep breath and sank into the cushy chair in her station, where her clients sat while she applied permanent makeup. This was her bread-and-butter job, seeing as the love of her heart job—working as a tattoo artist in the Canvas Shop right next door—didn't pay enough yet. And maybe it was silly and frivolous, but she'd grown fond of eating.

The problem was, all the hours on her feet working way too many hours a day left her exhausted.

And maybe the teeniest bit cranky. "Mom, it's not that easy."

"To think positively? Of course it is. You just do it. Take your sister . . ."

Sadie closed her eyes and caught a few Z's while her mom kept talking about her perfect sister Clara . . .

"Sadie? Yes or no?"

"Hm?" She sat upright, opening her eyes. She'd missed a question, but pretending she knew what was going on at all times was her MO. If she couldn't blow her family away with her brilliance, her plan was to always baffle them with her bullshit. "Sure," she said. "Whatever you guys decide."

"Well, that's very . . . sweet of you," her mom said sounding surprised. "And very unlike you."

Hoping she hadn't just agreed to wear a frothy, pink Little Bo Peep bridesmaid dress, she shrugged off the sarcasm and let her gaze shift to the window. The Pacific Pier Building had been built around a cobblestoned courtyard that each of the ground floor shops and businesses opened to, making it convenient for people watching.

One of her favorite pastimes.

But it was January in San Francisco, specifically the Cow Hollow District, and a thick icy fog had descended over the early evening with the promise of rain. The courtyard was lit with strings of white lights and lined with potted trees and wrought iron benches around a hundred-year-old fountain, and was usually a hub of activity.

Tonight only the faint glow of the lights was visible behind the wall of fog. The courtyard was empty. Except . . . wait a minute. A form moved through the fog. A tall, leanly muscled form, his overcoat billowing out behind him like he was some sort of super hero.

She called him Suits.

He had a real name, she knew. Caleb Parker. But she'd never said it out loud, preferring her nickname for him, since, with the exception of the one time she'd run into him at the gym, she'd never seen him in anything but a suit. And though she wasn't a suit kind of girl, she could admit there was something about watching him move in the clothes that had clearly been made to fit his rangy build and probably had cost more than an entire year's rent.

"Mercedes?" her mother said in her ear. "You still there?"

Being full-named always got her back up. It wasn't that Sadie had anything against it per se—okay, so she sort of did, because who named a kid after the car where that kid had been conceived?—but more than anything, she had a whole lot against her mother's tone. "Yes, I'm still here." She searched her brain for fragments of what her mom had said. "I'll be on time for Clara's wedding dress fitting appointment."

"Speaking of that, don't forget you need to find a date for the wedding next month."

"*Mom.*"

"What?" her mom asked, playing innocent. "It's a wedding, you'll need a date. And you're past due to find your Prince Charming. Way past due."

"I don't need Prince Charming," Sadie said. "Forest animals who clean, yes, but it's a hard pass on Prince Charming." She made her way from one window to the next in order to keep Suits in her sights. It was misting now and his dark hair shimmered with the droplets every time he passed beneath a lamp post.

Then he abruptly stopped between the day spa and the Canvas Shop, which was only twenty feet from her.

He didn't move.

"Mom, I've gotta go," she said.

"But—"

"I'll call you back."

"You always say that and you're lying. You're not supposed to lie to family."

Sadie found a laugh. "Tooth fairy, Santa Claus, and the Easter bunny," she said, and at her mother's gasp, she gently disconnected, squelching her grimace because she'd most definitely pay for that later, big time. Her mom had a lot of talents and one of them was the ability to hold a grudge for a hundred years.

Sadie had a few talents herself, such as not sleeping at night, and enjoying chocolate just a little too much. And okay, she was also talented at drinking tequila in the form of margaritas, preferably frosty lime.

Slipping her phone away, she went back to window, gazing to see what Caleb Parker was up to. He'd crouched low, easily balancing on the balls of his feet, looking at something she couldn't quite see as the wind and now rain pummeled his back, seemingly unnoticed.

What the actual hell?

She knew a few things about him. Such as he was physically appealing with his height and build, and that women tended to fall over themselves when he smiled. He had lean muscles everywhere a woman wanted a man to have muscles. His eyes were a beautiful caramel, with flecks of gold. They sparkled when he laughed and he laughed often. He was some sort of tech genius and used to work at a government think tank. He'd invented a bunch of stuff including a series of apps that he and his business partner had sold to Google, and more recently the two of them had created a way of getting meds and medical care into remote developing nations via drones.

Oh wait, there was something else she knew as well—that the two of them didn't like each other. She wasn't even sure how it'd started. They had a lot of mutual friends, which often landed them at the pub together. She couldn't explain it, but there was an energy between the two of them she didn't understand. At best it made her uncomfortable. At worst, it sometimes kept her up at night.

Her close friend Ivy, who ran the taco truck parked outside the building, said it was unrequited animal-istic lust.

But Ivy was wrong.

It wasn't lust, because Sadie no longer gave in to lust, animalistic or otherwise. Personally, she attrib-uted it to one simple fact—she and Suits didn't like each other and never had.

But what was he doing all hunkered down like that in the rain? Was he hurt?

Driven by curiosity and the inability she had of let-ting anything go, she unlocked and opened the front door of the day spa and stuck her head out. "Hey."

Staring at the brick wall, Caleb didn't turn her way or glance over. He didn't do anything except say, "*Shh.*"

Oh, no. No, he did *not* just shush her. Clearly, he was *asking* for a blast of her temper and all too happy to give it to him, she stepped out the door.

Keeping his gaze on whatever was in front of him, he held up a hand, silently ordering her to stop where she was.

No, really, *what the actual hell*?

Then he reached out towards the wall and she re-alized through the wind and rain she could hear him talking quietly to something.

Something that was growling at him fiercely.

"Don't be scared," he said softly. "I'm not going to hurt you, I promise."

The growling got a little louder, but he didn't back away, he just held eye contact with what sounded like a huge dog that she couldn't see in the dark shadows.

"Okay," Caleb said. "Come here. Slowly."

Sadie realized with a start that he was talking to her. "What? No way. What is it?"

"Come closer and you'll see."

Dammit. She stepped out from beneath the spa's overhang and immediately got wind and rain in her face. She pulled out her cellphone and accessed her flashlight app, which she aimed at the wall.

"Don't—" Caleb reached up and wrapped his hand around her wrist, bringing the phone down to her side. "You'll scare it."

"Better that than getting eaten." She shrugged off his warm hand but went still when the growling upped a notch.

"I think it's hurt," Caleb said just as the matted, drenched shadow scooted away from the wall. She could see now that it wasn't nearly as large as she'd thought. Not a young puppy, but not a grown dog either. It had a way-too-skinny, tan-colored body and a black face with black eyes. "Looks like a young, oversized pug," she said.

"Too big for a pug. It's got some bullmastiff in it though."

A bullmastiff with three legs, Sadie realized as it shifted closer, and her entire heart melted. "Oh my God." Moving towards it now without hesitation, she got only a few steps before the dog took a leap in Caleb's direction.

With a surprised grunt, Caleb fell to his ass on the wet cobblestones. "Okay," he said, backing up on his very fine butt cheeks as if suddenly terrified of the dog. "Okay, see? You're safe now, right? Stay. Stay and sit."

The dog didn't stay. Or sit, for that matter. Instead, it leaned on Caleb, leaving dirty, beige fur sticking to his coat.

Caleb sucked in a breath and seemed to hold it. "I'd really like be your person, but I can't."

The dog looked up at him and gave a single bark, like *too late, you're totally my person* . . .

"No, you don't understand," Caleb told it. "I literally *can't.*"

Undeterred by this news, the dog continued to lean on his new human, even as that human shifted back, trying to avoid contact.

Finally, Caleb lifted his head and looked at Sadie. "Help."

Fascinated by this unexpected show of weakness in the man who'd always come off as invincible, she shook her head. "I think he or she thinks you're its mama."

He glanced around the courtyard as if to see who the dog might belong to, but there was no one. In the meantime, the dog gave another loud "ruff" and sat on Caleb's foot.

"I hear you," Caleb said. "And we're going to help you, I promise."

"We?" Sadie shook her head. "Because *we* are most definitely not a *we.*"

Sliding her an unreadable look, he got to his feet. Ignoring her now, he lifted his hands at the dog, giving the universal gesture for *stay*, but the minute he raised his hands, the dog squeaked and leapt back as if Caleb had propelled him with a push.

Off balance with only three legs, the dog fell to its back, exposing its underbelly and the fact that it was most definitely a she.

Sadie didn't easily attach. In fact, she hadn't attached in a very long time but right then and there she fell in love. Not partially, but all the way in love because neglected and mistreated meant they were soul mates. "I'm going to kill her owner," she murmured, absolutely swiping a drop of rain and not a tear away.

"Not if I get to them first." Caleb's eyes were flashing total fury, though his voice remained low and calm. He once again squatted low, as if trying to get his six-foot-plus frame as nonthreateningly small as he could. "It's okay," he said softly. "We're together now, for better or worse, even if you're going to kill me."

"She wouldn't hurt a fly, much less kill you," Sadie said.

The dog had listened to all this intently before slowly scooting back towards Caleb, head down but her hind-end a little wiggly.

The sweet hope of it had Sadie's heart pretty much exploding in her chest as the dog crawled into Caleb's lap and set her oversized head on his broad shoulder.

With a sigh, he wrapped his arms around the dog and hugged her close.

"Yeah, that's some killer," Sadie said.

"I'm allergic."

He said this so nonchalantly, she blinked. "Is that some sort of euphemism for 'I hate dogs'?" she asked.

"No."

"You're kidding me, right?"

"Reach into my front left pocket."

She snorted. "Are you kidding me? Does anyone actually fall for that?"

"If I pass out," he said, still all quiet calm, "the EpiPen is in my pocket."

She paused, staring at his face. No sign of joking—very unusual for the charming, easy-going Suits she knew.

"I'm trusting you to use it before I die," he said as if he was discussing the weather.

"Stop it."

He met her gaze, his own serious, more serious than she'd ever seen him. "Listen, if you don't use the EpiPen, at least make up something really good for my funeral, okay? Like, I died heroically saving your sexy ass and not because a sweet dog like this one hugged me."

"Okay, I'm starting to think you're not kidding," she said.

"I never kid about dying."

*G*ive in to your Impulses!

These unforgettable stories only take a second to buy and give you hours of reading pleasure!

Go to *www.AvonImpulse.com* and see what we have to offer.

Available wherever e-books are sold.

AVONIMPULSE

IMP 0811